DANCER
AN EYE FOR AN EYE

OTIS MORPHEW

Order this book online at www.trafford.com
or email orders@trafford.com

Most Trafford titles are also available at major online book retailers.

Printed in the United States of America.

ISBN: 978-1-4907-4612-8 (sc)
ISBN: 978-1-4907-4611-1 (e)

Trafford rev.   09/08/2014

www.trafford.com

North America & international
toll-free: 1 888 232 4444 (USA & Canada)
fax: 812 355 4082

PROLOGUE

For my loving wife, Connie

The New York State coastline and seaport has always been the immigration capitol of the free world. Its doors were open, welcoming peoples of every race, creed and color, from every country on earth to enjoy the fruits of free enterprise. Although a majority of these new residents were, for the most part, illiterate and non-skilled, there were others that were of the most vicious and cruelest criminals in the world, coming to the Americas to assert themselves in their chosen trades. These were those who had left their own country to avoid prosecution, or most times, a rival death sentence.

Never the less, they were here, and they stayed, the stronger ones becoming leaders, or bosses, while the weaker ones did their bidding,... thus forming Crime Syndicates that exist to modern times. These crime organizations defied all laws, except their own, murder and extortion was commonplace, and daily,...and the worst of these Crime Syndicates were of Irish descent, and were usually smart enough to stay within the boundaries of civilian law,...to avoid breaking Federal Laws.

Sometimes these Crime Lords, being accustomed to bullying their way over those too weak or afraid to fight back, found themselves face to face with someone who was not afraid, someone who believed in justice and an eye for an eye,...and demanded it at any cost. When this occurs, the Crime Boss knows only one way to combat it,...power through hired killers, called Soldiers, or Enforcers. But occasionally a Boss will make a mistake, a sometimes, fatal one. Allan McCleary made two mistakes, the first in 1875, when he brought Organized Crime to Dallas, Texas. The second mistake would happen only three years later, when he sanctioned the death of a gunfighter's son,...one for which he would pay dearly!

Seth Dancer had not worn his gun since the war ended,...he had not killed a man in more than eighteen years, getting married had changed all of that. The guns he had always loved so much, he seldom thought about once his sons were born. He had found his niche in life, with the only surviving reputation being one of a very good husband and father. The gunfighter, killer, and holdup man was a forgotten past now,...there were no wanted posters on him. Those few who once knew, or ever heard of Dancer had all but forgotten him,...even believed he was dead!

Seth Dancer was Seth Mabry now, had been for more than eighteen years. Dancer was dead and forgotten to all but him and Laura, until now! His oldest son was dead, and his youngest in jail for the crime,...and this devastating tragedy would resurrect a long forgotten past. Seth Mabry had been wronged, he was owed the life of a son, whom he adored,...and he was owed for cruelty to his youngest son.

And Dancer would collect the debt,...an eye for an eye!

CHAPTER ONE

New York City was the first Capitol of then, a New United States, this in 1788,...and even then it was an economic center. It became an Atlantic Seaport to the vast agricultural markets in North America by 1825. After the Revolutionary War, thousands of New England Yankees moved into the city, and by 1820, far outnumbered the pre-war population. A dominant city was New York City.

In the 1840s, amid this Protestant, middleclass society of Stockbrokers, guildsmen, bankers, artisans and shopkeepers, thousands of illiterate and unskilled Catholic Irish immigrated to New York, so many that by 1850 the Irish comprised one quarter of the city's population, adding even more merchants, shippers, porters and well-paid laborers to the population. The city grew in wealth and power and it was only natural, as well as inevitable that Organized Crime came to enjoy a power and wealth of its own.

The immigration of Europeans to the city prior to the Civil War brought further social upheaval, as Old World criminal societies quickly exploited the already corrupt municipal machine, while local American Barons of industry exploited the immigrant masses with ever lower wages and crowded living conditions. They did so by using cheap foreign laborers from dozens of nations. This created a hotbed of revolution, syndicalism, racketeering and unionization and forced the upper class to begin using partisan handouts, organized crime groups, heavy policing and oppression to try and undermine these Barons.

Crime Syndicates recruited members from the ranks of the unemployed, the oppressed, and the angry, thus war was being waged in the Nation's largest city, a war for supremacy, power and wealth. This war created very powerful Crime Lords, who ruled parts of this city with threats of murder, depravity and torture,...and created a type of insurance that would later be coined The Protection Racket! This insurance was for the protection of business owners, and even laborers from molestation and robbery,...for a price. If these shopkeepers and laborers refused this insurance, they learned the hard way of their mistake. On the payrolls of these Crime Lords could be found Police Chiefs, street cops, Councilmen, Politicians, and even Judges.

Prior to 1860, Crime Boss, William (Boss) Tweed controlled most all of New York City, and his grip on the Nation's largest and wealthiest city was maintained by murder and ruthlessness on the part of his Tweed Ring of cutthroat thieves and assassins. Tweed lorded over his kingdom with a heavy hand, and continually pushed the smaller Syndicate Bosses farther away as he acquired more and more territory for himself,...forcefully taking what he wanted.

But there was one Irish Crime Boss who refused to be pushed, and the war for supremacy of New York City continued,...and by the late 1860s, the Irish Syndicate was almost as strong as the Tweed Ring. However, Jesse O'riely wanted it all and continued to push, and be pushed as soldiers on both sides continued to be killed. Even though New York City and Manhattan remained a battleground throughout the war years, the Irish immigrant bided his time to eventually become the most ruthless of all the Crime Lords in the city,...and its suburbs, a powerful individual who would have it all,...at any cost!

The ensuing gang wars continued for years, until the depression of 1873, when the great city all but went bankrupt,...along with the rest of the country. Money stopped coming in, depleting the millions these bosses were used to as store owners and shopkeepers went broke and began closing their doors. Some even began fighting back, even killing the collectors when they came to collect their extorted money! Shipping ports were closed, no European goods were coming in, and none being shipped,...because all of Europe was experiencing the same recession. Paper money was next to no good at all, worth less than half of its face value, and the scarcity of gold and silver in the Nation's vault was fast diminishing America's chances of regaining it's feet, so to speak,...because Europe, having sponsored the Civil War with loans of enormous proportions, were demanding repayment and President Grant had no choice but to repay the Nation's debts with our diminishing supply of gold and silver. This, however, was throwing the United States into a vicious turmoil of unrest and unemployment. The greatest country in the world was broke, the largest, and wealthiest major city in the country had been all but brought to its knees!

This did not sit well with the Crime bosses and especially with Jesse O'riely, who by this time had hundreds of Henchmen and territorial bosses to pay and to now, had paid them well for their loyalty and deeds. Something had to be done, and quickly,...so he derived plans to make up the difference. Since Boss Tweed and Company was a burr under his saddle, so to speak, and because his sources informed him of Police efforts, as well as the Federal Government's effort to find a way to rid New York of Tweed and his ring of mobsters, he began putting his plan into action. This was a plan that would incriminate Tweed and his men, and he did this by laying blame on the ring for each crime committed by his own soldiers,...doing this with anonymous tips to the Police, or by leaving clues at the crime scenes.

However, this was only one of two well thought out plans. The second was to expand his Crime Syndicate to other large cities in the country, towns that could be controlled and bled of their hard to come by, and hoarded gold and silver,...and even currency, as he believed that it would regain its value in time. So, using his most loyal and ruthless Lieutenants, he began moving to these cities to set up shop. Both plans were well on their way to completion by the mid-seventies, and by 1877, the first of his plans came together when William "Boss" Tweed was arrested and jailed for his New York City crimes, crimes committed by his "Tweed ring" of killers and enforcers.

*   *   *

Dallas, Texas,...already a very large and thriving village prior to 1856, was granted a town charter during the regular session of the sixth Texas Legislature of that year, electing a Doctor by the name of Pryor as it's first Mayor. They also elected a Constable, Treasurer/Recorder, and six Aldermen. By 1860, the town's population reached 678, including a hundred African Blacks, as well as Belgians, Frenchmen, Germans and Swiss. That same year found the railroad approaching from the South, and several stage lines were already passing through the town. Dallas was a city destined for greatness.

That year, a fire broke out in the square, destroying most of the business district, and many believed that slaves were behind it all, so they ran two Abolitionists out of town, hung three slaves, and all the others were whipped for the crime of arson. On June eighth of that year, a state of war was declared, and the town's citizens were avidly supportive. Men and boys alike enlisted in the effort, ranch hands, farmers, laborers, even those who owned businesses, and even landowners. These men left their families at home to fend for themselves, leaving them at the mercy of foreclosures, and with no place to go if they were evicted. Cattle Ranches were largely left unattended, their cattle roaming free, easy pickings for rustlers and wild animals.

Although Dallas was very far from the actual war and received very little damage from it,...it never the less suffered the consequences of defeat when it was over. The rights of most Texans were stripped from them, most of the homes and businesses confiscated as spoils of war, and the land offered up for grabs, to be bought up by the greedy Carpetbaggers. Returning Confederates had nothing to come home to,…and found their homes, land and sometimes even their families gone. The larger cities and towns in the South were under Martial Law, and under the victorious Union's heavy hand.

The Reconstruction period brought big challenges for Dallas. In June of '65, Texas slaves were liberated, and many more blacks poured into Dallas because the city was still prosperous compared to many other southern towns. Certain areas of Dallas were called Freedmen's towns because those areas were made up mostly of African Americans.

Dallas, Texas legally became a city in 1871, and prosperity was escalating by leaps and bounds, only to be hit hard again in '73 by the worldwide Recession, a Depression that many were blaming on President Grant. The whole country seemed to wake up in financial ruin but again, though it did feel the pain, Texas as a whole was not hit as hard as the rest of the country. The Houston and Texas Central Railroad, and the Texas and Pacific Railway intersected in Dallas that same year, and insured Dallas' future as a commercial center, and also sent the population soaring, shooting up from 3,000 people in '72, to more than 7,000 in '73. Daily appearances of new buildings and businesses made Dallas the epicenter for new markets of raw materials, like grain and cotton to be shipped south and East.

This is why Jesse O'riely chose Dallas as one of the likely places to send his most prized friend and under-boss,…and thus began the onset of a major Crime Syndicate on an unsuspecting, sleeping giant of a city, Dallas, Texas.

CHAPTER TWO

Allan McCleary was not a tall man being just under five feet, ten inches, however, he was a raw-boned and muscular Irishman with a round almost ruddy face, clean shaven and smug looking under his full head of reddish-brown hair. He sat behind the long, wide desk in his New York style gray pinstripe suit and smoked his large imported cigar while Yancy McGuire counted out the proceeds from the two saloons he owned. He was relaxed as he thought about his life and took in the extra large room he had converted into his personal office space. The furnishings was of European design, a long hand-carved and cushioned settee sat snuggled between two cushioned arm chairs along one wall, and above it, two large Frederick Remington oil canvasses depicting cattle drives.

On the wall behind his desk were several more paintings, along with as many windows overlooking the rooftops of other business places along the long, wide expanse of Elm Street. Next to one of the windows stood a suit of Spanish armor, adorned with shield and war-axe, this was where he placed his hat when in his office. The wall next to the front door consisted of a tall Mahogany High-boy dresser with heavy double doors, an item that was already there when he took over the saloon, and had never been opened. Along that same wall stood a coat rack where he hung his dress-coat, and on the wall more paintings depicting bear hunts, animals and Indian fights, and all by noted painters of the day. The other wall was much the same, and it all glistened with colorful beauty when all the French-style lamps on the low-hanging Chandeliers were lighted.

He never tired of the room, the hand crafted, many-colored Navaho rug that covered almost half of the middle portion of hardwood floor, and the tall twelve-foot high ceiling of the same hardwood. Sighing, he brought his attention back to the job at hand, blowing a cloud of strong, sweet-smelling smoke as he watched his underling friend, and cohort.

"Fifteen hundred and sixty-two dollars in gold and currency last night from liquor sales." Sighed Yancy McGuire looking up at him. "We could more than double that, Allan, if we set up our own distillery, don't ye know?"

"Yancy, me boy," He grinned. "I have come to know for a fact, that when it comes to drinking whiskey, this is not New York City! The drinking people here would know the difference. Ahhh, but I do admit there be some good Corn Liquor being made here already, and much milder than me good Irish Whiskey,...but we want people coming back to gamble as well as drink, they can buy bootleg whiskey anytime they wish. So, it is better we serve them good Irish Whiskey, don't you think?...Sure, and by Godfrey, you do, Lad, we think alike, you and me!....So,...what be the gambling take, me good man?"

"Fifty-two hundred, that be from both establishments!"

"That be the one we need to be doubling, lad!"

"I don't know how, Allan," Sighed Yancy. "Most are gambling with their egg-money now."

"Well, they'll just have to sell more eggs, won't they?...Any I-owe-you notes we might deal with?"

"No, Allan,...none last night,...nothing but local people last night."

"We must double our efforts, Yancy, me boy. There be seven thousand people in Dallas, could be even ten thousand by now and they all have money that we should be having. Ahhh,...but then this awful Depression is ruining everyone, and we do have to consider that!...Now, what of the working girls?"

Yancy stared at him blankly then shrugged his wide shoulders. "That, Allan, is something of a mystery,...most of my rooms are being used for sleeping lately, not for fucking....And talking with the whores is not helping,...they say the clients have no money."

"Nonsense, lad,...if there be money for drink, there be money for fucking!"

"My thinking as well, Allan. But I have had Mister Butcher talk with a few of the girls,...but that only resulted in them missing work,...it was a mistake!" He shook his head. "No, Allan, that is not the answer, me thinks. The girls are trying hard, I have watched them at work,...and they know what will happen if they do not!"

"Ahh, and I know that, lad!" Sighed McCleary. "But Jesse will be wanting money soon, and he will not understand our problem, why,... because he will not care! With paper money at half its value, there be not enough to make him happy with our results. No,...Jesse will not be happy,... and neither am I, Lad. We must put our heads together. We must look at this problem like it was New York City,…we must go after the gentlemen who do not visit our great establishment, and the streets are full of them!… Does that give you any ideas, lad?"

"Are ye forgetting the ordinance, Allan?…No soliciting in public places."

"Aye,…that be a problem all right,…but is it a Federal law, lad,…that be my question?…Don't forget, the City Councilmen work for us, and laws can be changed,…or overlooked. Aye, but that do be a fine line and I will need to look into it.…But in the meantime, lad, here is what you will do. Pick the youngest and prettiest whores to work the streets, dress them to look like everyday loving housewives, not the thin, see-through clothing they wear inside. Have the dresses buttoned down the front so they can show off their wares, otherwise they will look like any other woman on the street!…What do you think, lad?"

"I have already thought of that, Allan. But I know, as do you, that we cannot chance breaking the law too severely. We may have the law in our pocket, but with a Federal Judge here, and the Army so close, I don't know!… Besides, putting girls on the street that are too young could be a disaster,… experience, don't ye know?"

"Aye, and they might not handle themselves properly, I know. But there be not a man on that street out there that has not thought of bedding down with a wee girl, they find it exciting!" He rolled the fat cigar around in his mouth before grinning. "Then we will have to go about this in another way. How many girls do you have, lad?"

"Twenty three, Allan,…what are you thinking?"

"I am thinking we will put fifteen fresh young girls on the streets of Dallas, me boy,…sweet young things with every day dresses to wear, and with nothing but themselves underneath. We will remove the buttons on the dress from the crotch downward,…showing their slender young legs as they walk will make every man out there beg for their company."

"We don't have fifteen girls that young, Allan,…and if we did, none would be willing to bed with a man, you know that!…They be too young,… virgins!"

"Then put fifteen of your experienced whores with them to show them how?"

"That would leave me short handed in the brothel."

"Then so be it, me friend!…The whores that are left inside will stay busy that way. Yes, lad, that is what we will do,…that will bring in much more money, you'll see. With experienced girls with them to help peddle their wares, it cannot fail. If they still don't produce, we can always replace them."

"What with?"

"Yancy,...lad, you be doing this sort of thing in New York for years, this be no different!...They be all kinds of young girls in Dallas,...Chinks, Negro, German, Mexican,...pussy be pussy when a man is horny, lad,... and almost every family in this fair city is broke!...And if they be broke long enough, Yancy, me friend,...they will have children to sell, because they can not afford to feed them. That is exactly the way you recruited the whores you have already, have you forgotten that?"

"I have not forgotten, Allan,...but I believe that one day, that will all come back to haunt us!"

"Nonsense, lad, we have the money, these families do not. Use your imagination, like you did in the Bronks!...If they refuse to sell, you'll know what to do!...It be just another business deal,...like buying property!...The good Judge, McAllester with see to the legality of it."

"You be the Boss, Allan,...of course, I will do it!"

"Good man,...tell you what, dear friend," Sighed McCleary removing the cigar from his mouth. "You choose your best whores to accompany the new recruits, and I will talk with them, you know, to explain the dangers of not doing their jobs well!" He smiled wickedly and chewed on the cigar again.

"And by the way, me boy,...I think it is time we up the price of insurance to the good people of Dallas, they can afford a few dollars more, of which by the way, it be collection time again!"

"I will put Silva and Butcher on that tomorrow, Allan." He nodded. "Now, about the gaming tables, especially the card tables. Don't you be thinking we need dealers who can keep the games in our favor?"

"Crooked card games, Yancy?...Poker is a game that is always in favor of the dealer. Straight tables will always pay off, lad. Granted, sometimes a man will get lucky and win, but that only serves to bring him back to gamble some more,...but the odds are always against him!"

"Not always, Allan,...There be a young cowboy downstairs right now, and he is the same cowboy that won five thousand of our dollars last Saturday night,...and two thousand a week before that!...A month ago, he was in my saloon, and if you will remember, he won another five thousand!... To be in a depression, Allan, this cowboy is doing quite well for himself on our money!...So much for straight tables!"

"Who be this cowboy?"

"From what I can find out, he be the son of some rancher, somewhere south of the river. No one actually knows him, but he has a younger brother who is always with him and that one likes to drink!"

"Are they armed?"

"Oh, yes, both be armed, and I have no doubt they both can use their weapons quite well."

"Well that be strange, all right, I know,…but winning could just be a streak of luck on his part!…Then again, maybe not! Let us do this, lad,… when you go back downstairs tonight, change the dealer at his table and then watch him. Should he continue to win anyway, the lad could be cheating,… but if he is not,…and he continues to win, come and tell me,…because you be right, too much luck can be bad for us."

"Would it be wise to be rid of him, Allan?…A lot of people know he is lucky at cards! He has a crowd watching him play as we speak."

"Then we will use the brother, should we need to, Yancy! Use your imagination, lad,…brothers do kill brothers sometimes, it happens in Ireland quite often!"

"All too often!" Nodded Yancy. "But if need be, I will take care of it!"

*   *   *

Thomas Mabry was a year older than his brother, Gregory, who had just turned seventeen a couple of months ago, and they were inseparable. If you saw one of the boys, one could bet the other was nearby,…and this was to the delight of both Seth and Laura Mabry because they knew the boys would always be there for each other. Both young men were quite able when it came to using a sidearm, Seth having taught them the art of shooting at an early age. This was not the worry they shared when the boys went to town, however, what did bother them was that though inseparable, they were totally different.

Both Seth, and Laura had talked with Thomas about his joy of gambling, tried to make him understand all the dangers involved,…but it was of no use and he was, after all, a full grown man with a mind of his own. But not Gregory, he was only seventeen, and while his brother liked to gamble he liked the taste of drink and both was a dangerous vice to have!

Although they knew that Greg drank a lot on these trips to Dallas, he never seemed to be drunk, never seemed to drink to the excess,…and not only did Thomas gamble, but he always seemed to come home with a large amount of money to give to his father,…and it was always accompanied by a large grin on his face. They had to admit, the money was responsible for stocking the ranch with good prime stock, increasing the herd considerably and not only that,…the ranch its self was in better shape than ever before, a new barn, corrals, wagons. The Circle S-M was becoming prosperous and all because of Tom's gambling!

However, they were still glad Seth had began sending their only hired hand to town with them on Saturday to keep an eye on them. They felt somewhat better knowing that Trey Mathers was a level-headed man who didn't drink all that much. But they still worried, after all, they were parents..

CHAPTER THREE

Thomas Mabry buttoned his pants and adjusted the gun belt back in place then waited for Greg to do the same, and then they both waited for the half-dozen or so men in the saloon's rear alley to go back inside before he gave Greg the wad of currency to hold. "Stick that in your boot, little brother!"

Greg took the money and pushed it down into his boot-top. "How long we planning on staying tonight, Tommy,...it's already after midnight?"

"I'm on a roll, Little Brother!" He laughed then, and with his arm across Greg's shoulders steered him up the steps to the rear door. "I'm gonna give Pop ten thousand dollars when we get home, Greggie-boy!"

"How much did you just give me?"

"Damn if I know, Bubba, it's bad luck to count it, now come on!" They made their way back through the milling conglomerate of women and drunks and threaded their way past the stairwell toward the poker table,... and the noise was tremendously loud as everyone seemed to be trying to be heard above the banging of the piano keys.

"How can you stand this noise, Tommy?" Yelled Greg as they neared the table. "It's deafening!"

"That's called excitement, little Brother!" He laughed then raised his hand to rub his fingers against his thumb. "Money,...That's what it's all about!"

"They changed dealers on ya, Tommy." Voiced Greg as they got to the table.

"Look's that way, don't it?" Grinned Thomas. "Watch 'im, Bubba,...let me know if you catch him double dealing!"

"Sure." Sighing, Greg shouldered his way back to the bar and ordered another shot of Rye then sipped it while he leaned against the bar and watched the game.

The hours passed slowly, and the stack of chips in front of Thomas Mabry continued to grow larger as the night progressed until finally, along toward three in the morning the place began to clear some, even at the roulette tables. Greg did notice there was still a substantial crowd around both Tom's table, and the blackjack tables,…and no one was drinking as they watched Tom win pot after pot.

How much longer was he going to play? He wondered as he shook his head and ordered another drink not realizing that it was Yancy McGuire that served him, and not the bartender.…He sipped at the concoction and continued to watch the game,…and it was not long until he began to feel somewhat nauseated, and then very sleepy,…and not understanding he shook his head to try and clear it then drained his glass and almost fell over.

He didn't understand what was wrong, but as he became more and more dizzy-headed, he knew he'd better let Tommy know he was sick and pushed away from the bar,…and almost immediately he realized that someone must have done something to his drink, as it was becoming a task just to keep his feet as he staggered the twenty feet or so to the table,…and he had just touched his brother's shoulder when he collapsed.

*   *   *

Seth Mabry had not been a rancher all his life, had in fact been raised on a farm a few miles West of Nacogdoches, Texas. His father had been a hard working man who broke his back every day in the fields to feed and clothe his family,…and it was not an easy way of life, to fight a drought one year, and too much rain the next, and sometimes Indians in between. Most of the Indians were tame enough, but now and then a few would band together and raise a little hell and the Militia would have to quell the uprising.

Eli Robert Dancer was a good man who never knew anything other than hard work, and he taught that way to Seth Joe-Bob Dancer, who at an early age had learned to work the fields as well. But like it, he did not! He would much rather spend his time caressing his father's old 1812 Martial, Revolutionary flint-lock pistol, pretending to be a road agent, or Indian fighter,…and the day his father let him fire the 65 caliber weapon for the first time, it sparked a love for firearms unequal to anything since.

Eli Dancer had been awe-struck the afternoon he taught young Seth how to fire the awkward weapon, unable to believe how accurate the boy was as he was able to place almost every lead projectile exactly where he wanted it to go. After that, the younger Dancer was never without the relic.

But then came the day Eli Dancer was killed in the fields by a drunken Caddo, and before the Indian could get away from the scene, young Dancer had placed a well-aimed ball through the back of his head, thus beginning a life of crime for the fourteen year old Seth Dancer who, after his father's untimely death took to leaving home on his own, leaving the crops and fields unattended. Once the young Dancer had his first holdup under his lean belt, he became more and more aggressive in his pursuit of money until finally, he left home for good, leaving a Mother that had now lost both of her men.

Seth Dancer was eighteen years old when in the summer of 1847, he found the arrow-riddled, and scalped corpse of a gun salesman. The body lay face down in a dry creek bed, and on searching the area he found a leather case that had obviously fallen into the protection of heavy, thick grass,... probably as the man was thrown from his horse....And when he opened the case, he found the new Walker Colt 44 pistol, extra powder and shot, and a tin of percussion caps.

It did not take him long to learn how to load and fire the six shot revolver, thus beginning his career in earnest. By 1851, even lighter percussion pistols were on the market, and hip mounted holsters to carry them in,...and that was how he developed his fast draw and marksmanship even more. He quickly became a wanted man after that, wanted in three different states for armed robbery. It was at that point that he dropped all of his given name, except Dancer, and that is what he became known by. Even his wanted posters carried only the name of Dancer! He was a gunfighter now, fast on the draw, and quite deadly,...and he liked it! He never returned home to see his now aging mother, never knowing that she had died of heartbreak,...and all alone.

Dancer's reputation continued to grow, and he was now wanted in New Orleans, parts of Texas and Arkansas,...and it was there, in a town called Little Rock that he was thrown for a loop. He met Laura Whittaker, a passenger on a stagecoach he was robbing, and from the first eye contact with the young woman, was lost in her beauty. Dancer was in love. When he released the coach that day, he quickly changed his shirt and followed the stage on into Little Rock,...and he was there to help her from the stage and carry her luggage.

He was in love with her, and her with him, and she had known he was the man who had robbed the coach from the moment she stepped down,... and as the days turned into weeks, they made plans to be married. Once she said yes, robbing and killing was the last thing he ever wanted to do again. They were married somewhat secretly in a small chapel in Hot Springs, Arkansas, and it was there that he did away with the name, Dancer, and gave his name as Mabry, which was his Mother's maiden name.

They immediately purchased wagon and a team of horses and left for Texas and two months later, after resting for two days in the village of Dallas, talk of a Civil War prompted them to leave and look for land elsewhere to settle on. They found that land just ten miles to the South of there,...and having saved most of his unearned wealth, Seth and Laura found the old settler and his wife in a small log cabin nestled amid a stand of tall, Elm and Firs, and with a running creek in back,...and they didn't look any further.

Seth Dancer was no more, he was Seth Mabry now and he paid the old couple one thousand dollars for their four hundred and fifty acres of grass, a few livestock, and thousands of trees,...and had never looked back as they worked to build their new home there in the trees by the creek. Being in what most would call a wilderness the war passed them by unnoticed, even amid the period of Reconstruction and now, a Recession that had left the country devastated! But still they lived and raised two sons without molestation from Union troops, or the hated Carpetbaggers! Finally in 1877, Dallas officially became a township and that's when Seth took his family to town for the first time, registering the deed to his land, and his brand, officially calling it Circle S-M Ranch,...which was only a circle with the initials SM in the middle of it.

Being only three miles from the Republic of Texas Road, a trail that stretched across Texas from San Antonio, past Dallas, and on to the Red River,...it was therefore convenient for them to use it when going to town, even though it was quite dangerous at times, what with Road Agents being a major threat,...and the traffic most times was constant.

*   *   *

Laura Mabry yawned as she opened her eyes, and lay for a minute to look through the window at the dawn. It was Sunday morning and she found herself wishing for the hundredth time that she could attend Church today. But it was so far to town. She sighed and rolled over to look at her husband's empty pillow and thought it odd that he wasn't there. Curious, she threw off the covers, swung her legs off the bed and slipped her feet into soft, fur-lined, hand made house slippers before getting up and walking out of the bedroom into the spacious sitting room.

She smelled the coffee then and walked on past the fireplace and settee into the kitchen. The large pot of coffee was sitting atop the back of the wood cook-stove to keep it hot and sighing, she reached down a cup, poured it full then went back through the sitting room and out onto the wide, wrap-around front porch where she found Seth sitting in one of the rocking chairs there, his booted feet propped atop the long railing.

"I thought I'd find you out here," She smiled. "Good morning?"

"Good mornin', honey." He sighed.

"What time did you get up, Seth,…it's Sunday?"

"Th' boys ain't home yet, honey," He sighed again. "They're always home before now!"

"Well, it's a long way to town,…they Probably got a late start back, don't you think?...And they could have stopped to sleep, too!"

"Yeah,…you're likely right. But I woke up at three o'clock this mornin' with a chill runnin' up my spine, Laura!...That's never happened before."

"I'm sure it means nothing, honey.…They may have gotten a hotel room and slept over."

"I hope like hell you're right!"

"I am!" She smiled then drank some of the coffee. "You want some breakfast now"

"Maybe when th' boys get home,…I'm too worried right now!"

The large porch was their favorite place to sit, and were usually there late in the afternoon to watch the setting sun. But early morning was a rarity to just sit and watch the sunrise, they were always up and getting ready for the day's work, usually missing the event. But they sat and watched it today as they waited patiently for their children to return from their night in town.

It was up in the morning, and they were still sitting there, having left their seats only to go relieve themselves. They had finished the coffee several hours ago, and having run out of anything much to say were silent, and they had been for a while now with their eyes still focused on the winding, overgrown wagon road in hopes of seeing them riding out of the distant trees.

It was almost noon when they saw the rider and, what looked to be a pack animal appear out of the trees and Seth got to his feet and strained his eyes at them.

"Who do you think it is, Seth?" Whispered Laura as she also stood up.

"Can't tell yet," He sighed. "But that almost looks like Trey's brown horse from here."

"It can't be Trey, honey,…he'd be with the boys."

"I know, honey." He sighed worriedly, but after a couple of minutes. "But it is,…and that's Tommy's Sorrel." He quickly pushed past her and went down the steps into the yard, with her on his heels.

"Dear God, Seth," She shrieked. "It is Trey,…Oh, my Goddd,…what's that on Tom's horse?"

They were standing there arm in arm when a heartbroken Trey Mathers stopped his horse unable to look at them and then sighing heavily, dismounted as Seth went quickly to Tom's horse and lifted the blanket from his eldest son's lifeless head. When she glimpsed her boy's chalky face, Laura screamed and fell to her knees,…and her wailing came from her very soul.

Seth wiped the tears from his own eyes and reached to touch his son's face before lowering the blanket,…and holding back his sorrow went to help Laura to her feet,…and she was still wailing great ragged sobs of despair while he helped her back to the porch then urged her up the steps and eased her back into her chair. He turned back then as a silent Trey led the horses on to the porch and tied them there.

"What happened, Trey?" He choked.

Trey broke down then and cried for a minute before bending over and puking, staying that way for several long seconds while he heaved,…and when he finally straightened up again, he ran a sleeved arm across his mouth then wiped at his eyes as he stared sadly at him.

"He was stabbed to death, Boss!" He gasped. "I don't know what happened, I was waitin' at th' stables like always, and when they didn't show I went lookin. I saw three men carryin' Tommy to a wagin and stopped 'em!…He was all covered in blood, Boss!…I should'a been there, boss!"

"Slow down, Trey, take a breath!…Where's Greg?"

"Greg's in jail, Boss,…Sheriff says he's th' one done it!" He broke down again. "I'm sorry, Boss. Oh, God Damn, I'm sorry!"

"It's not your fault, Trey." He sighed, once again holding back his own sorrow. "You up to usin' a shovel, man,…he has to be buried?"

Nodding weakly, Trey untied the reins and slumped off around the side of the house leading the horses and still sobbing brokenly. Seth watched him go then reached to wipe at his eyes again before squatting down to console Laura.

"My son is dead, Seth!" She wailed loudly. "Whyyy?"

"I don't know, honey."

"Oh, my God, Greggory!…Where's my baby?"

"Greg's okay, honey,…pull yourself together now, we have to bury Tommy!…He would want you to be strong, okay?…He's home now." He sighed heavily as he hugged her and fought back his tears again until she finally stopped crying.

"Yes,…You're right!" She sniffed. "I'll go get dressed." She got up and hurried around him to rush into the darkness of the house.

*   *   *

When the very hard and emotional graveside service was over, they all three went back into the house to sit silently around the kitchen table while a sniffing Laura cooked a late mid-day meal....After a while, Seth finally sighed loudly and looked at the downcast head of Trey.

"Is Greg all right, Trey?"

Shrugging, Trey looked up at him solemnly. "I,...I don't rightly know, Boss,...th' Sheriff wouldn't let me see 'im!...Said Greg was caught with a pocket full a money, and a bloody knife on 'im!...But somethin' ain't right about it all, Boss,...Greg would never a done that, never in a million years!"

"We know that, Trey,...and I want a thank you for bringin' Tommy home."

"I might be in trouble for it!" He shrugged again. "I pulled a gun on th' Undertaker."

"You did what?"

"He wouldn't give me Trey's body, boss!...Said it was evidence, or somethin'," He shrugged then. "So I took 'im!"

"You done good, Trey,...and I wouldn't worry none about that...I'll see to it!"

"Thanks, Boss."

Laura placed the heaping platter of eggs, sausage, potatoes, biscuits and grease-gravy on the table, and they all filled their plates from it and ate in total silence, their minds on the sorrow of the day's heartbreaking events. Once the meal was over and the coffee consumed, Seth pushed back his chair and got up, and then without a word walked back through the house, leaving Laura and Trey to stare at their plates dejectedly.

Several long minutes passed before Seth came back to the kitchen door, and when Laura saw him with his gun on, she gasped loudly.

"What are you about to do, Seth?"

"I have to see about this, honey!" He looked at Trey then. "I'm expectin' you to look after things here, Trey. Don't let Laura out of your sight!"

"You can count on it, Boss."

"Seth,...honey, you left all that behind you!"

He half smiled at her then. "I didn't have any sons then, Laura,...and one of 'em wasn't dead. I do now,...and Greg didn't do it!...Somebody else did!...And I'm gonna find th' Son of a Bitch!...I have to."

"But,..."

"No buts about it, my love, Greg's bein' railroaded,...somebody's framin' 'im!...Don't worry, Greg will tell me who done it!"

"Th' Sheriff won't let you see 'im, Boss,...he almost threw me in jail for tryin'!"

"He'll let me see 'im!" He said flatly. "No man keeps me away from my own son,...no man!"

*   *   *

"I love you, Seth!" Sniffed Laura as he stopped his horse by the porch.

"I love you, too, honey." He nodded. "I'll be home in a few days,...and Greg will be with me!" He reined the horse around and spurred it into a trot down the wagon road.

"Dear God!" Moaned Laura aloud, causing Trey to frown at her in puzzlement.

"I'm sure sorry, Miss Laura!" He sighed. "But they won't let him see Greg,...they might even arrest 'im for wantin' to!"

"Oh, no!" She sniffed. "He'll see Greg all right."

"How do you know that, Miss Laura,...that Sheriff near-bout arrested me?"

"If he don't let him see our son, he'll be dead!"

"I don't understand, Ma'am."

"I know you don't, Trey. But you would if you knew who he is." She gasped and looked at him quickly. "I'm sorry Trey,...forget I said that, okay, I wasn't thinking?"

"What do you mean, Miss Laura,...who is he?"

"Oh, Trey!" She sighed worriedly and began wringing her hands. "You wouldn't remember him anyway, it was more than eighteen years ago."

"I might, ma'am,...anyway, I already know he weren't always a cattleman, he ain't got th' walk of a man that's worked cows all his life.... Who is he, Miss Laura?"

"He's Dancer, Trey!" She sniffed. "He's a gunfighter."

"Good Lord, all mighty!" He grinned, turning to watch the now small figure of Seth disappearing into the trees.

"You remember him?" She asked incredulously.

"Yes, Ma'am, I do!...I never seen 'im,...but my daddy did, said he was greased lightenin' with a pistol!...I sure wouldn't a believed it, ever'body said he was dead!"

"I'm afraid there's going to be more killing now." She sniffed. "Someone will surely die if he doesn't get any answers, Trey!...So please don't tell anyone who he is, or that I told you, especially not him?"

"Oh, not to worry, Miss Laura,...last thing I want is Dancer mad at me!"

*   *   *

As he entered the trees, and was out of sight from the rambling ranch house, Seth could not hold his heartbreak in check any longer and stopping the horse in the overgrown road, leaned forward on the animal's neck and cried loud and long, and was unable to stop for several long agonizing minutes. And when the heaving and the wracking sobs finally subsided, he removed the bandana from his neck, uncapped the canteen to wet it down then washed his face with it before tying it back in place.

After another few minutes, he breathed deeply of the sultry, humid air and urged the horse into a gallop along the wagon trail and was trying to push the picture of his eldest son's dead face from his mind,…to no avail,… and by the time he rode out onto the well-traveled, and semi-crowded Texas Road he was mad! He spurred the horse into a mile-eating gallop, passing freight wagons loaded with cargo, and others with families heading toward unknown futures. Light wagons, buckboards and even horsemen, some in groups and some alone, some coming from and others going toward Dallas,…he passed them all, having to leave the road at times to get around cowboys riding abreast, ignoring the angry comments from men already aggravated about something, or nothing in general. He didn't hear them because his mind was on the problem at hand, and that problem was his youngest son, in jail for a murder that he could never have even thought of committing!

Somebody murdered Tommy, he thought sadly, and that same somebody was framing Greg for it,…and that same somebody was going to pay a heavy price for it! At that moment, he fleetingly remembered his mother, and almost broke into tears again. How she must have felt when he left and never returned,…and when he finally did, all he found was her grave and the sign left by the headstone, saying she had died alone and heartbroken! He shuddered inwardly and this time, managed to shake the thoughts from his mind and concentrate on the dusty road, thinking briefly, that for a Sunday there was a lot of traffic.

Five o'clock found him urging a tiring Buckskin horse onto the long bridge spanning the Trinity River and slowed the animal to a walk as he crossed, noting that she was breathing normal again as he rode off on the other side, and then stopped to give the gallant horse a breather, as well as to get his bearings. He knew the town's square was in the approximate center of the city's business district and so was the Sheriff's Office, having seen it there on their trip to register his deed. So, with the taller grouping of buildings in sight, he urged the horse onto the road again only to turn off again onto an intersecting road and headed for the town's square, still a good two miles away.

It was close to dusk by the time he turned onto Main Street and amid a conglomerate of pedestrians, men on horseback and spring wagons, clucked his horse along the wide rutted street toward the center of town. None of the shops were open, it being Sunday, but the eateries, and especially the saloons were in full swing. The shrieking laughter of women coming from open doors of the saloon, and along the boardwalks, men cursing and guffawing drunkenly as they staggered back and forth across the wide street causing traffic to either stop, or veer away to avoid hitting them. He had passed, and even marveled at several lighted lamp poles on the street's corners,...and one was even being lit by a man on a ladder, having opened the door of a glass box and inserting a lighted match to the wick.

He was finally riding into the crowded square and the noise from the Dollar saloon was loud through the open, swinging doors, blending itself with the off-beat banging of a piano,...and shaking his head, he spotted the Sheriff's office across the street and just two doors off the square and carefully reined the Buckskin over to the hitch-rail where he sat the saddle for a minute to stare through the shade-drawn lower half of the office window. Seeing the legs and chair of one man behind the desk, he sighed and made a quick scan of the busy square and street, and then along the crowded boardwalk before dismounting to loop the reins over the railing.

Waiting for three slow-moving men and a woman to walk past on the walkway, he stepped up and crossed to the door and finding it locked, knocked loudly.

"Who is it?" Came the muffled voice from inside.

"It's me, open up!" He returned, knowing that the man inside would be curious enough to open the heavy door,...and it paid off. He heard the bar being lifted from inside and once it began to open, he pushed the door inward causing the Deputy to utter a "Hey!" And have to take a step backward.

"Who th' hell are you?" Gasped the lawman. "Get your ass out a here, man,...th' Sheriff ain't here!"

Seth looked at him hard for a second then turned to close and rebar the door. "I ain't here to see th' Sheriff!" He grated. "Not yet, anyway!"

The Deputy reached and gripped the butt of his pistol. "Then what do you want?"

the noise from the Dollar saloon was loud through the open swinging doors, blending with the off-beat banging of a piano.

Seth turned and pulled the window's shade all the way down before answering. "I'm here to see my son,...and that gun won't help you none!"

The Deputy stared at him for a moment then removed his hand from the pistol. "Are you Greg's father?" And when Seth nodded, he went to the wall for the ring of keys. "Sheriff Gentry gave me strict orders nobody was allowed to see him," He sighed then. "But it ain't right, and it ain't right what they done to 'im, neither!" He opened the cellblock door and turned to look at Seth.

"I'm gonna be fired for this, Mister Mabry, I want you to know that! But there's things goin' on around here that I just can't stomach anymore!" He stared down at his boots for a moment then sighed. "You're not gonna like what you see, Sir, because I don't,...so come on in." He stood aside for Seth to move past him then followed as he went on to open Greg's cell.

"Take as long as you want, Mister Mabry."

"I'd like you to stay, too, young man!" He said tightly. "And I ain't askin'."

"I understand, Mister Mabry,...and I'll be glad to."

"I'll need some light." Nodded Seth, and the Deputy quickly lit one of the wall lanterns and entered the cell ahead of him.

Greg was laying on his side, his face to the brick wall,...and appeared to be sleeping....Sighing, Seth went to the bunk and gently rolled him onto his back.

"NOOO!" He yelled, his arms coming up to protect his already swollen, red, blue and purple-blotched face. "Leave me alone!" He screamed.

Seth grabbed the boy's flailing arms and held them. "It's daddy, Greg, I'm not gonna hurt you, son!"

"Daddy?" He gasped loudly, and then started crying as he reached up to hug his father,...and then continued to cry for another long minute, his trembling arms wrapped tightly around Seth's neck.

Once he had calmed down, Seth pushed him away enough to really see his face. "God Damn it!" He cursed. "My God, Son, who did this to you?"

Greg's face was unrecognizable, one side of his head and face was a puffy mass of red and purple bruises, his left eye was completely covered by the dark swelling,...and his right eye was open only a tiny bit as he cried.

"Tommy's dead, Daddy,...somebody killed him!"

"I know, son,...who did this to you?" And when Greg shook his head in obvious fear and peered up at the deputy. Seth looked up at him also.

"You know about this?"

"No, sir, I don't!...Sheriff Gentry just said I should watch 'im, and that's all!"

Seth nodded and looked back at Greg."What are you afraid of, son,...you have to tell me!"

"They'll come back and kill me, Daddy!" He sniffed.

"No, son,...they will not!...Now, who did this to you?"

"I,...I don't know who he was, Daddy,...but he was real big! They kept askin' me why I killed Tommy?...I tried to tell 'em I didn't, but they wouldn't believe me!...He just kept hittin' me, hard!...I couldn't take anymore, daddy!"

"They made you confess?" And when Greg nodded. "You see who killed your brother?"

Greg shook his head. "I think somebody put somethin' in my drink, daddy,...I passed out! I barely remember Tommy helpin' me outside!...I woke up in here!...What's gonna happen to me, daddy?"

Seth was seething with anger when he looked up at the wide-eyed Deputy. "If you know anything about this at all, you'd best tell me!"

"All I know is what th' Sheriff told me. But I think I might know who did this to 'im."

"Who?"

"They call 'im Butcher,...he works for Yancy McGuire over at the Commerce Theater and Whorehouse!"

"Butcher, huh?...Tell me this,...would your Sheriff happen to work for this Yancy, fella, too?"

The deputy shrugged. "I only know I don't!"

"H,...he was here, daddy." Said Greg as he winced in pain.

"The Sheriff was in here?...When, Son?"

"When I was beat up,...h,...he let 'im in! Will you get me out of here, Daddy?"

"I'll see about it, son,...but not tonight. I'll be back tomorrow, okay?"

"What if he comes back, daddy?...I had to tell 'em I did it, I couldn't take anymore!"

"He won't be back, son,...I promise! Now, you just lay here and rest, I'll bring a Doctor to see you tomorrow." Greg nodded and lay back down.

"I love you, son!" Said Seth grimly. "Everything's gonna be okay!" He stood then motioned the Deputy out and followed him.

CHAPTER FOUR

Back in the office, he turned and waited for the deputy to lock the cellblock, and when he came back toward the desk. "You got Greg's belongings, Deputy,...what do I call you anyway?"

"Name's Richard Hurd, Mister Mabry,...just call me Ricky, everybody does,...and, Sir,...I sure am sorry about all this!"

"I believe you, Richard. Now what about those belongings?"

"Yes, Sir!" He went around the desk and opened a bottom drawer, then removed Greg's gun-belt and pistol and placed it on the desk.

"That'll do." Said Seth and quickly unbuckled his own belt, placing the older Navy Colt percussion revolver on the desk, picked up Greg's new version and buckled it on. "He have any money on him?" He asked as he tied the holster to his leg.

"I don't know, there's none here."

He nodded and readjusted the gun rig on his hip. "I like this one better." He grinned then pulled the gun to check the loads. "Richard,...you might not ought a say anything about my bein' here tonight, not if you want a keep your job....Besides, your Sheriff will find out soon enough, I'm here!"

This job ain't that important to me anymore." Returned Hurd. "Not after today. But then again, as hard as times are right now, a job's a job!... But, if you're thinkin' of goin' up against Yancy McGuire's bunch, I got a tell you, he's a Syndicate Boss from New York City,...and there's two of 'em! His boss run's Ringerman's saloon and gambling parlor on Elm Street. Yancy does th' dirty work for 'im, rather, he has Butcher do it!...Him and that Mexican, Silva have beaten up lots of folks in town, especially when they don't pay up!"

"Pay up,...for what?"

"Protection Insurance!...Least that's what folks call it....I call it extortion!"

Seth nodded. "And of course, they can't go to th' law for justice!...Is there any honest law in Dallas at all?"

"I think so,...Rod Dempsey's an honest man, he's Town Marshal. But most of the City Councilmen are bein' paid off by McCleary,...he's Yancy's boss,...and they have pretty much tied th' Marshal's hands."

"What about the Army?"

"Wouldn't know about that!...But Dallas does have an honest Federal Judge, famous man, too!...But I don't think he meddles in th' town's business."

"Any others?"

"Sure, town's full of 'em,...but most are barely surviving, while th' rest are just afraid of McGuire."

"Makes a man wonder how it happened, don't it?"

"Money happened, Mister Mabry. Nobody had any, but when Allan McCleary came to town, he began bailin' folks out a debt!...They been under his thumb ever since, too."

"I want a thank you, Richard,...you're a lawman, and a good one I think. You damn sure didn't have to tell me all this,...but I do appreciate it!"

"I just wish I could do somethin' to fix it all?"

"Well, don't give up hope!" He sighed. "Nothin' lasts forever, no matter how bad it gets....There some place I can hold up till I'm done here, I got a lot to do, and no place to start?"

"Yes sir, there's several Hotels near by....A couple a roomin' houses, too!...And there's always th' Dollar Saloon, Mason Cooper's a friend a mine, and he's got rooms to let!...He's also not on McGuire's payroll!"

"That'll work!...Watch after Greg for me, will you?"

"I'll do my best,...but Sheriff Gentry will send me home in th' mornin'."

"When does th' good Sheriff get here?"

"Seven, seven thirty, usually."

"I'll be here at eight o'clock with a Doctor....Has Greg eaten anything?"

"Not today, Mister Mabry,...Sheriff said he wasn't to be fed."

"Son of a Bitch!" He sighed. "That'll change, too!...Do you know a good Doctor?"

"Doctor Mitchell." He nodded. "Got an office on Commerce,...next street over!"

Nodding, Seth looked sadly at the cellblock door then sighed. "Good night, Richard!"

"Good night, Sir,...and call me Rick!"

He opened the door and stepped out onto the boardwalk, hearing the bar dropped in place behind him as he studied the darkened street. Urgency was like a wolf gnawing at a bone in his gut, and he knew he had to start somewhere,…and grinning, he thought he knew exactly where….It was still fairly noisy at the Dollar Saloon across the way, he noted, but then again it was early yet and sighing, he crossed the sagging boardwalk and stepped down to pull the reins free,…and his mind was on something else as he pulled himself into the saddle. He reined the Buckskin around and into the street where he stopped another cowboy on horseback.

"Can you point me at th' Livery, friend?" And when he was told. "Much obliged!"

*   *   *

He urged the horse through the double doors and dismounted, spotting the dim light coming from the door of the tack-room and that's where he headed. The skinny little man was eating a plate of cold beans and crusty bread as he opened the door and looked in. "You th' Hostler?"

"That I am!" He grinned. "If ya need a stall, it'll be a dollar and six-bits a day, fifty cents extry for grain!"

"I'll take it!…Now,…how much to rent me th' whole place for one night?"

The Hostler almost choked as he swallowed, and when he was through coughing, stared at Seth almost numbly. "What?" He uttered hoarsely.

"I'll put it another way, old timer!…How much is this McGuire bunch takin' you for,…twenty-five, fifty dollars a month?"

"Twenty-five," He answered, still peering at him. "A week!…You work fer 'im, do ya, you come to collect?"

"No, sir, I do not work for 'im!…But I'll give you thirty dollars to let this place to me for th' night!"

"What are you, some kind a crazy Dickhead,…what you gonna do with it?"

He grinned at the old man's sarcasm then shook his head. "I don't know what a Dickhead looks like, old timer,…but I'm gonna use this place to meet with a gent,…and I'll need it to be a private meetin'!…And you'll have to do somethin' else for me, too!"

"Uh-huh,…and whut might that be?"

"Look up a friend a yours, that's all,…and tell 'im I want a see 'im."

"Ha!…only friend I got is a bar-fly named Gus!…So cut out th' horse-shit, why don'cha, and tell me what ya want?"

"Just what I told you,…I want you to go to that cathouse on Commerse Street and look up a man they call Butcher!"

"You what?" He Gasped. "I was right, you are a fuckin' Dickhead!…No way in hell, I'm gonna go anywhere close to that Fucker,…he's meaner'n shit, and twice as curly!...Uh-uh, I want no truck with 'at Fucker, Son a fa Bitch near-bout broke my arm, he did,...said he would, too, I didn't buy that God damn pertection insurance!"

"Old timer,...all you got a do is tell 'im I want a see 'im here at th' Livery?"

"Oh, is 'at all,...well just who th' hell are you?"

"Just tell 'im this, okay?" Seth breathed deeply then placed a foot inside the doorway and leaned his arm across his bent knee. "Tell 'im a man rode in here tonight,...and he was braggin' about seein' some fella stab a man last night! Tell 'im that man is still here drunk and passed out in a stall....He wants to know why you're tellin' him about it,...just tell 'im you don't want to get in trouble, or somethin', he'll believe you!"

"Do you have any idea what th' fuck you're a doin?...He's a fuckin' killer!"

"So am I, old man!" He reached in his shirt for the money and held it up in front of him.

"That's all I got a do fer thirty dollars?"

"In advance!" He nodded.

"You got a deal,...but it's your funeral!" The Hostler grabbed the money and counted it. "How long you want th' place for?"

"Just don't come back till mornin', old timer." He grinned. "Oh, one more thing,...I'll need a piece a stout wood, about four feet long." He added.

"Plenty a fence posts against th' wall back yonder."

"Thirty foot of chain?"

The old man peered at him with a puzzled look. "Outside wall aroun' there. What ya gonna do with chain?"

"Keep an animal from gettin' away,...got a lock and key?"

The Hostler continued to stare hard at him, but then a wide grin appeared on his lean face. "You gonna kill 'at Son a fa Bitch?"

He smiled and shook his head. "What you don't know, won't come back to hurt you, old man!...Just do what I told you, friend,...and don't come back here before mornin', you hear me?"

*   *   *

Leaving the light on in the tack room, he set about preparing for his company. He placed the lock and key in his pocket, took the chains he thought he would need and placed them on the floor beside the floor-to-roof support column, in the center of the dung covered barn's floor. Then he found some thick, but flexible pieces of old leather and cut thumb and finger holes in them before trimming away the excess,...he was ready!"

Picking up the three-foot length of petrified post, he moved to the dark side of the open doorway and leaned it against the wall before going to tie his horse to the first stall. Then checking the barn's interior again, he was satisfied as he went back to the dark side of the door, sat down on a bale of hay and then waited.

It was most of an hour before he heard the approaching horse fleetingly hoping it was him and not someone else. After all, he had not thought about the fact, that the stables was a place of business and was open to anyone!

He breathed a sigh of relief, however when the large horse and rider came into the dim light from the tack-room, and almost gasped aloud at his size when the giant dismounted in the doorway, stood for a minute to look around then hitched up his pants and walked inside. Spying the saddled horse, Butcher had just started toward the stall when his lights went out! Seth swung the length of hard wood at the man's head as hard as he could, hearing the dull crack as Butcher went to his knees first, then fell forward in the dung and hay,

Unable to move the man's weight, he went to his saddle and shook out the rope, tying it around Butcher's thick torso, then brought the Buckskin over and tied the rope to the saddle-horn and allowing the horse to drag the body to the center column…and fifteen minutes later, the Butcher was sitting with his back to the thick post, with thirty-odd feet of chain locked around his upper arms, body and the column. Breathing hard from his efforts, Seth straightened and looked down at the man as he thought of how strong he must be,…and sighing again, went to tug an old crosstie across the room and slide it across Butcher's outstretched legs….It took even more chain, but he tied the man's thick, lower arms to the crosstie, palms down then satisfied, went out to bring the other horse inside and close the heavy doors.

He had never seen a man quite that large before, he thought as he looked down at him,…and thinking he might still be stout enough to move the crosstie, grabbed more chain and tied the crosstie to his legs and thighs,… and breathing deeply of the smelly air, he picked up a pail and went to dip water from a barrel, came back and dumped it on the giant's head.

"Wh,…what th' fuck is this?" Sputtered Butcher angrily, then tried to lift his arms up from the heavy railroad tie. "Get these fuckin' chains off a me, God damn it, I'll tear your fuckin' heart out!…Who th' hell are you,… you tie me up like this?"

Seth grinned at him as he pulled the pieces of leather over his hands, and without a word, slowly walked over to the glaring giant, leaned over him and hit him as hard as he could in the face and with his left hand, he hit him again.

"OWWWW, God damn it!...I'll kill you, man!" He roared, and then spat blood from his mouth as he groaned and heaved mightily at his bounds again.

"That was my son in that jail cell, you piece of shit!" He yelled, and then hit him again in the eye, then again, then began raining blow after blow to the man's shaggy face, beating him until his beady eyes began to close on him....And still breathing hard, Seth straddled the giant's legs and continued to rain blows to his face until Butcher's thick lips were a cut, and bloody mass of flesh.

"No Son of a Bitch beats my son like that!" He yelled and puffing hard, hit him again. "If he does," He puffed. "He won't do it but once!" He backed away from him then to get his breath, and after a minute walked back to the tack-room, picked up the iron mallet and came back to stare down at the gasping Butcher.

"You know what I ought a do with this thing, man?" He asked as Butcher spied the hammer and whimpered, having to lean his head backward to be able to see it with his puffy eyes. "I ought a beat your lousy head to a pulp with this thing, but I won't!...I ain't gonna kill you, man, but I God damn sure want to!...No, I'm just gonna do this!" He suddenly swung the mallet and crushed the bones in Butcher's ham-like hands, first one then the other, hearing him scream and cry like some woman might.

Breathing hard again, he dropped the sledge on the floor and waited until Butcher regained some composure. "Now, if I was you, big man," He panted weakly, stooping to loosen the chains around his arms and legs. "While I still had good legs,...I would walk my nasty ass right out a Dallas and keep goin'!" He moved around him and opened the lock to let the chains dangle loose.

"Cause if you don't, somebody's liable to just finish what I started, you bein' th' likeable fella you are,...cause I hear you made a lot a friends here!... And think about this too, while you're at it!...You ain't no good to your Mister Yancy McGuire anymore, you got no hands, and besides,...I'm gonna have me a little talk with him, too!" He was still breathing a little heavy as he stared down at the man.

"But it's up to you, man, I collected my debt!" He laughed then as he went to open the doors again and come back. "But it was me, I'd be some worried! You must know a lot about McGuire's business, and I'm willin' to bet he wouldn't want you talkin' too much!" Still grinning, he coiled and replaced the rope on his saddle, mounted and reined the Buckskin around to look down at the killer as he pulled the pieces of leather from his hands and dropped them.

"By th' way, Mister Butcher! If you don't leave, and I see you again,...I'll kill you myself!" He turned the Buckskin and rode out of the barn, leaned to close the heavy door behind him, then galloped back toward town.

         *   *   *

"Come in, Lad!" Nodded Allan McCleary when Yancy was let in by the half-naked, young woman. "Rebecca, bring us a bottle of me Irish whiskey my love, then leave us alone." She quickly went to the small bar along the wall, took bottle and glasses from it and brought them to his desk.

"Thank you, me darlin'." He smiled then ran his hand seductively along her naked bottom as she turned away. "Stay in the bedroom, Darlin!" He laughed wickedly as she suddenly began crying and ran from the room. "And clean yourself, Love!" He yelled after her,...then shaking his head with a smile, looked back at his cohort, and friend and smiled even wider at Yancy's expression.

Yancy McGuire watched the very young girl leave in her flowing, see-through nightgown, then shook his head sadly and sat down across the desk from McCleary as his boss poured their drinks. "Where did you find the lovely, Allan?"

"Oh, you can stop drooling, lad,...that one is not for your stable of whores." He grinned widely again. "This young lovely, I will keep for myself,...your Mister Silva brought her to me this afternoon! It seems she is the daughter of the good Reverend Muenster in Lewisville, don't ye know?... And pray, do not be angry with your Mister Silva, I ask him to find me a young woman suitable for a man in my position....Now, me friend,...what brings you here so late on a Sunday night?"

Yancy tossed off his drink and placed the glass down. "We just might be having a problem, Allan,...Mister Butcher is missing!"

"Missing,...and how do you know this?"

"Me Bartender,...He said a man came into my place and spoke with him, and shortly after that, he left without a word to anyone!"

"Ahhh, Yancy,...I would not worry too much. I am acquainted with your Mister Butcher, and I am truly satisfied that the man can take care of himself!"

"This is true, and I know it!" He nodded. "Still, I have a feeling about it, Allan. He has been gone for more than two hours, and the Butcher is a man who will do nothing unless he tells me first."

"Two hours ago, me boy,...you were here with me going over the books."

"Yes,…I was!…That is why I have a bad feeling about it. Whatever this man told him, it must be something he thought he had to take care of himself, since I was not there!"

"Then what be your feeling, lad?" He sighed, reaching to pour more whiskey into their glasses.

"For one thing, Allan,…it be too soon after the death of the young cowboy last night….I am thinking it could be revenge!…Butcher beat the younger lad pretty bad to make him confess this morning."

"I see," He mused. "Do you have people looking for Mister Butcher?"

"Silva." He nodded.

"Then I would not worry, me good friend,…Silva is a very thorough enforcer."

"Yes,…he most certainly is, and I'm sure he will find him!" Draining his glass, Yancy got up. "I will go now, Allan,…thank you for the drink, me friend."

"As always, the pleasure is mine, dear boy,…but do keep me informed?… And Yancy,…I do not believe I have ever seen you worried about anything,…is this all that be bothering you, lad?"

"It's nothing, Allan,…just me feeling about all this. They be people who saw Mister Silva and me follow the two cowboys out that night."

"But did anyone see you kill him?"

"No,…I don't believe so,…Mister Silva was watching the street."

"Then you have no problem, lad,…and do not worry, Mister Butcher will show up, and you will see how foolish you are, and Yancy, lad,…thank you for telling me this?"

*   *   *

After having taken time to eat a hot meal, it was late by the time Seth rode up to the hitch-rail, and after studying the dark faces of several men in the light from the saloon's large windows, he dismounted and tied his horse,…and with another look along the long boardwalk, turned and scanned the busy street before climbing the steps to the walkway then stopping to study the men along the outside wall again before walking across to the swinging doors where he pushed inside to stand and survey the small crowd in the room for a minute more before shouldering his way to the bar.

Leaning on the long, polished counter-top, he once again scrutinized the room noting that most of the tables were occupied, some were gambling, others just talking and drinking, and satisfied he had drawn no attention to his self turned his eyes to study the men along the bar for a minute.

"What'll it be, Gent?" Came a man in an apron from behind the bar.

"Mason Cooper?" He returned.

The man eyed him narrowly for a moment then leaned closer. "You workin' for McGuire, Mister,...cause if you are, he ain't available?"

"I work for myself, friend!...And I'd like to talk with Mister Cooper."

The bartender eyed him a moment longer before he nodded his head at the end of the bar. "Door at the end, there, come on, I'll see you in."

Pushing away from the bar, Seth moved along behind the patrons and met the man at a door marked, Office and waited while the bartender knocked.

"Wait here!" Said the man and went inside to close the door behind him....After a couple of minutes, he came out again and held the door open for Seth to enter.

Mason Cooper was a man in his mid-fifties, almost six feet tall in his black pants and walking shoes. His shirt was white, and his vest was also black. His face was not what one would call fleshy, and the mustache was not too large for the friendly smile he flashed.

"Come in, sir and have a seat?" He smiled, turning a chair around for him then watched as Seth nodded and sat down. "Now,...who am I talking too?" He asked as he held out his hand. "I'm Mason Cooper!"

"Seth Mabry." He replied as he shook Cooper's hand.

"I see,...You kin of that boy in jail?"

"He's my son." Nodded Seth.

"Then you have my condolences for your loss, Sir!...I'll never know what turns brothers against each other that way."

"My son did not kill his brother, Sir!" Grated Seth.

"But, I heard he confessed?"

"It was beaten out of him!" He sighed heavily then. "Greg would have confessed to killin' Lincoln, if they'd told 'im to!...No, Sir,...Greg said his drink was messed with,...he was out cold when his brother was killed!"

"That sounds like McCleary,...were they gambling?"

Seth nodded. "His brother was,...at th' Casino!"

"Then he was probably winning a little too heavy." Sighed Cooper. "Don't get me wrong, Mister Mabry, I'm not laying accusations on anyone in particular....It's just a mite suspicious, mind you!...Your other son,...did he tell you who beat him?"

"Fellow named Butcher!"

"I might have known!...That is one vile, beast of a man!...So, what can I do for you, Mister Mabry?"

"First off, Mister Cooper,...I need a room for a few days, young Deputy Hurd tells me you ain't on this Yancy fella's payroll, so I figure you for a man I can trust!"

"Ricky's a good boy," Nodded Cooper. "He's right, too!...I've had several run in's with Mister McGuire!"

"Then maybe you can tell me how men like that can get so much control over a town and th' people in it,...where's th' law in all this?"

"In their hip pocket, that's where!...Only decent lawman we got anymore is Rod Dempsey, and his hands are tied!" He sighed heavily then. "I have tried to sway the rest of the City Council to allow him to do his job, but I'm always out voted!...And before you ask, yes,...They're all under McGuire's thumb!...I'm the minority."

"Does this Rod Dempsey know what's happenin' here?"

"Of coarse he does, and he tries to do something,...but every time he does, he's threatened with being fired! The City Marshal's job is under the control of the City Council,...we hired him to do the job, and now we won't let him do it!"

"Then I'm on my own, looks like."

"On your own?...I don't understand."

"It's simple," Sighed Seth, shifting his weight in the chair. "I aim to prove my son didn't kill his brother!"

"Oh, I see!...Mister Mabry, Be it far from me to offer any advice,... but McGuire and McCleary have got the Mayor, and the Sheriff on their payroll,...and you had ought to be careful!...Yancy McGuire is a killer from back East, although he doesn't have to get his hands dirty any more,...he's got Butcher and that Mexican, Silva to do his dirty work for him!"

"Well I don't think Mister Butcher will be givin' folks any trouble for a while!" He grinned. "As a matter of fact, I think he might a left town."

"Where did you hear that?" He gasped with surprise.

"Told me his self!...Mister Cooper,...I'm here to prove my son's innocence, and I aim to do just that!...But I'm gonna need a friend or two in Dallas, folks I can depend on....Can you be one of 'em?"

Mason Cooper eyed him narrowly for a minute then nodded his head. "I can, and I will!!...Sometimes it takes an outsider to do this sort of thing,... but you are biting off a large chunk of trouble, Mister Mabry!"

"Seth, sir,...call me Seth!...Now how about this Dempsey,...can he be trusted?"

"Marshal Dempsey?...I trust him, yes, his deputies, too!"

"Then I'd like to talk with 'im, to be sure?"

"I can have him here in the morning, if you like?"

"No, Sir,...I'll go see 'im tomorrow, him comin' here could draw attention. What I would like, though, is for you to have a Doctor meet me at th' Sheriff's office tomorrow mornin', say eight o'clock?"

"Consider it done, Seth!...Now, other than something like that, I don't know how much help I can be to you,...I'm not much of a fighting man any more,...I guess I care a lot more about living than I used to....Anyway, I have grown soft!"

"Appears you earned that right, Sir,...and I would not ask you to fight, it's my son that was killed! In fact, Sir,...fighting is somethin' I ain't done in eighteen years, and it's also somethin' I ain't crazy about doin' now!...But I'm owed,...and I will collect!...But I do want a thank you, Mister Cooper!...Now, how about that room?"

*   *   *

He was awake early, and pouring water from the pitcher into a cracked, well-used crock basin then with a towel, washed his body before getting dressed. Looking around the room he buckled on the gun belt and tied it to his leg then opened the door to look out along the hallway,...and seeing no one closed the door behind him and went to the railing overlooking the saloon's main floor. There was a man with a large straw-broom sweeping up last night's debris, while yet another man was behind the bar washing shot-glasses and beer mugs. But there was no sign of Mason Cooper anywhere.

Sighing, he turned and walked the length of the hall and out onto the second story stoop, looked up and down the alley then descended the outside stairs to the ground and leisurely walked to the end of the building then down the side alley to the boardwalk,...and without losing any momentum, leaped up to the walkway and grunted as he all but ran into a slender Mexican that was stepping down onto the lower walkway,...the near miss causing the smaller man to almost trip on his own feet.

"Sorry amigo,...I didn't see you!" Grinned Seth apologetically.

The Mexican glared hatefully at him, his dark eyes flashing,...and for a second he thought the man was going to draw on him.

"I said I was sorry, amigo!" He repeated as he met the man's angry stare,...and his own hand was only an inch away from the Navy Colt on his hip. "What's it gonna be, friend, I said I was sorry?"

"You watch where you go, Gringo!" Said the Mexican and pointed a finger at him,...and that gesture made Seth angry.

"Or what,...Amigo!"

"Or, Silva will kill you!" With that, the Mexican turned and walked on down the walkway.

"Touchy Son of a Bitch!" He said aloud then shook his head and walked on across the boardwalk and down into the street, but then got mad at himself when he saw his Buckskin at the hitch-rail with drooping head.

Shaking his head angrily, he stopped momentarily to turn and look for the Mexican along the boardwalk, but he was nowhere to be seen. So that was Silva, he thought, remembering Mister Hurd as saying McGuire and Silva brought Greg to jail that night. Maybe he should have a talk with him about all this?...And sighing, he turned back and continued on to his horse.

"I forgot all about you, old son." He said as he walked up, and then grinned when he received a responsive greeting from the thirsty animal. He pulled the reins loose and led the horse to a watering trough pumped fresh water into it then checked his watch while the animal drank.

Seven o'clock, he thought as he mounted and clucked the Buckskin down the street toward the Sheriff's office, but then, thinking it a bit too early to call on the man decided to have a good breakfast and wait for the Doctor to arrive. He reined the animal over to the hitchrail and dismounted in front of the small Cantina, and as he tied his horse, stared for a minute at the two horses at the hitch rail in front of the lawman's office before climbing the steps and opening the door.

The first person he saw on entering the small eatery was the old Hostler from the stables, and grinned as he watched him wolf down his steak and eggs, and then studied the other patrons as he walked over to stop at the old man's table.

"Hey there, old timer!" He grinned, placing a hand on the man's bony shoulder,...and causing the Hostler to jerk in surprise.

"Huh,...oh, yeah,...Ho,...how you doin' man?" He grinned toothily.

"I'm well, old timer....I just wanted to thank you for last night, you done real good!...You been to th' stable yet,...everything okay?"

"Uh-huh, yeah," He grinned. "You left th' doors open!"

"Oh, no,...I closed th' doors when I left,...your friend likely left 'em open....He was gone, right?"

The old man quickly looked around at the other guests before nodding. "Oh, yeah, he was gone,...but th' God damn doors was wide open!"

"Was that a problem?"

"Hell, yeah, 'at's a problem,...town's full a crooks, 'at's th' problem!"

"I never thought a that!" He shrugged. "Anything missin', you know of?"

"Nope,...none I could tell!" He leaned toward Seth then, and after looking around. "Weren't nobody there,...So I cleaned up real good, nobody knows nothin'!"

"In that case, I want a warn you not to talk to anybody about it, it'll be just like it never happened,...like I was never there!...Do we understand each other?"

"You got my word on it, Mister!" He nodded. "But now I got a warn you about somethin'!" He leaned closer to Seth again. "A Spick name a Silva is out lookin' fer th' Butcher,…they're Cronies, ya know,…and that Mex is a mean Son a fa Bitch, so you best watch 'im,…he throws a knife!"

"I already met 'im, but thanks, I'll remember that!…Think you can take my horse down to the stables and grain 'im for me?" He took three silver dollars from his pocket and dropped them on the table.

"Yep,…soon's I get done!"

"Much obliged, he's at th' hitch-rail, Buckskin!" He nodded and moved on to an empty table leaving the little man to finish a steak that looked bigger than he was. Shaking his head, he grinned and sat down, thinking that the Hostler seemed a little jumpy for some reason, but guessed he was just a little afraid.

Ordering a meager dish of eggs, potatoes, sausage and coffee, he finished it in short order,…and when the girl brought him fresh coffee, ordered the same breakfast for Greg, telling the waitress he would wait on the boardwalk out front,…and after she promised to bring it out when ready, he walked outside to smoke and watch for the Doctor to arrive.

He was sitting on the boardwalk with legs dangling,…and was on his second smoke when he spotted the black carriage rounding a corner at the end of the block and got to his feet. Flipping the spent butt into the already busy street, he was about to reenter the café when the girl came out with the tray,…and promising to return it, he took the tray and walked across, then down the street just as the Doctor was stepping out of his buggy.

"Doctor?" He queried as he walked up.

"Why, yes,…I'm Doctor Mitchell. Do I know you, Sir?"

"Name's Seth Mabry, thank you for coming." They shook hands and he went on to knock at the office door,…and when it opened, quickly pushed past the startled Deputy and into the office.

"Heyy!" Blurted the lawman. "You can't bust in here like that!"

"It's okay, Jordan!" Said the medium-built, almost short man as he stood up behind his desk. "What's goin' on here, Doc?" He asked quickly. "Who sent for you?"

"I did!" Said Seth in return.

"Well, who th' hell are you?"

"Name's Seth Mabry, Sheriff,…that's my son you helped beat up yesterday mornin', and I'm havin' a Doctor treat 'im!"

"Th' hell you are,…that killer don't get no Doctor!…No visitors, neither, especially you!"

Seth's jaw tightened at the insinuation, but fought down the anger and stared at the lawman for a minute. "Sheriff,…I'm a pissed-off man right now!...You threw my son in jail and then you let a man twice his size beat 'im half to death,...now in my mind that was th' wrong thing to do, Mister, and it's somethin' we're gonna have to talk about!...Now, will you open that cell block door,...or shall we have your deputy do it,...don't matter none to me?"

"Nobody opens that door!" Spat the Sheriff angrily. "Not for you, not for anybody!...And you know what I think, I think you know where th' victim's body is, too,...and that's called tamperin' with evidence!...Now, you want a tell me about that, do ya?"

"That victim was my oldest son, Sir,...not evidence, and he's home now,...we buried him there!"

"You're under arrest!" Growled Gentry and streaked his hand for the gun on his hip, but immediately froze and in wide-eyed disbelief, suddenly found himself looking down the cannon-like bore of the forty-four pistol. Breathing deeply, he released his grip on the gun and quickly raised his hands.

Gritting his teeth to quell his anger, Seth nodded grimly."Tell your deputy to drop his gun belt, Sheriff,...and do it now, Sir,...I'm about two seconds away from shooting your sorry ass!"

"Do what he says, Jordan!" He stammered his wide eyes still fastened on the drawn pistol. "You won't get away with this, Mabry!"

"Seem's I already have!...Now, pull off that gun belt and put it on th' desk." Once the lawman obeyed, he motioned with the pistol. "Now, come on around here you asshole and open that door!" He backed up a step to let him pass then looked at the Deputy.

"Jordan, is it?...Bolt that front door and move over here by your boss!" Once he complied, he ushered them both inside then nodded at the Doctor to follow them.

"Open th' cell door, Sheriff, and both of you go inside." He went in ahead of the Doctor who quickly went to where Greg was sitting up on his bunk.

"Somebody light a lantern." Breathed the Doctor as he looked closely at Greg's face.

"Do it Jordan!" Ordered Seth then watched him as he went out for the lantern, lit it then came back in. "Give th' Doctor some light."

"Who did this to this boy?" Gasped the Medic as he examined Greg's very discolored, and swollen face.

"Ask our friendly Sheriff here." Returned Seth. "He played with his self while it was bein' done!"

"Is that right, Gaylon,...you condoned this?"

"I didn't condone any fuckin' thing!" Growled the lawman.

"No, he didn't!" Grinned Seth. "He just followed orders and watched!"

"Well, get everyone out of here, Mister Mabry,…I'm gonna be a while!"

He went to place the tray of food on one end of the bunk then motioned with his pistol again. "You heard th' man, get your asses back in th' office, we got us some talkin' to do!" He followed them back into the front and made them sit down then holstered the pistol and walked to the window to peer out at the street.

"Who killed my son, Sheriff?" He queried as he rolled and lit another smoke.

"Your other son, that's who!"

"Now, we both know you're lyin' to me, and I'll tell you somethin'. I hate liars!...Now, who killed my boy?"

"Your son did!" He spat.

"You know he didn't do it!" Said Seth tightly. "And so do I,…you know how I know?...Butcher told me, you remember him, don't you,…you stood in that cell in there and watched 'im half kill my son, you sack of shit!"

"You don't even know th' Butcher!" Stuttered the lawman.

"Sure I do,…I beat 'im half to death last night, and you know what else,…he was happy to tell me all about it! So now, th' question is,…am I gonna have to do th' same to you?...Think you can outlast my boy in there before you confess? You will confess, you know, cause I'll beat ya till you do, just like you allowed Butcher to do!...And because he did that, Mister Butcher,…well, let's just say, he'll never hurt anybody anymore!"

"You,…you killed him?"

"You'll never make me confess, Sheriff!" He shrugged. "But no, not quite! He just saw the error of his ways and left town. Said he might even go to Church!...Yeah,…I think we both know who killed my son, and all I got a do now is find out why?...And when I do, I'm gonna kill th' Son of a Bitch, just like I would a snake!" He shrugged then and shook his head.

"Damn, you're good, Sheriff, I just confessed!...Well,…you know I can't leave any witnesses, now!" He shrugged again. "I didn't want it to come to this, neither."

"What are you gonna do, Mabry?" Blurted the lawman. "You can't kill a Sheriff, Texas Rangers'll hunt you down!"

"I don't think so,…not after Mister Yancy McGuire tells 'em it was you who done it, and not him,…and we both know it was him!...Don't we?" He watched Gentry's face make a change then from one of hostility and surliness, to one of helplessness and futility. The man seemed to shrink in stature right before his eyes.

Gentry looked at him then and nodded. "Yeah, we do, Mabry….It was either him, or Silva that done it, maybe both of 'em…they both brought your boy over here."

"How could you let somethin' like this happen, man,…folks depended on you?"

"McGuire owns me, Mabry!" He sighed. "They wouldn't hesitate to murder my whole family if I refused to take orders!"

"What happened to you, man?"

"I was losin' everything we had to th' bank three years ago," He sighed. "I was dead broke,…owed th' bank more than my holdings was worth! Then, Mister McGuire walked in here one mornin' and dropped my paid in full notes on my desk, said that now I could pay him back, instead a th' bank,…and that I could do it when I could, with no penalties or deadlines!… Only, I didn't know that the interest was goin' to double and triple each month. Hell, it wasn't long till I owed th' Bastard four times what I owed th' bank!"

"How'd you come to work for 'im?"

"He came in one day with that, Butcher, and his sidekick Silva. Told me I could erase my interest charges by working for him when they needed me, you know, do 'em favors!…They said that I really had no choice in the matter,…said Butcher and Silva would make my family disappear without a trace!…He gave me a contract to sign,…and I signed it!"

"God damn it, Man!" Cursed Seth going back to peer out of the window again. Then sighing, he turned around to look at the silent Deputy. "What about you, you in hock to th' Fucker, too?" And when Jordan nodded. "Jesus, God!"

"They pretty much run th' town, Mister Mabry," Continued Gentry. "They got me, Grant Richards, and damn near all th' Town Council in their pocket!…I had no choice but to take their word for it and lock your boy up!… McGuire dropped a bloody knife on my desk and some money with blood on it, said it was evidence th' boy knifed his brother….I put 'im in a cell and they left,…said to come tell 'em when he woke up!"

"And that was when,…when did he wake up?"

"Bout daylight yesterd'y mornin'. So when I got here, I sent Jordan there to tell 'em."

"That when they beat 'im up?"

Gentry nodded. "They brought a Lawyer with 'em to make his statement legal, and made me watch th' whole thing to bear witness."

"God damn you, man!" He voiced loudly. "This kind a shit makes me want a kill your sorry ass, both of ya!…Your're th' law, for Christ sakes, you could a stopped this bunch three years ago!"

"Maybe I could a stopped it," Sighed Gentry. "But, I didn't!...And after a while, it was easier just to do what they wanted!...Weren't much two men could do to stop 'em, anyway, Mabry,...and you ain't gonna do it by yourself, neither!...You might a killed Butcher, but they got twenty guns workin' for 'em, and Silva,...well that Bastard can cut a man up in a heartbeat!" He looked up at Seth then with tears in his eyes. "I didn't want a be murdered, man,...and I didn't want my family killed!...They're gonna kill you, too, ya know,...you and your son!"

"Well, that boy in there is my family,...so was th' boy they murdered!... And Mister Sheriff, come hell or high water, I'm here to collect for it!"

"Well, Sir," Sighed Gentry wilting in his chair as he looked down at his badge. "I'm sorry as hell for your pain,...and your loss,...but all I can do about it is this." He tore the badge from his vest and tossed on the floor. "I ain't been a law man in nearly three years!...And I ain't been a man since I was forced to frame an innocent man for th' Ringermans!" He dropped his head down on folded arms and sobbed brokenly for a minute.

Seth shook his head and wondered just what he'd gotten himself into? How could a gang of killers get such a stranglehold on a town as large as Dallas, but he knew the answer,...it was the Depression the country was in. There was no money, and as it was now, McGuire was taking what money some of them could earn away from them!...And with the law, and the Courts in their pocket they were getting away with it! He gritted his teeth then. Somebody had to put a stop to it, but how? Maybe he could get some real proof of what they were doing, maybe then the Army would step in?"

He sighed heavily then, knowing that would have to wait! He had to clear Greg first, and then get him to safety,...but after that, Mister McGuire was going to pay for Tommy's death with his own,...of that one thing, he was certain! He was pulled from his thoughts then as the Doctor came back into the room.

How is he, Doc?" He asked anxiously.

Doctor Mitchell shook his head. "Well, Sir,...I have never seen a boy that young, beaten that badly and live!...But He'll eventually be all right I think. Right now though, he's spooked pretty bad,...but he is eating the food you brought, and that's a good sign."

"Thank you, Doctor,...now I'm gonna need your help again, if that's okay?"

"I guess so, what's going on?"

Seth looked at Gentry's tear-stained face and made up his mind. "You got a wagon, Mister Gentry?"

"Yeah, I got a wagon." He whispered. "Why?"

"I'm gonna give you a choice here, that's why,…one you don't deserve, by th' way!…But I want you out a my way,…so, I want you to get up from there right now and go home, load your family up in that wagon and get 'em th' hell out a Dallas! Take 'em anywhere you think they'll be safe and stay with 'em,…there's gonna be hell to pay around here!…That's th' choice you got, Sheriff!"

Nodding, Gentry got up and came around to face him. "Thanks, Mabry!" He muttered and then nodding again, looked sadly at each of them and left.

"What is going on here?" Queried Doctor Mitchell.

"I'm gonna ask you a question first, Doc, and it might make you mad!… Are you on Yancy McGuire's payroll?"

"I am not!…Is that what,…Don't tell me Gaylon was?"

"I'm afraid so." Nodded Seth. "Deputy Jordan there, too! Where do you stand now, Mister Jordan.…you want a leave town, too?"

"I've wanted out for a long time, Mister Mabry,…but without help, I couldn't bring myself to quit!" He shrugged then. "What can I do to help you?"

"If you're serious, buckle on that gun belt, son,…but if you're not, I can kill you, remember that!"

"Mister Mabry," Interrupted the Doctor. "Surely, you're not planning on taking on that Syndicate all by yourself,…Yancy McGuire has twenty gunmen on his payroll. Men that are dangerously notorious!…You won't stand a chance, Sir!"

Seth looked at the floor and sighed. "I won't if I don't try, Doc." He looked back at him then. "They murdered my son, Sir, It was either Yancy McGuire, or that Puke of a Silva, but they used a knife on him, and now I'm gonna use one on him! It's just that simple, an eye for an eye, Doc,…that's what th' good book says!"

"You'll have to fight that whole bunch, you know that?"

"Yes, sir, I do!"

"Then God bless you, son,…now, what can I do?"

"Mister Jordan," He said, watching the deputy tie his holster to his leg. "Would you please help my son in here, and be gentle with 'im, please?"

"Name's Jordan Hicks, Mister Mabry, and I'll be glad to!…And I know somebody else who can help us, too."

"Richard?"

"Richard Hurd, yes, sir,…you know 'im?"

"I was here last night." He nodded. "He got a family here?"

"Neither one of us."

"That's good to know." He grinned. "Army's are built, one man at a time,...now get Greg, okay?" When Jordan went back into the cellblock, he turned back to the Doctor. "Doc, I hear the Town Marshal is a good man, you know 'im?"

"Rod Dempsey?...Of course, I know him. He is a good man, a true Lawman, why?"

"I'm gonna put Greg in his care till this is over, and I'll need you to drive us there in your buggy, and if you don't mind, stay while I have a talk with him?"

"I will be glad to do that!" He nodded. "Besides, Rod Dempsey could just be the ally you need!"

CHAPTER FIVE

Allen McCleary got up from his chair as Yancy and Silva told him the news, and as he listened he took a fat cigar from his desk and lit it.

"Where did you find him, exactly, Mister Silva?"

"No more than one half mile from the stables, Hefe,…in the yard of a Gringo!"

"Would that be Jenson's Stables, Lad?" Queried McCleary incredulously.

"Si, Hefe,…on Main Street!…The Butcher was murdered, Hefe,…his face was mashed like a bug, and his rope was around his neck!…He was dragged behind his cabayo!" He said viciously. "He was murdered!"

"That be quite obvious, Lad." Nodded, McCleary with a sigh. "But by who, was he murdered?"

"No, Allan," Returned Yancy. "Who be they?…No one man can do what was done to Butcher!…Me thinks it was revenge,…he was a very mean man, ye know!"

"Aye,…and I know it well, Lad,…and I know about revenge all too well. But if these men were going to kill him, why beat him that badly?"

"The Cabrones broke his hands, Hefe!"

"That be making my point, Lads!" He sighed. "But you be right, too,… it was revenge,…but a bit more than that, too, I think!…No, our Mister Butcher was made to suffer greatly for his crimes, he was not meant to die!… The man, or men who did this vile thing to his hands did not kill him, Lads, they only wanted him to be helpless, to suffer,…that be why he was beaten so badly!"

"I do not follow you, Allan." Returned McGuire. "What are you saying?"

"I be saying that perhaps these men did not kill Mister Butcher!" He sighed, rolling the cigar around in his mouth before gesturing with his hands. "Perhaps someone else came along to finish the job, after he was beaten,...after all, lads, he was helpless to defend himself?...Now tell me, have you though of that?"

"No, Allan, I have not!...What I be saying is that I do not understand how this can be,...the Butcher could whip a dozen men, the likes of what be in Dallas!...No man has ever even dared to complain about the man!"

"That be because alone, they are afraid!...No lads, this deed was done to send us a message,...someone else killed Mister Butcher, Yancy, I be convinced of that!...Do ye know where he might have gone last night?"

"Si, Hefe!" Interrupted Silva, before McGuire could respond. "He went to the stables!"

"That be right." Nodded Yancy. "According to me bartender, the man from the stables came in and talked with Butcher, then they both left."

"Again, are we talking of our Mister Jenson?"

"Si, Hefe,...Jenson's stables."

"Have you spoken with Mister Jenson about this?"

"We have, Allan. It seems that a stranger rode in there very drunk last night. Mister Jenson says that this man was saying that he saw what I did to the cowboy Saturday night,...and that was when he came straight to tell Butcher,...after the man passed out of course."

"And you believe him, do ye,...could he be afraid to tell the truth?"

"He is more afraid to lie, Hefe!" Smiled Silva. "He knows I will kill him!"

"Mister Jenson says he did not return to the stables until this morning." Continued Yancy. "And he says the man was gone and there be no sign of Butcher. The little man is much too old and weak to lie about such a thing!"

McCleary nodded. "Then this drunken stranger be the man we have to find, because he was obviously not drunk at all,...and he obviously had help waiting for Mister Jenson to leave. But how did the stranger know of what you did to this cowboy, if he did not see you?...And he obviously knew that Mister Jenson would be frightened enough to come and tell someone!...But why Mister Butcher and not you, me friend,...Mister Butcher was not there with you?"

"Because I was here with you, Allan,...and Mister Butcher obviously thought he could take care of this man for me,...and with Mister Silva also away, he went to the stables alone!" He shrugged then. "That be my only explanation, Allan."

"And a most logical one, dear friend." Sighed Allan, clamping the cigar in his teeth as he thought over the situation, and after a minute he took the cigar from his mouth and peered at them.

"Lads," He sighed loudly. "We must put every man we have on this,... someone in this great city has to know who did this terrible thing!...And when you find them, I want them brought here to me,...we must make an example of them and send a message of our own!...Otherwise, it will only beget more of the same, as it did many times before in New York City! But tell me, lads,...do you believe this just might be all because of what we did to this young cowboy,...and of course his brother?"

"Yes, Allan!" Nodded McGuire. "I do believe that, and it be what I have said!"

McCleary nodded. "Mister Silva,...I would like to speak with our good friend, Sheriff Gentry, would you arrange that, please?...I would also like to speak with our dear friend, Judge McAllester!" He watched the slender killer leave then reached to pour two glasses of Irish whiskey before giving one to McGuire.

"What is your plan, Allan?"

"It is quite obvious to me," Sighed McCleary. "We have that cowboy's kin to deal with here,...and whoever they are, they are quite capable of doing us damage,...they have proven that!...We must bring whoever they are into the open, and the only way to accomplish that, be with the brother our Sheriff has in custody. I am going to have the Judge set the Court date, and the hanging for this Thursday. That should make his kin show their hand.... Now drink up, lad, you have work to do!"

*   *   *

Roderick Dempsey looked up from his desk as Deputy Marshal Jake Tulane opened the door. Doctor Mitchell entered first then Seth and Jordan Hicks, with their arms around Greg to half carry him through the door.

"Hello, Doc," Smiled Dempsey as he stood and came around his desk. "What have you brought me, Sir?" He shook the Doctor's hand and then eyed Seth as him and Jordan eased Greg down into one of the chairs.

"Well, Roderick,...This man is Mister Seth Mabry, and the injured boy is his son, Greg,...and he has a problem!"

Dempsey turned and shook Seth's hand as he studied him. "Mabry," He mused. "That was your son that was killed the other night?"

And when Seth nodded. "My condolences, Sir!" He then looked at the bandaged head and face of Greg and then back at Seth. "Is this the Accused?"

"Yes, Sir, he is," Nodded Seth grimly. "And he didn't kill his brother!"

"I heard he confessed," Sighed Dempsey. "But I think I can see why." He nodded. "This has got to be the Butcher's handiwork,...am I right?"

"That it is, Sir,...and Mister Hicks here will testify to that!"

Dempsey sighed again as he looked each of them in the eyes. "Why are you here, Mister Mabry?" He asked as he looked back at him. "I know nothing about your boy's case,...and why is Deputy Hicks here, where's Sheriff Gentry?"

"Th' Sheriff resigned!" Came Seth in an impatient tone. "Deputy Hicks, too,...that's why I'm here!...I was told you're th' only honest lawman left in Dallas, Marshal, and that bein' th' case, I want a leave my son in your care while I look into my other son's death!...Can I use one of your cells, Sir?"

"In other words, you intend to take the law into your own hands!"

"Unless you're willin' to do it for me, Yeah, I do!...But if you know another way, I'd be more than glad to hear it!"

Dempsey sighed and went back to his desk then shook his head as he sat down again. "Unfortunately, I don't!" He sighed. "What happened with Gentry?"

"He admitted being on McGuire's payroll, Roderick." Nodded Doctor Mitchell. "Mister Mabry gave him the option of leaving Dallas,...and I guess he took it. He dropped his gun and badge and left."

Dempsey nodded then looked back at Seth. "Mister Mabry,...did you kill that man, Butcher?" The question was point blank and took Seth by surprise..

Seth stared at him for a moment then realized that something must have happened that he didn't know about since last night. He shook his head then. "No, sir,...I didn't!" He said firmly. "I did beat th' Bastard half to death,...but he was alive when I was done!...And I did tell 'im to leave town!...He beat my son almost to death, Marshal, so I did th' same to him,...but that's all I did!" He continued to stare at Dempsey's questioning eyes with a frown on his face both surprised, and angry at the point-blank question.

"Marshal, if that Son of a Bitch is dead, it is not by my hands!" He continued. "And you can take that for what it's worth!" He sighed heavily then and reached down to grip Greg's shoulder. "There was a time I would have killed him, Marshal,...but not now, he was alive when I was done!"

"None th' less, he is dead." Returned Dempsey with a sigh. "McGuire's man, Silva found 'im an hour ago. Mister Tulane there saw th' body as Silva brought 'im to th' Undertaker,...seems somebody tied his own rope around his neck and spooked his horse." He grinned then. "But don't worry about it, Mister Mabry,...it was just a question. In my opinion, it was a long time in coming."

"Again, Marshal," Nodded Seth. "Th' Bastard was alive when I left 'im!"

"Oh, I believe you," Sighed the Marshal. "I just don't know how much help I can be to you at th' moment....I will accommodate your son, however, but not in a cell. I have a room in th' back where I sleep sometimes,…it's got a bed and a lavatory. He can stay there.…Mister Tulane, please show, Mister Mabry th' way, will you?"

"Yes, Sir!" Tulane gave Seth and Hicks a hand with Greg, and together, they walked the boy slowly into the cellblock then into the Marshal's spare room.

Doc," Sighed Dempsey as he watched them leave. "Is this man for real?"

"I'm afraid so, Roderick, and it's about time someone with guts took a stand against this bunch,…and please don't feel offended, I know your situation?…But I believe that before this is over, you will have to take a side in this."

"I'm already on his side, Doc!…I'm just waiting for th' chance. Hell, I've been ready for a long time,…but I need proof of what's going on before I can justify going up against th' Mayor,…and that Chicken-livered Town Council!"

"I know that, Roderick, and God willing you'll get it!"

"What do you think of Mabry, Doc,…personally, I mean,…who is he?"

"I don't know, Roderick, I just met him this morning. But I think he's just a father with guts, and that's all I know,…only he does know how to handle himself,…he beat Gentry to the draw this morning, disarmed him!"

"How bad, Doc,…did he beat him, I mean?"

"Gentry didn't get his gun out!" They both looked up then as Seth and the two deputies returned to the office.

"Doctor," Sighed Seth stopping in front of him. "How much do I owe you, sir?"

"Your bill was paid at the Sheriff's office, Mister Mabry!" He smiled, reaching out to shake Seth's hand. "I am most glad to make your acquaintance."

"Well, thank you,…can you keep tabs on Greg for a day or two?"

"I always tend to my patients."

"Then you'd best go, Sir,…don't draw any attention to yourself. If Yancy McGuire finds out you helped me with Greg, it might go bad for you."

"You are right." He nodded. "But come calling if the need arises." He looked at Dempsey then. "Do what you see fit, Roderick!" He shook their hands again and left.

"Marshal," Said Seth as he pulled a chair up and sat down, prompting Dempsey to do the same. "Marshal, you don't know who th' hell I am, so I'm gonna lay it on th' line for you!…First off, I'm an honest man, if I was not, I could a walked in and shot Mister Gentry and taken my son home!… My sons came to town this Friday night past, to gamble and drink,…I'm sorry to say!…But them both bein' law abidin' and honest boys, I let 'em come, just like they been doin' for several months now! Only this time, my oldest son was murdered, and my youngest blamed for it!"

"Greg says that his drink was spiked with somethin', and he passed out in th' Casino, Ringerman's, I think it is....Anyway, he woke up in jail, he didn't know anything about what happened to his brother, or how he come to be in jail. What he does know, is that the Sheriff and this, Butcher came into his cell yesterday morning with a lawyer and beat him into confessin' to his own brother's murder!...The man that beat him has paid for that crime now,...and before I leave Dallas with my son, I aim to kill th' man who knifed my oldest,...and Sir,...nobody will stop me from doin' that!...Not even you!"

Dempsey leaned forward to rest on his elbows atop the desk. "Who do you think did kill your son?"

"Accordin' to th' Sheriff, Yancy McGuire and that Mex, Silva brought Greg to jail, along with th' planted evidence. But My money's on McGuire!"

"You do know he's got twenty guns workin' for him, and that several of them are noted gunfighters?"

"So am I, Sir!"

"I thought you might be!...Just who are you, Mister Mabry?"

"Somebody that died a long time ago, Marshal, and I aim to keep it that way!...Now,...I hear your hands are pretty much tied when it comes to keepin' th' peace around here!...I also heard that th' reason is because most of th' Councilmen are on McGuire's payroll, includin' th Mayor,...so I won't press you for any help. But I would like your word that Greg will be safe in your care,...he's all his mother and me have left?"

"You have my word on that!...Now, I'd like to make you an offer, Mister Mabry!...You get me proof of this whole operation, enough that I can take th' law into my own hands,...and I'll side you till hell freezes over, with both guns blazing!"

"What kind a proof, are we talking?"

"Well, Sir,...gettin' folks to speak out against McGuire and his bunch is out of th' question, I've tried!...They are too afraid to say anything, so,... that leaves only one way,...their books. They must keep records of what they do, likely in a safe in McGuire's office, or that of his boss, McCleary. Somewhere, there are record books!"

"Well," Sighed Seth. "I'll keep that in mind. But in th' meantime, Sir, do not be surprised at what happens here!...I am a firm believer in an eye for an eye, and if I'm owed, I will collect!"

"I believe you will!" Sighed Deppsey. "A word of caution though, this man, Silva,...it's said he can pull and throw a knife as fast as a man can pull his gun!...There's another man, too, who's said to be even faster,...his name is Gerrard Roachman....Rumor is that even Wes Hardin shuns him."

"Never heard of 'im, Marshal,...don't know Hardin, neither. But thank's for th' warnin'!...Now,...I've got two men willin' to help me, one is Mister Hicks here, th' other is Richard Hurd, do you know 'em?"

"Yes, I do." He nodded at Hicks as he spoke.

"Then I'd like to leave them both here to help watch over Greg, if that's okay?"

"But, Mister Mabry," Interrupted Hicks. "I'd like to help you fight?"

"I'm better alone, Jordan, right now, anyway! But I'm sure I'll need you later. Right now, I'd like you to go find Mister Hurd and bring 'im back here."

"What about Tindall and Simpson, they worked for Gentry, too?"

"Find them, too. Tell 'em their job has been terminated,...but don't tell 'em about me!...We don't know whose side they're on."

"All right, Mister Mabry." Sighing, the Deputy left the office.

"They'll be lookin' for you and your son, you know!"

"Yes, Sir, and they likely already know who I am!...But that's okay, I want 'em to know who's comin' for 'em!"

"Then I wish you good luck!"

"Luck is a random thing, Marshal, one a man has to make on his own."

"If you should find that proof we talked about, I'm sure Federal Judge Emmit Castle will call in th' Rangers to help corral this bunch."

"No promises there." Sighed Seth. "But I do appreciate your help, Sir." He got up and shook the Marshal's hand firmly, nodded at Tulane then left.

"What do you think of that, comin' from an old man, Jake?"

"He might be a little long in th' tooth, but he ain't a bit afraid of the odds, Marshal,...and I wouldn't want 'im after me, I think!...Anybody that can take that Butcher out has got my vote, I'll tell ya that!"

"Yeah," Sighed Dempsey. "That's what worries me!"

"Are we just gonna stand by and let 'im do this on his own, Boss,...ain't this what we been waitin' on?"

"Let's see what happens first, Jake!...We get all hot and bothered now, we'd prob'ly just get in his way!...When Hicks, and Hurd get back,...I'd like you to find Derrick and keep an eye on Mister Mabry....Don't interfere unless he's in need of help, though, he's goin' up against an army of killers!"

*   *   *

Yancy McGuire knocked at McCleary's door and when bade entry, walked in as Allan was lighting his cigar. "That was quick, Lad!" He smiled. "Have ye got results already?"

Yancy walked across the large room without a word and deposited the Sheriff's badge on his desk. "Silva brought this to me, Allan, it was on the floor in Gentry's office. The Sheriff is gone, and so be our prisoner!"

McCleary studied the tin star for a moment. "What do ye think this means, Mister McGuire?"

"Who would know that, Allan?" Sighed Yancy. "But I believe we have trouble coming!"

"Aye,…it would appear that we do, wouldn't it?" He nodded. "It must be the boy's father that is behind this!…So now,…where do you think he has taken the boy?"

"I would not know that, either, Allan,…perhaps home?"

"That be hard to say, lad,…and I say this because our Mister Butcher is dead,…and he is dead because of the beating he gave young Mabry,…that is the cowboy's name, is it not?"

"Mabry, aye, Allan."

"That tells me that our Mister Mabry will be coming for you next, me lad,…so, where might our Mister Silva be right now?"

"I sent him to Gentry's home to find him."

"Good thinking!" Sighed McCleary. "Gentry be the key to finding this Mabry, me thinks. But do this as well, dear friend,…when Mister Silva returns, keep him close to you!"

"I can take care of me self, Allan!"

"I know that, lad!…But our nemesis is a very capable man, and very wise,…as Mister Butcher would surely agree,…if he was still among us? I can not afford to lose you, my dear friend!"

"I have twenty men out looking for him, Allan, but without knowing what the man looks like, he will be hard to find!…No one seems to know him."

*   *   *

"Hello old man." Said Seth as he walked through the Livery doors.

The attendant leaned on the pitchfork's handle and nodded. "Come fer yer horse, did ye?"

"Why would I do that, I'm not through yet?…Naw, I really came to ask you why you killed that Butcher fellow?" And the wide-eyed look on the little man's face, told him his assumption was correct.

"Why,…I,,,I never done that!" He stuttered. "I don't know who done that!"

"Yeah, you did,…and I ain't here to do nothin', but to tell you to keep your mouth shut about it.…My reason for not killin' 'im, was to make 'im suffer!"

"Well, I hated th' Son a fa Bitch!...Damn near broke my arm, he did!"

"You saw what I did to 'im, didn't you,...you watched th' whole thing?"

A wide grin appeared on the little man's bewhiskered face, and he nodded his head. "Yep,...Damndest thing I ever seen, too!...Uh-huh, I slipped in back yonder and watched. I know you told me not to but I didn't know you from Adam, or whut you had in mind?...Hell, you could a burnt th' place down, all I know!"

"Well, you'd best keep your story straight,...his Boss is mad now, and they're all lookin' hard for me!...And you, old man, you are th' only one who knows what I look like!"

"You ain't got a worry none about me!...They done been here, and I told 'em nothin'!"

Nodding, Seth walked on into the barn, after first checking the street and stopped beside the Hostler. "What do you know about this Mexican, Silva?"

"Silva's a mean Son a fa Bitch, 'at's whut he is! I don't want no truck with 'im, no, Sir!...He just left here twenty minutes ago, too, came in fer his horse!"

"He say where he was goin'?"

"Sheriff Gentry's house,...asked me if Gentry had been here? I told 'im he came in fer his wagin this mornin' and left,...is 'at okay?"

"Yeah, that's okay,...will he be back?"

"Oh, yeah, Dickhead leaves his horse here!...Why you askin'?" He frowned.

"I'm gonna have a little talk with 'im about his boss."

"Jesus Christ, Mister,...Silva ain't th' Butcher, he's meaner!"

"That's what they tell me." He sighed. "Tell ya what, old Timer,...I'll wait for 'im in your tack room there. "He peered at the old man then. "And just so you'll know,...you give me away, I'll shoot you!"

"You ain't got a worry none about me, I told ye, I want 'em all dead!...But ya better watch his right arm, I hear tell he's god-awful fast!"

"I heard that, too,...now go on about your business and don't let on!" He went into the tack room and almost gagged from the stale, musty smell, but then saw the old chair and moved it into position before he sat down to wait.

He had no idea what to expect from the slender Mexican, but if he could find out exactly who did kill Tommy, he might end the whole thing a little quicker,...and it would help to know what he was up against. If nothing else, maybe Silva could tell him where McGuire keeps his record books, because he knew it was going to be hard to get to the man, especially now!...The Mexican might even own up to Killing Tommy himself, and he could end that part of it right here!...But somehow, he knew who killed Tommy, he thought, remembering the old adage that said, "If you want something done right, do it yourself", and McGuire was likely one of those men!...What he should do is take Greg home first and then come back,...but the thought that McGuire might slip away rejected the idea. No,...if need be, he'd take the hired help out one at a time, and then go for McGuire,...but whatever he had to do, one way or the other Tommy would have justice done!...Sighing, he removed the loop from the hammer of Greg's pistol and checked the loads in the dim light filtering through the door before putting it away again.... He had not killed a man in eighteen years, he thought bitterly, and until now had not even thought about it,...but Thomas was dead now, killed without mercy, and likely over the money he had won and now,...now that man had to pay!"

Several patrons had come and gone in the half hour it took for the lean killer to return to the stables, and as Silva rode through the doors, Seth, who was watching him from the darkness of the tack-room, saw Silva stop his horse suddenly and look around as if he could sense that something was wrong.

"Light down, Mister Silva, I'll take 'im!" Voiced the old man somewhat shrilly and came on to take the reins.

Still scanning the roomy barn's interior, Silva slowly dismounted and followed as his horse was led toward its stall.

"Somethin' wrong?" Queried the old man as he lifted the stirrup and loosed the cinches and then shrugging, lifted the heavy saddle off and hefted it with a grunt to the top rail of the stall.

Silva continued to study the barn's darkness while the Hostler worked. "Who else is here, old man?" He asked tightly. "Someone is here,...I can feel the eyes watching me."

"Ain't nobody here, 'sides me!...But I'm always here!"

His senses working overtime then, the little Mexican turned around and momentarily stiffened when he saw Seth standing in the tack-room's open doorway. "You say no one is here, old man!" He said this with malicious intent, never taking his narrow eyes off of Seth.

"Well,...nobody, but him!" Cackled the attendant, who quickly left the stall to get out of the line of fire.

"Who are you, Gringo?" Voiced Silva, his narrow black eyes sparkling. "What do you want from Silva, Cabrone,...to die, is that what you want?"

Seth stepped out into the large room and moved toward him for several feet before squaring himself, his hand dangling loosely just below the grip of the Colt pistol. "You use th' word dyin' a lot, don't ya?" He grinned, still watching Silva's narrowed eyes....."Well, that's somethin' we'll need to talk about directly! But first, my name's Mabry, Mister Silva, Seth Mabry,…and I got a couple questions to ask you!"

"Silva does not answer questions, Cabrone!" He sneered.

"Cabrone?" Repeated Seth, slightly shaking his head. "You got that all wrong, Amigo, I had me a daddy!…Now why are you callin' me names, anyway, you don't even know me?…You should show a little respect for your elders, man!"

"Silva does not respect Gringos!"

"I'm truly sorry to hear that!…But that's okay, most Mexicans think they're inferior to us Gringos!…Anyway,…I just wanted to know if you found th' Sheriff?…I heard he left town, or somethin'!" He shrugged then. "Can't blame 'im none, I guess,…well, did you find 'im?" And when he didn't get an answer. "Okay then,…can you tell me who killed my son Saturday night, I know you was there?…Come on, Silva, was it you killed my boy, or was it Yancy McGuire, you both was there?"

"Don't guess you're gonna tell me!" He sighed. "But that's okay, I already know!…Anyway, maybe you'll tell me where your boss man keeps his books, I'd like to take a gander at 'em?" He shifted slightly onto the balls of his feet as he watched Silva grow even angrier. "I guess you no habla American….is that it, Silva?…Or has th' gato got your tongue?"

"I know you, Gringo!…one day past, you bump into Silva on the street, why you do that?"

"Now, how do you expect me to answer your questions, when you won't answer mine?

"If you do not, you will die!" He sneered.

"Are you real sure a that, Amigo, you said it twice now?…Seems to me you think way too much a yourself….But okay, since you're a nice fellow!…Bumpin' into you was an accident, amigo,…seein' you today, was not!…Did you kill my son, Cabrone?…If you're not gonna tell me, I'm gonna think you actually helped your Hefe kill 'im!…Is that right?"

"You will never know this, Cathrone!" Sneered Silva. "Because you are about to die!"

"You ain't givin' me no choice here, Amigo,…so I'm gonna give you one!…Why,…because I don't think you killed my son, I think McGuire did?"

"What is this choice?" He sneered.

"Take off that gun belt and leave Dallas, you're Hefe is a dead man anyway!"

"You kill Butcher, Gringo?" He asked, suddenly dropping his hand to hang at his side.

"Butcher?…Oh, was he a big man,…very tall and ugly,…was that his name?" Seth stared at Silva until his serious expression turned slowly into a half grin. "Yeah," He nodded. "I killed th' Bastard!" He saw the Mexican's right cheek twitch with seething anger then drew and fired, the slug striking the slender killer high in the right shoulder just as he made his draw,…the slug's impact spun him around before slamming him face-first into the stall-post behind him.

The explosion was ear-shattering in the hollow barn, but soon echoed away. He had beaten the slender gunman handily, and was some surprised, after all the hoopla. He wondered also why he didn't used his knife, since he was notably so good with it? Sighing, and with the cocked pistol in hand, he walked over to Silva and toed him in the ribs. "Roll over, Silva, you ain't dead!"

Gasping loudly, the Mexican rolled onto his side to glare up at him hatefully. "You will not live to kill Hefe, Gringo,…you will die like the dog, you are!"

"HEE-HEEE-HEEEEE!" Cackled the skinny attendant as he squatted down beside Silva. "How's it feel, Pepper-Belly, huh?…Ain't so fuckin' tough now, are ye, Dickhead?"

"That's enough, old Timer," Sighed Seth. "Better pull that knife from his belt before he decides to try and use it."

"Yes'ireee!" He cackled, reaching to slide the thin stiletto from its sheath. "Yes'iree, Bobtail!…OOOOH, look at this Frog-sticker?" He held it up for Seth to see, but then suddenly reached down and laid the six-inch blade against Silva's throat, causing the Mexican's eyes to widen. "Why don't I go ahead and kill th' Dickhead?"

"Move th' knife, old timer, I don't want 'im dead!" Seth squatted beside Silva then and shook his head. "What happened here, Amigo, I heard you was fast on th' draw,…I was actually scared of you for a time?…Well, looks like I didn't die after all, don't it?…You up to talkin' now?"

"Pincha Cathrone!" He groaned then reached to hold his shoulder and glare at him. "Hefe will kill you a thousand ways, you dog!"

"You can do better than that, Silva,…you can't kill me with words!…Hell, you can't kill me at all, look at ya, you're whimperin' like a whipped dog!…Hey, now!" He laughed. "Guess that makes you th' dog, instead a me!…Tell ya what, Silva, you talk to me, I might get you a Doctor, man,…course you prob'ly won't like 'im, he's a Gringo! So, come on,…who really killed my son?…Okay, Is there another way to your Hefe's office, without goin' through th' saloon?…these are simple questions, Cabrone,…how about it?"

"I will never tell you, Cathrone!…If you kill me, I will laugh at you!"

Sighing, Seth looked up at the attendant's smiling face. "What is your name, anyway, old man?"

"Gus!" He shrugged. "Name's Gus Jenson, anybody could a told ya that!...Now, why are you grinnin'?"

"I thought your only friend was a bar-fly named Gus?"

"It is,...Me!...I'm th' only fuckin' friend I got!" He cackled mirthfully again.

"Give me that knife, Gus." He took the very sharp, long-bladed dagger and slid it into his vest's inside pocket. "Now, go get Doc Mitchell for me,... and tell 'im to bring his buggy."

"Heyy,...I got a biz'ness to run, why don't you go get 'im?"

"Cause I want to keep this one alive!" He looked back at the street then. "You think that shot was heard, Gus?"

"Aww, hell no!...Nobody cares anyway, shots are heard around here all th' time....Somebody could come in, though, maybe more a McGuire's bunch!"

"Then let's drag 'im into th' stall here." He got up and moved to Silva's shoulder, grabbed him under the arms and dragged him, cursing into the stall alongside his horse.

"Okay, I'll go get th' sawbones." Nodded Gus. "But ya should a kilt th' Buzzard! God damn Spick hurt lots a people here, him and that God damn Butcher!" He got up and tramped out through the doors, leaving a grinning Seth still watching the hate-filled face of the Mexican.

Silva's right cheek twitched with seething anger, and Seth drew and fired.

"What will you do with Silva, Gringo?...Hefe will look for me, and he will kill you,…he has many guns!"

"Oh, I wouldn't worry about that, Amigo,…I ain't hard to find!...In fact, I want 'im to find me,…but somehow, I don't think he has th' guts to come lookin' his self! He'll send somebody else, like you, to look for me."

"Then you are muy-loco, Cathrone!" Sneered Silva.

'You're prob'ly right about that!" He sighed.

CHAPTER SIX

"He gonna live, Doc?" Breathed Seth as he watched Silva being bandaged.

"He'll live," Nodded Mitchell, getting to his feet. "Very few men die from shoulder wounds. What will you do with him?"

"Take 'im to th' Marshal, I guess,…that's why I asked for your wagon."

"You know McGuire has men out looking for you?…I'm surprised they didn't show up during all this!"

"Yes, Sir, me, too!…I knew they likely was lookin' for me….Would you happen to know any of 'em?"

"Three or four, I treated them once,…but I couldn't describe them well enough for you to recognize on sight. They're locals mostly, the rest came from all over!…What I'm saying is, sooner or later someone is bound to see us depositing prisoners at the Marshal's office."

"What else can I do, outside a killin' 'em?"

"Why not keep them here,…you can put a guard on them,…old Gus could watch them!"

"I don't think so, Doc, I need 'em alive!" He grinned and looked down at the old man, who had come into the stall to squat back down beside Silva, still cackling his intimidation of the killer.

"How about it, Gus,…you got a spare room back there somewhere, one with a door on it?"

"Sure I do, keep feed in it!…Can't see it from here, neither!"

Seth nodded and looked back at the Doctor. "That's what I'll do, Doc, thanks. He looked back at Gus then. "Let's get 'im up, Gus,…show 'im his new home!" And once they had the cursing Silva on his feet. "When you goin' to check on Greg, Doc?"

"Going over there right now." He nodded.

"Fill th' Marshal in for me,…and have 'im send Mister Hicks over here for guard duty."

"Be glad to." He closed his bag, took his horse's reins and turned the buggy around, smiled back at Seth and climbed aboard.

Nodding, Seth and the still cackling Gus half carried the Mexican gunman toward the rear of the large barn.

*   *   *

"Good to see you, Jordan." Grinned Seth when the ex-deputy Sheriff entered the barn. "Anybody follow you?"

"No, Sir,…but with all that traffic, I doubt I would see anybody."

"Tell me, would you know any a McGuire's men by sight?"

"One or two, maybe,…but I can't say I know 'em, they came to th' office a time or two, that's all."

"You see anybody you know, anybody that might a seen you come in here?"

"A dozen or so, maybe." He grinned. "Don't worry, Mister Mabry,… none of 'em worked for McGuire, I can vouch for that!"

"It's been fairly active around here, too!" Sighed Seth. "But tell me,…you would know a McGuire man if you saw 'im, wouldn't you?"

"I think so, yes, Sir. I have pretty much seen 'em all at one time or another,…and they all keep their horses here, or at McGreggor's Livery on Jefferson Street. All of 'em are pretty tough-lookin'!"

"Okay," He sighed, giving Hicks the key to the pad-lock. "Find you a place to hide back there, one where you can watch th' goin's on in th' barn here. Old Gus there won't give you away, not on purpose anyway,…but there's always th' chance he might!…Is Mister Hurd still in with Greg?"

"He is,…and Doc said tell you his face is already healing real well."

"Thank God for that!" He sighed. "Jordan,…do you know if there's a back way into McGuire's office?" And when Hicks shook his head. "There any guards inside?"

"Two,…one at th' stairs in the saloon, one at th' stairs on th' second floor. That whole second floor is for th' whores, and they're constantly usin' 'em with their customers. Th' Saloon guard pretty much let's them pass, once th' client pays 'im!"

"We're talkin' about McGuire's place, right?"

"Yes, sir,…Commerce Street Theater and Bar!…It ain't nothin' but a saloon and whorehouse anymore….But back in it's day, it's said that Lilly Langtree sang there a couple a times,…that was in Seventy-one, I think,… before my time!"

"Come on," Said Seth, nodding. "I'll walk you back….What about this Ringerman place?" He asked as they walked. "Tell me about McCleary."

"Don't know much about 'im, nobody ever much sees 'im,...we just know he's there. He's th' big boss of th' outfit!"

"Top floor, I guess?"

"Same as McGuire." Nodded Hicks. "Just how are you gonna get to these men anyway, Mister Mabry?...The only time McGuire leaves his place is to go to McCleary's, and he always has three or four gunmen with 'im when he does?"

"It'll be tough, I guess." He nodded as they reached the dark corner of the barn. "Do you know any a them whores,...personally, I mean?...One that might be unhappy?"

"Believe me, sir, they're all unhappy! Why, you got got a plan?"

"Just givin' myself some options, and there ain't that many."

"Well, they're all unhappy, Seth,...scared to death, too!...McGuire said he'd kill them if they didn't produce!...Corine Brewer told me that!" He shook his head then. "Her own daddy sold her to McGuire a year ago, made 'em all sign a contract,...th' same with th' rest of 'em, I hear!...Anyway, they're nothin' but Slaves, Mister Mabry, plain and simple!...But Corine's the one who won't be too afraid to help you. Just ask for Baby." And when Seth frowned. "None of 'em use their real names."

"That's good to know, Jordan, thanks. Now here's what I'd like you to do,...if any of McGuire's men come in for their horses, I'd like to know about it!...Just keep that door key with you and come find me, I'll be somewhere between th' Marshal's office, and th' Dollar saloon. You can't find me, don't worry just come on back here. I'll have Mister Hurd relieve you tonight, him or one a Dempsey's men, and keep out a sight!...And thank's, Jordan."

"Yes, Sir!...Thank you, Seth,...and you know why?"

*   *   *

"Missus Mabry?" Queried Trey Mathers as he walked up to the grave, and his hat was in his hand when she looked at him. "Are you okay Missus Mabry?"

Laura Mabry pushed herself unsteadily to her feet from where she had been kneeling. "Yes," She responded hoarsely, having to clear her throat a time or two. "I'm okay, Trey." She sniffed.

"Well, I'm sorry, Ma'am, but,...you sure don't look okay to me,...you was out here all day yesterday, and in that front porch rockin' chair most all a last night,...and here you are again out here!...Missus Mabry, you ain't et nothing in two whole days, that I can tell!"

"I haven't been hungry, Trey." She sighed.

"No, Ma'am, I understand,…but if you was to make yourself sick over this, th' Boss'll kill me, he told me to look after you!"

"I apologize, Trey,…I haven't made you anything to eat in two days, either, I'm so sorry?"

"That's okay, Ma'am, there was plenty a leftovers. I'm just worried about you, I was left in charge."

"I know,…but I just miss Thomas so much." She sniffed. "He was our first born, and so much like his father!…I'm sorry, Trey," She sniffed. "Come on in the house, I'll fix us something to eat."

"Thank you, ma'am. But I have to say Tommy wouldn't want you makin' yourself sick this way, and I know th' Boss wouldn't!"

"I'm worried to death about him, Trey!" She said as they walked out of the trees toward the house. "I haven't seen that look on his face in eighteen years, and it scared me just as much as it used to."

Trey climbed the steps to the rear porch ahead of her, and held the back door open for her to enter the darkening kitchen. He went around her again to quickly light one of the two lamps that were sitting on the dining table. "I'll make a fire in the stove, Ma'am!"

"Thank you, Trey,…and thank you for being such a good man, I don't know what we'd do without you."

"Shucks, Ma'am,…this is home to me. I don't know what I'd a done, you folks hadn't took me in?"

"Did you ever hear from your family after that, Trey?"

"Never did, no, Ma'am!…Don't know whut happened,…guess Loretta took th' kids back to Iowa, that's where she was from."

"It's a shame, Trey,…I'm so sorry."

"Yessum, me, too!" He sighed. "Reckin th' boys are plumb grown now!…Anyway, I wouldn't worry too much about th' boss. From th' stories my daddy told, your husband can take care of his self!…I'd sure hate to be that killer if he finds 'im!"

"Oh, he'll find him!" She sighed. "He's like an Indian, when it comes to finding someone….He won't let go until he does find him!…But he hasn't worn that gun since the war ended, and that's what worries me!…I just wish I knew he was all right, if Gregory was all right?…I can't stand the waiting!"

*   *   *

"Mister Mabry!" Grinned Mason Cooper as Seth was shown in. "How was your room last night, you left before I returned this morning?" He shook Seth's hand and motioned at a chair.

"Th' room was just fine," He sighed as he sat down. "Slept like a rock!"

"Good!...Heard they found Butcher's remains yesterday, that your doing?"

"Partly, yeah,...I beat hell out of 'im,...but somebody else done 'im in!"

"Could have been anyone!" Shrugged Cooper. "He beat up a lot of folks in town. That sidekick of his was in the bar this morning, asking everyone if they knew anything, even me!...Must be lost without the big man."

"Not anymore, he ain't!" Sighed Seth. "Got 'im locked in th' feed room down at Jenson's stables."

"What happened?"

Seth shrugged. "Man wanted to fight!...Mister Cooper, what do you know about McGuire's whorehouse? What I mean is,...th' Marshal said if I could come up with some proof of what's goin' on in Dallas, he could maybe step in and help me do what I came here to do?"

"Well, I don't know, Man. I have been in the place,...but that was back when it was actually a theater and saloon,...even saw Lily Langtree there once. No,...I was there a time or two,...let me see, I bought this place in sixty-nine, it was called the Gold Piece then,...widow by the name of Ryker owned it, Judith Ryker,...she was a beautiful young thing, too!...Said she didn't want it after her husband was killed saving her from a rapist,...and on their wedding night ta-boot!...Anyway,...at that time the theater had three stories like now, except now, the whole third floor is used for McGuire's office space, and the second floor for the girls and their clients."

"Any back way in?"

"Sure, but only to the second floor, but I think that outside door was nailed shut when McGuire took over, I don't know!"

"How about Ringerman's?"

"Same thing, I'm afraid."

"Well, it was a thought." Sighed Seth.

"Both places are well guarded inside." Nodded Cooper. "Are you planning something?"

"I'm always thinkin', Mister Cooper!...How th' hell did these men get their hold on this town so easy, that's what I can't figure?"

"A good question....It was said this fellow, McCleary came in here with a million dollars to lend to anybody that needed help getting on their feet again,...and everybody needed help!...Except for a few, Ringerman and myself included. We managed to plan for the future!"

Seth breathed deeply then. "Yeah, I heard all about how he paid off notes and such,...that makes th' man smarter than most folks when it comes to gettin' his way!...But this Ringerman,...you said he was smart enough to plan for th' future, so how'd they manage to get his place?"

"Ringerman's house burned down on him and his family, two o'clock in the morning, it was,…all of them died in the blaze!…It wasn't a week afterward that McCleary produced a bill of sale for the gambling house, dated two days before the fire,…legal, too, forged, but legal,…and signed by Judge McAllester!"

Seth nodded with a slight grin."That's what th' Sheriff was talkin' about, I guess." He saw Cooper's frown then. "Gentry told me he hadn't been a lawman since what happened to th' Ringermans, I didn't know what he meant….Anyway,…I heard they had a Judge in their pocket, too,…would that be McAllester?"

"It would, him and a Lawyer or two, even the Mayor!…But I don't think any of them like being under McCleary's thumb, they're just too afraid to go up against him. The man is too powerful, and he has too many killers working for him."

"Why hasn't he got you, Mister Cooper,…no offense, you told me you planned for th' future,…but so did Rimgerman?"

"No offense taken." He sighed. "It isn't like he hasn't tried to buy me out, he has. But then, I guess I don't pose that big of a threat to him,…and I don't have a family he can threaten me with!…Anyway,…he knows where to draw the line, I think, because he stops just short of making his activities a Federal Crime!…I'm afraid you are up against a stone wall, Seth,…Dallas has upwards of seven thousand people, and those of any means are controlled by McCleary, and McGuire."

"Sure sounds like it." Sighed Seth. "But they murdered my son, Mister Cooper,…and that was their big mistake!" He sighed again then. "But I'd like to ask you a favor now, Sir?"

"Of course, anything."

"If I don't make it,…do everything you can to help my son?"

"You have my word, Sir!"

Seth nodded. "Marshal Dempsey's a good man, I think he'll see that Greg stays alive and maybe, between the two of you, you can get 'im a fair trial!"

"I wish I could help you, Mister Mabry, But,…I'm just not a fighting man!"

"It's my fight, Mister Cooper, it's me has to do it!"

"Just what will you do, Seth,…what can you do?"

"Get a couple of hours sleep first, after that,…I'll think of something." They heard the knock at the door then and Seth got up to move back against the wall beside the door before nodding at Cooper.

"Come in!" Said Cooper loudly, and when the bartender stuck his head inside. "What is it, Leon?"

"Couple of McGuire's men just came in, they want a see you."

He cast a furtive glance at Seth and on seeing him nod again. "Send them in, Leon. But stay close, I might need you!"

Leon nodded and closed the door.

"I'm gonna take 'em down, Mister Cooper,...is that okay with you?"

"Yes, Sir, it is!" Nodded Cooper. "It's the least I can do to help you."

Two minutes later, Leon opened the door again to admit the two gunmen. The first man into the room was close to six feet tall, dressed in black pants and matching boots, and sporting two holstered guns tied to his legs. His shirt was black beneath a matching cowhide vest and his face was lean, with close-set, narrowed and steely eyes that peered hard at Cooper.... His movements suggested he was a gunman with confidence. The second man also had a sneering swagger about him, but his clothes were more the garb of a cowpuncher, than a gunman,...but his weapon was worn low on his hip and also tied down.

The man in black came on to stand in front of Cooper, stared at him for a moment then reached up to push his black hat off his eyes with a thumb.

"What do you want this time," Asked Cooper tightly. "You already searched my place once?"

"We're gonna search it again!...We're lookin' for a man, name of Mabry. We know he's hold up in Dallas somewhere and he ain't in none a th' hotels, so,...Mister McGuire thinks he might be here....Is he here, Mister Cooper?"

"Well now,...You can just go on back and tell your Mister McGuire that if Mister Mabry is here, he's my guest and it's none of his business!...This is my place of business, not his! You can also tell him that I have a new partner now, and he's also my body guard,...and I will not stand for any more of his rough housing tactics!"

"Now, ain't that nice!" Nodded the gunman. "But McGuire don't give a rat's ass what you got, Cooper, so answer my question!...Is Mabry here?... And before you lie to us again, I have to warn you,...I will have my answer!"

"No," Grated Seth. "You already got your answer!" He stepped away from the wall as his voice caused both men to whirl around and stare at him, their hands dangerously close to their pistols.

"Your name, Mabry?" Queried the man in black.

"No," Said Cooper quickly. "This is my body guard, Gentlemen. Meet Mister John Wesley Hardin!"

Both men's eyes grew a little larger then as they continued to stare at him.

"Is that right?' Asked the man in black. "You Wes Hardin?"

Seth walked further into the room to square off at the men before speaking. "Who are you, Sir?"

"Names Charlie Devlin," He grinned. "And I been hopin' to meet up with you!"

"Well you got a couple a fancy lookin' Remingtons there, Charley Devlin, you any good with 'em?"

"I'm better than you, I think," He grinned. "Would you care to find out?"

"How about your girl friend there, she any good?"

"I'm good enough to take you, ass hole!"

Seth drew his pistol then, taking both men by surprise as they stood mutely to stare at the cocked and ready Navy Colt. "Why don't you both get rid of all that weight you're packin around,...go on now, unbuckle th' hardware. Just drop th' rigs on th' floor there,...or you can draw and be dead!...It's the only two choices you got!"

"Come on, Hardin," Growled Devlin. "Why don't you holster th' gun and give me a chance, somethin' like this don't sound like you?"

"If I did, I'd have to kill you!" Grated Seth. "And th' name is Mabry, not Hardin,...now do it!"

"But he said…"

"I lied!" Chuckled Cooper. "Now, I suggest you do what Mister Mabry says, he does mean business!"

Seth was watching the eyes of Charlie Devlin, and suddenly realized the man might actually take the chance. "Don't be a fool, Mister Devlin, I can kill you in a heartbeat, man,...and I don't want to! I'm only interested in takin' McGuire down, not you two. Once I'm done, you'll be free to go!"

"It's better than dying, Gentlemen!" Voiced Cooper. "Mister Mabry just beat your friend Silva, not two hours ago,...and he will surely kill you."

The standoff lasted a couple of more minutes before Devlin finally shrugged and slowly reached down to untie the leather strings from his legs. "You win this round, Mabry." He smiled. "But when this is all over, I'm gonna come lookin',...you know that!"

"Man's got a do what he thinks is best!" He shrugged.

Still grinning, Devlin unbuckled his belt and lowered the rig to the floor, and then cursing loudly, the other man did the same.

Cooper came around his desk and gathered up the weapons.

"What now, Mabry?" Queried Devlin.

"Now you get hogtied!" He grated. "Mister Cooper, you got any rope, Sir?"

Nodding, Cooper went on to the door and opened it, allowing Leon to enter with his shotgun, but he lowered it when Cooper told him it was okay. He told the bartender what he wanted and closed the door again.

"McGuire knows we're here, Mabry." Said Devlin. "We don't come back, he'll send more men lookin'!"

"Then you'll have company." Sighed Seth. "Now tell me, Charlie Devlin,…you ever been in McGuire's office?"

"Yeah,…so?"

"Where does he keep his records, you know, his books?"

"You don't really expect me to tell you that?"

"Why not,…you don't owe th' man,…do you?"

"I'm loyal to th' man that pays me!…And McGuire pays well!"

Leon was back shortly with the rope, and between the two of them, tied the two men up while Seth covered them with his gun.

"What now, Seth?" Asked Cooper as he tied the gag in Devlin's mouth.

"We take 'em to th' stables." He looked at Leon then. "Can I trust you, Sir?"

"Any day of the week!" He nodded.

"Then I could use your help."

"Have Dennis watch the bar, Leon, and come on back." Said Cooper.

"And bring that Greener." Added Seth.

"Yes, sir!" Leon left the room and several minutes later, was back with his shotgun.

"Now we wait till dark," Sighed Seth. "It's a little too light out yet, we might be seen by somebody."

"Good idea." Nodded Cooper. "Leon, please go out to the hall and extinguish the lamps, we'll want it to be dark in there when you leave."

*   *   *

"What's happening out there, Jake?" Asked Dempsey as Tulane came in and closed the door behind him.

"He took out Silva, Marshal. I watched it from Rankin's wagon yard, never seen anything faster!"

"Where'd he hit him?"

"Shoulder,…Silva barely cleared leather! Marshal,…this Mabry's for real!"

"It appears he is, don't it?…You see Deputy Hicks go in?"

"Doc Mitchell, too." He nodded. "He fixed up Silva."

"I know, he was here a while ago!…Doc said they locked Silva up in th' feed room, is that right?"

"Maybe, he didn't bring 'im out when he left!…Anyway, we followed Mabry to the Dollar saloon, and about a half hour later, two of McGuire's gunslingers went in, that's when I hustled back to check in with you!...Derrick's still watchin' the saloon."

"And you're sure he hasn't spotted you?"

"Don't see how, we're usin' your telescope!"

"And you was able to see all the way into that Livery when he shot Silva?"

"Doors were wide open, yes, sir!...We seen it all. Why,...somethin' wrong?"

"No!...Go get your supper, Jake....You say Derrick's still at the Dollar?"

"I left him across the street," He nodded. "He'll be somewhere between th' saloon and th' Livery, I guess."

"Good,...when you finish your supper, Jake, go on back to Rankin's, keep an eye on that stable. That old man, and Hicks will need help if McGuire's men come lookin'!...And if they do show up, go ahead and take 'em down! I don't want our own men hurt, old Gus neither,...he's stickin' his skinny neck way out by what he's doing!" He sighed heavily then. "But somebody has to, it seems....Anyway, when you see Derrick, send 'im to supper and then home, tell 'im to relieve you in th' morning....Go on now, get your supper!"

He watched the deputy leave then got up and walked to the window. The street was crowded, as well as the boardwalks as most of the shops were still open for business,...and it was not yet dark, he noted. He stood for a minute to watch the old lamplighter climb his ladder and light one of the street lights, then rolled and lit a smoke before walking back through the cellblock and into the spare room. "Mister Hurd," He nodded, closing the door as he entered. "How is he?"

"Wide awake, Marshal,...ask 'im yourself."

"How you feelin', son?" He asked as he sat down on the foot of the cot.

"It's,...a little hard to talk yet, Sir,...but I'm doing some better, I think....Have you seen my daddy?"

"Not since he brought you in. I will tell you he's all right though, Deputy Tulane is keeping an eye on 'im for me."

"What's he doing,...he do,...he don't know these people, they'll kill him, Sir!"

"I don't think so, son,...now stop worryin', okay, I'll keep you posted!...Now,...would you mind tellin' me what happened Saturday night?"

Greg was silent for a moment, trying to remember any more than what he had already told his father then shook his head. "I really don't know, Marshal,...I felt sick!...I tried to tell Tommy, but I passed out before I could!...I barely remember him helping me outside!...I don't remember a thing after that,...not till I woke up in jail, being accused of killing my own brother!" He almost broke down then, having to breath deeply to keep from crying.

"It's okay, son....Why were you there so late,...at Ringerman's, I mean?"

"Tommy wanted to win ten thousand dollars for daddy,...I think he did, too, there was a lot of chips on the table in front of him, money, too!"

Dempsey mashed out the spent smoke beneath his boot and sighed. "They say they found five hundred dollars in your pocket, along with the murder weapon."

"I don't know how it got there, Sir,...I did not kill my brother!"

"It's okay, boy,...I believe you."

"My boot, Marshal!" Said Greg quickly. "Tommy gave me some money to hold for him, said he was going to win the rest before we went home."

Dempsey reached down and lifted Greg's foot then worked the boot off, and spotting the lump in his sock removed the wad of currency. He smiled at Greg then, and held it up for Hurd to see. "Mister Hurd, help him off with th' other boot, will you,...he might as well be comfortable."

"That's all he gave me, Marshal, I swear!"

"I know that, Son,...and don't worry this money will be in my desk, you'll get it back!...Now,...just to satisfy my curiosity...do you know who your father was,...say,...before he married your mother?"

"I,...I don't understand the question, Marshal?"

"Let me explain,...I feel like I know your father, or I knew him a long time ago,...but if I did, he had a different name!...Like I said, I was just curious."

"Well his name has always been Seth Joe-Bob Mabry."

"Okay,...I appreciate that, Greg!...Don't guess you know where he's from, originally, I mean?"

"I'm sorry, Marshal,...He never talks about any of that!"

"Well, it was a thought." He mused. "Seems there's always somethin' to keep me awake!...Mister Hurd?" He said, looking at the Deputy. "I'm goin' out for a while, you might want a bolt this door behind me, just in case."

"Yes, Sir, I will."

"There's blankets on th' table there, you might want a get some sleep later,...I'll be bringin' a pail of stew for th' both of you when I come back, and come mornin', you can go get yourself a hot meal and clean up a little." He looked down at Greg then and nodded.

"Don't worry about your daddy, son, he can take care of himself, and I'll get to the bottom of all this, too,...I promise."

"Thank you, Marshal,...please help my daddy?"

Dempsey nodded and left the room, and closing the door behind him thought again of Seth. Maybe he shouldn't have questioned the boy about his old man like that, he thought,…but the nagging idea that he knew the man just would not go away. He needed help, and knew he had already made up his mind to do so before going in to see the boy. Council or no Council, He was the law, he had a responsibility to himself, and to Dallas,… and if he lost his job for it, he was going to help Seth Mabry bring this bunch down. He stopped just inside his office, remembering the Ringerman fire, a fire that Gaylon Gentry investigated and ruled as arson. It was also a fire that murdered the whole family.

He knew Gentry had been right in his ruling, it had been arson,…but when an innocent cowboy was hung for the crime, he should have done something,…and when the City Councilmen ordered him to step down and keep away from it, he knew something was wrong!…He should have done something!"

"God damn it!" He cursed aloud. He knew the same thing was going to happen here, if Mabry couldn't find the proof he needed to the contrary,… and damned if he was going to stand aside and let it happen again! He walked across the floor and pulled all the shades, donned his hat and left the office, locking the door behind him.

CHAPTER SEVEN

The election of Rutherford B. Hayes in 1876, led to the end of Reconstruction in March of '77, and although a few of the railroads were still in operation,...and even shipping some produce eastward, there were still crops in the fields rotting due to booming speculations of the markets returning,...and they were, but at a much slower rate than hoped! But the Silver market was something else again. Before the Silver Act of '73, the United States had backed its currency with both Gold and Silver and now, because of the Depression, paper money had become almost worthless, this in '74, and '75.

Equine influenza in '72 had a pervasive effect on the economy, as well as transportation. Railroads came to a halt because coal and wood could not be delivered to power the locomotives. The United States Cavalry was reduced to fighting western Indians on foot, and even the Indian found his pony too sick to do battle. Men were forced to pull wagons by hand, while trains and ships full of cargo sat unloaded,...basic community essentials were not delivered. Silver was no longer bought from the public, and coins no longer made.

Bit the worst was supposedly behind them now, and even though Texas was not hurt as bad as the rest of the Nation, it had its woes. The paper dollar still was not worth its true value, but never the less hoarded by those that had it, because prospects were good that the new Gold Standard would prop it up again. Among those hoarding paper money was the Syndicate, who had millions of extorted dollars in iron safes,...and none of these crime bosses trusted banks enough to keep their money in them.

Now, in 1878, with Reconstruction behind them, the dollar was slowly regaining its value, being backed by gold, instead of both precious metals. People were spending again, not as wildly as before, because they were still forced to buy with gold to get their money's worth. But they were slowly turning loose of their paper money again, too,...and Mills in the North were operating again, though not yet at full capacity. The Farmers were selling their crops, and this ultimately meant more for the economy in Dallas, Texas, and more in the pockets of McCleary and McGuire.

Allan McCleary sighed his contentment as the pretty, nude teenaged girl got to her feet to stand docilly between his outstretched legs to gag until he pushed her away, then stood tearfully against his desk as he got to his feet and pulled up his trousers. Smiling, he clipped his suspenders in place and sat back down.

"Lass," He said, still smiling his satisfaction. "That was even better than the last time, I am tremendously pleased with your progress,...now run along, me darlin', I have work to do....Go on, now, I'll be there in a bit!"

"Ca,...can I go see my mama now?" She sniffed, not daring to look at him,...but allowing him to focus on her almost full, ripening breasts as her breathing caused them to rise and fall with each sniff. "You,...you promised?"

"Little Darlin',...me love," He sighed, and then opened a metal box on the desk, produced a fat cigar and lit it before devouring her nakedness again with a lustful glance. "I so much wanted to spare you this heartache,...but you be so insistant that I must tell you something for your own good now!... This is how it is, me lovely,...ye see, Darlin', you belong to me now,...your father, and your dear loving mother sold you to me for money!" He lied,..and then watched her expression of disbelief.

"It's true, Darlin',...you signed a contract with me, remember, Angel?... Of course, you do!...Well, your parents signed one also, breaking all ties with you, and you with them! What I am saying, me love,...is that I am your father, and your mother now so to speak. I am the only family you will ever have now!" He pulled his handkerchief then as she began crying and covering her face with her hands,...and that made him angry. He suddenly reached and grabbed her slender arm to jerk her roughly back onto his lap, and at the same time jerking a stifled shriek from her pouted lips....Once on his lap, he hugged her against him and pulled her hands away from her face to reach and gently dab at her tears with the kerchief.

"I do not like me women to cry, sweetheart so dry your eyes, here, take this!" Once she complied, he roughly turned her around on his legs and looked her in the eyes. "Little Darlin', it is true that I love you,...but I will only love you as long as you love me!...It will be up to you to see that I continue to love you,...because should I stop loving you, I will kill you!...And if I do not kill you, I will give you to my good friend Yancy for his stable of whores!...So you see, me Darlin', if you break your contract with me,...ahhh, well, you do get the idea, you be not such a baby that you do not know what I say!...Now run along, and keep yourself pretty for your Father!" He laughed wickedly as he pushed her to her feet and patted her adolescent buttocks, sending her sobbing into his bedroom,...and still smiling, he got up and bent to open the safe behind him, taking out several ledgers, which he placed on his desk before sitting down again to look at his pocket watch. He then sighed and placed a hand on the stack of books as he thought about their latest ongoing problem!

He knew that if this Mabry character was not stopped, his whole operation could soon be in jeopardy. A few merchants were already refusing to pay their protection insurance fees,...and all because they had heard of the Butcher's death. Mabry was trouble, and if he succeeded in taking out more of his men, he would have no choice but to order the man's death before all their soldiers were put out of commission. He also knew that if he was not careful, he could bring the Government down on him. It was a thin line he was walking now, and the wrong move either way could mean destruction!

He sighed heavily then, thinking of the wire he had received from Jesse O'Riely demanding that funds be sent to New York City immediately,... but that would mean he would have to go to the bank, deposit a large sum of currency, wire the Exchange Bank in New York City and transfer the money,...and that in it's self, was dangerous! He was suddenly finding himself between a rock and a hard place, and he did not like it! He was doubtful if the banks in Dallas were yet sufficiently funded enough to handle large transfers of cash cross-country, and he was even more afraid to ship it by rail,...and so had already decided to put it off until absolutely necessary. It was that, or ignore the request altogether!...He had been thinking of severing the ties with O'Riely anyway, and this could be a good time to do it!...But if he did, Jesse would retaliate, he might even send assassins to kill him,...and that made him shiver. He heard the knock then and shook the thoughts away.

"Come in, Yancy!" He called out briskly.

"Evening, Allan." Smiled McGuire as he closed the door and came on to sit down heavily.

"Well, now, Lad,...have we found our Mister Mabry yet?"

McGuire shook his head and sighed. "No, Allan, we have not!" He said dejectedly. "And now, three more men are missing."

"What on earth are ye saying, Lad,...three more?"

"Mister Silva never returned from Gentry's house, Allan,...and now, Charlie Devlin, and Jimmy Kidd are gone!...They were sent to the Dollar Saloon to look for Mister Mabry,...I have not see them since."

"Did you not inquire?"

"I sent two more men." He nodded. "Mister Cooper told them Devlin and Kidd had been there, but left after they searched his rooms!...I do not understand, Allan, Charlie Devlin was almost as fast as Mister Silva, and yet they are missing also!"

"This is strange indeed!" Mused McCleary. "But even stranger to hear of our Mister Silva. What do you suppose has happened, Yancy?...What are your thoughts?"

"I do not know, Allan!...The old man at the stable told Charlie that Silva returned hours ago and left his horse like always,...but he said he did not see him leave."

"Then likely he has met the same fate as Mister Butcher!...Are ye sure Mister Silva would have come directly back to report his findings?"

"Yes, Allan," He nodded. "All of them would have returned,...good men, all of them!"

"Then someone is most definitely hiding our Mister Mabry, Lad!...Who would you consider the most likely candidate here?"

"The one most likely to hide him?...Could be anyone, Allan, we are not among the most popular, ye know!"

"Putting that aside, think, lad!...four men are missing, one of them dead,...and the last two places they were all known to be was Jenson's Livery,...as well as the Dollar Saloon! Maybe our Mister Devlin, and Mister Kidd went to Jenson's after leaving the Dollar."

"Now why would they do that?" Shrugged Yancy. "Unless someone at the Dollar told them where to find Mabry?"

"Exactly, my dear friend."

"We will search both places again, then!" Nodded McGuire.

"But be careful, Lad,...send four good men this time, and instruct them not to inflict any unnecessary harm to these proprietors, we must remain inside the law, and not draw attention to our activities,...this is vital, Yancy!"

"Of course, Allan,...and if we find Mister Mabry?"

"Bring him, and that proprietor back here to me,...they will be dealt with severely!"

"Shall I go now?"

"Of course, Lad, the books can wait!"

*   *   *

Marshal Dempsey pondered the question of what to do as he jostled his way along the crowded block to Main Street and turned left on the boardwalk having to either stop or sidestep passing pedestrians along the way to the darkened windows of the Sheriff's office where on impulse, he stopped to try the door. Finding it open, he pushed it inward and in the dim light of fading day, entered and went directly to the desk to try the drawers.

Finding several papers in the top drawer of one side, he unbuttoned his shirt and slipped them inside. The bottom drawer yielded a stack of old wanted posters, and he took those before buttoning his shirt again. The drawers on the opposite side contained holstered guns, so he took these, buckled the belts together and laid them on the desk before scanning the room. The rack of rifles was unlocked, with the securing lock-rod dangling from a chain on one side, and he went to slide the iron rod back through the breaching levers to lock them in place again.

The cellblock door was locked, and sighing he went back to loop the holstered weapons over his shoulders,…and with a last look around, turned and left the office. Closing the door behind him, he stood on the boardwalk for a minute before stepping down into the street, having to wait for a passing wagon as he crossed to the tiny café and entered. Standing in the doorway, he surveyed the small room until he spotted Derrick Tinsley at a table and worked his way toward him.

"Hi ya, Marshal," Greeted the Deputy. "What's with th' guns?"

"Got 'em from th' Sheriff's office,…Jake at th' Livery?"

"Yes, sir, across th' road at Rankins.…I was watchin' th' Dollar when he told me what you said."

"Mabry ever come out?"

"Never saw 'im, if he did,…least not while I was there!"

"What about McGuire's men?"

"No, sir, them neither."

"Can I get you something, Marshal Dempsey?" Smiled the Mexican waitress.

"Yes you can, Marketta, but I'm in a bit of a hurry,…what have you got that's fast?"

"Beef stew!" She shrugged.

"That'll do,…you got plenty of it?" And when she answered. "Then I'll need enough for two people, you know in one a them pails you use, and wrap up a couple a spoons, too, and a few biscuits. I'll be back for it!"

"We close at ten, you know." She smiled.

"I know, sweetie,…just keep it hot for me"

"You takin' it to th' jail, Boss?" Queried Tinsley quickly. "I can take it over for you, it's on my way home?"

"You heard th' man, Marketta!" He grinned, laying the weapons on a chair to fish coins from his pocket. "Will that take care of his meal, too?"

"Yes, sir,…you even have change coming." She said as she palmed the money.

"Keep it, honey."

"Thank you, Marshal Dempsey" She smiled. "Be right back with your stew."

"Jake fill you in on everything, Derrick?"

"Yes, sir. This here Mabry fella, is he a gunfighter or something,…he sure is fast on th' draw, if he ain't?"

"I believe he most likely is." Sighed Dempsey. "But if he is, I never heard of 'im!...Course, a lot a men can use a gun if they carry one, and most men do!...But it's best you don't talk about 'im,…or about what's goin' on around here. Nobody at all, that understood?"

"Clear as rain, Marshal….But if you don't mind me askin,…you're actin' different, you feelin' okay?"

"As a matter of fact, I feel real good, Derrick!" He grinned. "Better than I have in two years….Now,…think you can manage these guns, and that pail a stew?"

"Sure, I can!" He nodded. "Where you off to, Marshal?"

"I'm gonna call on Mason Cooper at th' Dollar Saloon, I want a find out what Mabry's up to,…and I'll have new orders for you and Jake come tomorrow."

"Is this what I hope it is, Marshal,…want me to go with you?"

"Thanks, but there won't be any trouble, I just want a know where Mabry and McGuire's men are, none of 'em came out of th' Dollar yet."

"Maybe they went out th' back, Marshal, I could a missed 'em, if they did?"

"Guess I'll know soon enough." He nodded. "Derrick, identify yourself when you deliver that stew." He took the key from his pocket and laid it on the table. "Office door's locked, too."

"I'll take care of it, Marshal."

      *   *   *

It took the better part of an hour for Seth and Leon to take their prisoners to the Livery, having to dodge, hide, or evade those using the alleyways for things other than travel,…and once they were finally there, he knocked loudly at the barn's rear door and waited.

"Who's there?" Came the muffled voice of Jordan Hicks.

"Mabry,…let us in!" He heard the door's heavy latch being lifted and when Hicks opened it, found him-self looking down the muzzle of a pistol.

"Let us in, Jordan." He said as the gun was put away and hustled the two men inside. "Open th' door there, will you?"

He untied the two gunmen and removed their gags, and once the two were locked inside with Silva, he shook Leon's hand and warned him to be cautious then sent him back to the saloon.

"Any activity around here?" He asked as he turned around.

"Had a couple of McGuire's men come in." Returned Hicks. "Pushed old Gus around some. Said they was lookin' for Silva, but Gus played it smart,...showed 'em Silva's horse and told 'em he left!"

"Good,...whatever you do, do not try and take any of these men on your own,...not unless they hurt that old man....If that happens, and you do, shoot first and talk later, because they will!...These men are killers."

"I'll be careful, Seth,...I do know my limitations. Where you off to now?"

"Well, I was gonna bed down at th' Dollar,...till this happened!" He sighed. "Now, I ain't goin' anywhere!...But you are gonna go get yourself somethoin' to eat, and go home!...I'll see you back here in th' mornin'!"

*   *   *

He didn't know what it was, a horse, the wind, or what, but his eyes were open. He blinked away the dregs of a hard sleep and wiped at his eyes with his fingers as he raised himself up slowly from his bed of straw,...and listening intently, he first stared at the dimly visible feed-room door and satisfied that it was not the source, slowly surveyed the large interior of the barn full of stalls and hay for several long seconds before hearing the barely audible sound again.

Jerking around, he stared at the barn's rear door as someone tried it again, and then there was nothing,...and he knew that whoever it was had decided to go around to the front. He strained his eyes at the partially closed livery doors, and the lighting was something to be wished for,...and old Gus was obviously in the tack-room having his supper,...or sleeping!

On impulse, he looked at his pocket-watch and shook his head, barely nine, fifteen, he thought tiredly,...he had just closed his eyes! Replacing the watch, he sighed and eased himself out of the depression of hay and slowly made his way into the barn's interior by using the stalls to hide his movements. He slowly worked his way to the nearest occupied stall, eased the low gate open and moved inside with the Buckskin, running his hand along the animal's neck to keep it quiet,...and there in the darkness he watched the double doors in the light of the one lantern that Gus kept on the tack-room wall.

He thought his eyes were playing tricks on him when one of the large doors began to slowly creak open but as he watched, four gunmen slipped inside to begin slowly searching the stalls one at a time, each taking precautions not to go near the tack-room door. As he watched them come closer, he knew he had made himself vulnerable by hiding in the stall,... but he knew they would surely see him if he tried to leave now....Wanting to avoid the noise of any gunplay, he pulled the Colt and waited, and it took several long seconds for the men to reach his stall, and braced himself. They were moving slow, and when one of the gunman cautiously peered over the low gate, Seth quickly raised the gun,...and before the man could make a sound with his open mouth, he rammed the Colt's barrel in it and cocked the pistol.

The man's eyes opened widely as he gasped his surprise, but he didn't move. "Th' gun!" Whispered Seth. "Give it to me." And when the man complied.

"You men stop where you are!" He ordered loudly, and cocked the other pistol, causing them to whirl toward him and stare. "Drop th' gun-belts, or die, Gents,...and if you think you can beat me, you're wrong! You'll kill your own man here, and then I'll kill you!"

He watched them in their indecision, their feet shuffling nervously in the dung-encrusted straw of the floor. "What'll it be, Gents?"

"I was you Dickheads, I'd do whut he says!" Cackled old Gus loudly. "Cause you don't, I'll cut yer asses in half!"

"All right!" Shouted one of the gunmen as he quickly unbuckled his belt and let the rig drop. "Watch it with that thing, you old Coot!...Come on, boys," He said loudly. "We're out-numbered anyhow,...do it! You know what th' Boss said, no gunplay!"

"All right,...hold it right there!" Shouted Deputy Marshal Jake Tulane as he rushed through the open doorway in a crouch. However, he quickly saw what the situation was and straightened up as he came forward.

The other two gunmen dropped their gun-belts then and raised their hands,...and shaking his head, Seth removed the gun's barrel from his prisoner's mouth. "Move back, friend." He ordered, allowing the man to back away and join the others as he came out of the stall to peer at them.

"Just what are you men doin' here?" He asked as he stepped out of the darkness. "What did McGuire tell you to do, exactly?"

"We was lookin' for you," Returned one man. "We was supposed to bring you and the old man back to th' boss, if we found you."

"Well, you found me,...now what?"

"That's up to you, I reckon." Returned the man.

"Appears it is,...get some rope, Gus!"

"Rope?...Let me shoot th' Dickheads!"

"Get th' rope, old man!" He grinned as Gus turned to do as he was told then looked at the Deputy. "It's Tulane, ain't it?"

"Jake Tulane." He nodded.

"What are you doin' here?"

"Watchin' your back, Mister Mabry….Marshal's orders."

"Well,…I appreciate the effort, Jake, and thank th' Marshal for me, okay?…And that bein' said, my friend,…do not jump into somethin' like you just did again,…it could get you killed,…if not by these men, then by me!… Always know what you're doin, before you do it!"

"Yes, Sir,…and you're right!…I didn't even know you was here, I was worried about old Gus!"

"I understand, son, and I appreciate that,…but you got a lot to learn!"

"I know, Mister Mabry, but I am learning!" He shrugged.

"Yes you are, Jake, and you're a good man." He nodded, and then looked back at the gunmen. "Get on your knees, Gents." And as they did, Gus returned with the rope. "Mister Tulane, would you please tie these gentlemen's hands to their waist,…leave just enough slack for them to reach their chins,…they'll need to eat."

"I know exactly how to do 'at!" Cackled Gus mirthfully, and shaking out the rope as he moved in behind the gunmen. "You can help me, Jake, come on!"

"If you don't mind me sayin' so?" Replied Tulane. "They're just gonna untie each other in there!"

Seth sighed then nodded. "Sound reasoning, Jake, forget th' rope, Gus!" He waved the gun then. "Okay, Gents, get up and move to th' back of th' barn,…come on, move your ass!"

*   *   *

"What a surprise, Rod!" Smiled Mason Cooper getting up from his desk. He came around to shake Dempsey's outstretched hand. "Damn good to see you!"

"How have you been, Mason?"

"Good, I guess. Business is not as good as my competitors, obviously,… but good!"

"It's honest business, Mason,…that's th' good part!"

"Yes it is," He agreed. "What brings you out and about?"

"I'm looking for Seth Mabry, Mason,…he stayin' here?"

"Why do you ask, Rod,…has he broken the law?"

"No, Sir, he hasn't. I've had my Deputies tailin' 'im in case he gets in trouble,…but they lost 'im when he came in here tonight, and then got worried when McGuire's men came in!...When none of 'em came out, Jake came to tell me."

"I see,...well, Rod,...yes, they were all in my office here." He grinned then. "They wanted to search my establishment again, said they was sure Mabry was here. That's when Mabry got the jump on them, backed them both down, he did,...disarmed them without firing a shot!"

"Where are they now?"

"Well, according to Leon, they're locked up down at the Livery." Hearing the knock at the door then, he quickly went to admit Leon again.

"Four more McGuire men just came in, Mister Cooper, and they're comin' this way,...do I stop 'em?"

Cooper looked back at Dempsey then, and nodded. "Might as well get this show on the road, Leon, show them in." He closed the door, and looked back at Dempsey. "Rod, by you being here, I'm assuming you have decided to go against the council's orders?"

"Yes, Sir, I have!" He nodded.

"Good!" He smiled and opened the door as Dempsey moved back to one side of the room, then stepped aside as Leon showed the hard-eyed gunmen into the office. "That'll be all, Leon, thank you." And after closing the door, he came around the four to stand beside Dempsey.

"What can I do for you men?"

"We're here to search your place again." Replied one of the men as they each continued to eye the Marshal.

"Not even I can search a private business without a warrant!" Said Dempsey evenly. "Now, if you men will show us your badges and warrant, then, by all means, you can search the place!"

"You tellin' us no, Mister Cooper?" Queried the man.

"I'm tellin' you no!" Returned Dempsey. "I'm also sayin' you're all under arrest,...for being in th' company of a wanted felon!" He drew his pistol as he spoke, taking them all by surprise. "That felon bein' Mister Morgan Whitely there,...now drop your guns, all of you!" He cocked the gun as he spoke,...but they made no attempt to do as he ordered.

"Unless you think you can draw and fire before I kill you, know that I'll be able to at least get two of you before I go down,...and Mister Whitely, you'll be th' first. Now draw on me, or drop 'em!"

Almost as a unit the four men let their gun-belts drop at their feet. "A wise choice!" Nodded Dempsey. "Mason, would you please call Leon in?"

Nodding, Mason went to the door and called the bartender. "He's here, Rod, what do you need?"

"You got a shotgun, Mister Leon?"

"I sure as hell do, Marshal!"

"Then how would you like to ride shotgun while I take these gents back to my office?"

Leon looked at Mason Cooper then, and when Mason nodded his assent. "I would like that a lot, Marshal!" He grinned. "Be right back!"

He was back in a few short seconds with the scattergun and together, they ushered the four men out of the office and across the floor of the saloon, each smiling when they heard several people clapping their hands in approval.

Mason Cooper walked out of his office behind them to stand at the end of the long bar and watch, nodding his own approval when he saw several men stand and applaud the Marshal,...and it was moments like that, that kept his spirits alive because he knew his town still had people who were not corrupted living in it, men who were tired of being ordered around by a mob of killers that demanded their hard earned money.

But he had to admit, that under cover of his good feelings, there still lurked worry. McGuire would know now that he was involved, and was more or less responsible for six of his men disappearing,...and he found himself suddenly wishing Seth Mabry was still in the saloon.

"Can I get you somethin', Boss?"

"What?...Oh, Dennis, you startled me!...Yes you can. Would there still be a bottle of that old Brandy under the bar there?"

"Yes, Sir, a couple of cases,...want one?

"A bottle, yes,...I think I need a drink!" He nodded and surveyed the now half-empty room, letting his eyes travel up the stairs to the second floor landing and remembering when he had taken over the saloon. Jason Ryker's office had been there, as well as his living quarters, and the other rooms were used for his prostitutes and clients. He recalled the stories that surfaced after the man was fatefully killed and in his mind, knew that the story Judith Ryker had told him was an absolute falsehood. According to rumors, Jason Ryker was every bit as corrupt as Yancy McGuire, or McCleary,... committing murder, dealing in slavery, extorting money!...Yes, Sir,...his saloon had a history, he thought sadly....If only it could talk?...Anyway, he remembered that as why he only used the rooms for his help to live in, or to let one now and again to someone in need,...like Seth Mabry.

"Thank you, Dennis." He smiled as the substitute bartender poured his drink and left the bottle, and he sipped at it as he thought of Seth Mabry again. There was a man of moral stature, he thought, a dedicated family man,...a man, he was sure just might put an end to McCleary's stranglehold on the city of Dallas. He was a man with determination and a great desire for justice, one almost as strong as his own he thought with a sigh. 'Only I can't do anything about McCleary and his bunch!'...But why not, he wondered sadly, he knew how to fire a gun, he'd survived a war, killed his enemies? If enough people would get off their broken-spirited asses and fight back,....'I'd join them', he thought seriously. But he knew he could do nothing alone, and Seth Mabry did not need help anyway. 'At least, his being here has motivated, Rod', he thought. Maybe now, Rod will continue to defy the council majority and join' forces with him?

He tossed off the drink and scanned the room again, still worried at what this latest development might make McGuire do? He had now lost six of his men by sending them here to look for Seth,...and sighing, he motioned for Dennis to come back.

"Yeah, Boss?"

"Dennis,...son, I know your job here is not to put your life in danger. But when Leon gets back, I would appreciate it if you would hang around down here until closing, maybe keep your eyes open for any trouble,...can you do that?"

"Sure can, Boss,...what's goin' down, anyway?"

"Hopefully, McGuire and his bunch, Dennis,...but anything can happen!"

"Don't I know it,...I'm sure glad th' Marshal was here!"

"He may not be, the next time!...If any more come looking, Dennis,... you saw all four of those men leave on their own!...They searched the place, and they left, just like before!"

*   *   *

Seth padlocked the feed room door then rejoined Gus and Jake. "Thanks, old timer." He grinned, placing a hand on his bony shoulder. "I just might not a handled all four of 'em without you."

"Tweren't nothin'!" Grinned Gus. "I'd a had me some fun, you hadn't been here, though,...yes'ireee!,...I'd a kilt me some Dickheads, I would!"

"You wouldn't want a do that, old man,...hell, they might a been customers!"

"Customers, my ass,...they 'as legit, they'd a rung th' bell,...customers knows it's there!" He chuckled then. "Whut ye want I should do with all 'at hardware now?"

"Jake here can take it to th' Marshal's office." He placed a hand on Tulane's shoulder then. "Can you do that?"

"Yes, sir, I can!" He nodded glumly.

"And don't feel so bad, son,...I shouldn't a chewed you out like that, you done th' right thing to check on Gus,...and I want a thank you for it!...I chewed on ya cause you scared me, I damn near shot you without thinkin'!"

"Thanks, Mister Mabry,...but I didn't think!"

"But you will next time!"

"You got that right!"

"Then forget about it, son, I have!...You're gonna make a damn good lawman,...you got th' qualities!...Now,...if you two don't mind, I'm gonna finish out my nap and come daylight, I'd appreciate it if you'd maybe go to that little cantina, th' one across from th' Sheriff's office, and fetch us a pail of beans, soup, stew, or somethin',...we got prisoners to feed....Mister Hicks ought a be here by then and, oh yeah,...borrow some tin plates and spoons, too!...You need money?"

"I'll sign for it!...No problem,...Derrick will relieve me by then."

"Good man, now gather up these weapons, and Jake,...after you fill th' Marshal in on this,...come on back and watch th' place, you done real good!"

"I got vittles left, you're hungry, Seth?" Gummed Gus. "I just started to eat, I heard that door squeak."

"No thanks, Gus,...I just want a get some sleep right now."

"Okay,...but you need me, holler!"

CHAPTER EIGHT

"I have four men left, Allan," Said McGuire angrily as he paced the floor in front of McCleary's desk. "I sent eight men to look for Mabry, four to the Dollar saloon, and four more to Jenson's stable,...and none of them returned!...I am at me wit's end!"

"He be taking our soldiers away from us, lad" Sighed the Crime Boss. "Eight more gone now, you say,...and do ye think it was Mister Cooper's doing?"

"I do not know, Allan. Word on the street was that Marshal Dempsey arrested Mister Whitley and the other three men. Now, why would he be doing that, I ask you?...I thought we did not have to worry about the man?"

"I have no answer, Lad,...but I will have a long talk with our Mister Redman, and maybe show him the error of his ways!...Now,...assuming that these rumors be right, and four of your men are in jail, that leaves four that are unaccounted for,...and we know where the trouble now lies, do we not?"

"Jenson's stable." Nodded McGuire.

"Me thinks, perhaps our Marshal was only having a drink at the Dollar Saloon, lad,...perhaps one of your men was a wanted man, who knows?...We will pay the fine, lad, don't worry, I'll have Judge McAllester arrange it.... Now,...it appears our Mister Mabry is using that Livery barn to hide in, that is how he is able to take your enforcers away from you so easily, they keep their horses there!...We should have this Mister Mabry on our payroll, me thinks!"

"Dear God, Allan,...what a sickening thought, man!...Anyway, I am not willing to send more men there to look for him!"

"Me thinks we will not need to do that, lad, it is you he is after!...We will make no further attempts to find Mister Mabry,...all we have done to now, is help the man defeat our army!...No,...by doing nothing, mister Mabry will come to us, now!"

"I do not know what the man looks like, Allan, and neither do you!...So, pray tell me,...how do we prepare for him? Maybe we should just burn down the stables, and smoke the man out,...we got away with it once?"

"Now, Yancy,...my dear, dear friend,...we can not do that!...As it is, we be on the very verge of being destroyed, and by one man, mind you!...No, we have to be very smart now, because if we don't, we could lose everything!...I received a wire from Jesse yesterday, he wants our money sent to him right a way,...and I have not done so!" He sighed then. "The banks are not solvent yet,...maybe they are in New York, I have no way of knowing,...but not in Dallas, Texas!...As upset as he must be with me, with us right now, what would he do if we should start a war here, maybe bring the Federal Government down on all of us?"

"He would see us dead, for sure." Nodded McGuire.

"Exactly, lad, and he might be tempted even now!...Judge Castle would gladly call in the army if things get too far out of hand, and that would be the end for us, and quite possibly, for Jesse, too!...No,...we will wait for our Mister Mabry to come calling,...then we can deal with him quietly. Once this is over, I will wire Jesse some money and explain the problem to him."

"I am not so sure that will appease Mister O'Riely, Allan,...the man does hold a grudge once he is mad, even with an explanation....He has ordered men killed, even after they have been proven not guilty of wronging him!...But we will do it your way."

"I think it is best!...Just stay in your establishment, lad, and keep your men around you, and tomorrow I will send the four men I have to help you, because me thinks our Mister Mabry will come calling tomorrow night."

"Why would you be thinking that, Allan,...why not tonight?"

"He has just relieved us of four more soldiers, lad,...he thinks we will be waiting for him tonight, but tomorrow night our defenses will be more lax,...so he might think!...And you will be waiting!"

"And should he decide to murder you first, instead of me?...you will be vulnerable!"

"Not to worry, me friend,...one man is all I will need....Mister Roachman is the very best!"

"And if he is not?"

*   *   *

Jake Tulane walked into the Marshal's office with the holstered weapons over both shoulders, and sighed as he allowed them to slide off his arms onto the desk.

"Looks like you been busy, Jake, what's th' story on this?"

"Four of McGuire's men came lookin' for Mister Mabry tonight."

"You arrest 'em,…where are they?"

"No, sir,…I didn't know Mister Mabry was even there!…By th' time I could get there, he had all four of 'em corralled. They're locked in th' feed-room."

"Well,…I've got four of my own back there, Jake, they came lookin' while I was talkin' with Mason Cooper tonight!…Our Seth Mabry might be a gunfighter, Jake," He sighed. "But he ain't no killer,…not yet, anyway!"

"He will be," Voiced Tulane. "He's gonna kill Yancy McGuire,…and that's a fact!"

"I know,…and it's something I sure can't blame 'im for!…But hopefully, I'll be able to persuade 'im to let me bring McGuire to trial instead, McCleary, too!"

"Am I hearin' you right, Marshal,…you're stepping in now?"

"Don't you think it's time, Jake?"

"I'd say it is, yes, Sir!" He grinned. "But what about th' Town Council?"

"Don't know,…they'll be callin' on me tomorrow, I expect!"

"Why don't we move the prisoners over to th' Sheriff's jail, Marshal,… The Councilmen won't have a leg to stand on,…if you don't have any prisoners they'll think you released 'em already?"

"That, Jake, is not a bad idea." He nodded. "I'll think about that."

"We could do it now, while I'm here to help you?"

"People are still out and about, we might be seen….If I do, I'll wait for the early hours,…Mister Hurd can help me."

"Maybe you're right….Well, I'd better go, sir."

"Yeah, where?"

"To keep an eye on th' Livery,…I just came to bring the guns and to fill you in on what happened."

"Mabry still there?"

"Said he was going to bed." He nodded.

Dempsey shook his head. "He is a strange one." He sighed. "Nobody's lookin' for me, and I can't sleep!…I don't know what's botherin' me so about th' man?"

"Why,…you think he's wanted somewhere?"

"I wish I knew, Jake,…I've checked all th' old posters, both here and at the Sheriff's office,…and nothin'!"

"Then what's th' problem,…to my way of thinkin', he's just what we needed here?"

"Problem is, Jake,…I know th' man!" He sighed then. "Or I used to know 'im!"

"What if you do remember and you find out he's wanted,…what then, Marshal,…you gonna arrest 'im?

"I don't know, Jake,…I really don't know!...Anyway, to the problem at hand. Derrick's gonna relieve you tomorrow, right?"

"That's what you said tell 'im, yes, sir."

"When he does come on back here, will you, I need to go see Judge Castle before those councilmen come callin',…I need some legal advice now, and some help, if we can get it!"

"No problem, Marshal, but Seth asked me to bring food for the prisoners first, if that's okay?"

"Yeah, that's fine, but make it early, okay?"

CHAPTER NINE

"Roderick Dempsey,...as I live and breathe!" Smiled Emmit Castle when the Marshal entered his office. He quickly got up from his desk and came around to shake his hand. "It's been a while, Roderick, how are you?"

"You mean, other than frustrated?" He smiled. "I'm just fine, I guess,... how's th' wife and son?"

"Never better, Roderick, Gwendolyn is as pretty as ever, and Grant Cameron is growing like a bad weed!...What brings you to see me?"

Dempsey sighed. "You know what's goin' on in Dallas, Emmit," He shrugged. "What else would I be cryin' to you about?...Except that now, I think things are about to reach the boiling point....You heard about th' murder on Saturday night, didn't you?"

"As a matter of fact, I did, Marshal Griggs heard about it and informed me. He was killed by his own brother, right?"

"So they said, Emmit,...the confession was beaten out of th' boy,... badly!...But now th' boy's father is in town, and he's here to kill Yancy McGuire for th' murder!"

"I see,...Did McvGuire do it?"

"I believe that he did, yes, sir!...I believe they framed th' boy."

"The same as that Ringerman thing, a couple of years ago." He nodded, and when he saw Dempsey's facial expression. "Yes, Roderick,...I know these men murdered the Ringermans, I had Marshal Griggs do a confidential, but complete investigation!...There just was not enough proof to arrest McCleary and his bunch! They stay just inside the legal limits,...everything they do is backed by forged documents,...and I can not prove that, either!...I have heard also, that one of McGuire's enforcers was found dead, is that correct?"

"Th' one called Butcher, yes, sir." Nodded Dempsey. "He's th' one who beat th' boy."

"The father kill him?"

"He told me he beat hell out of him, but he said he didn't kill 'im,... and I tend to believe 'im! But anyway,...McGuire thinks he did it and that's why I'm here. They have had men looking for Mister Mabry since Sunday night,...and Mabry has been taking them out two, and four at a time,...he now has seven McGuire men locked up at Jenson's Livery. I also have four in my jail, I arrested them in Mason Cooper's office last night when they came lookin' for Mabry!"

"And you arrested them, why?"

"Morgan Whitely,...he's wanted in Arkansas for murder."

"Then you have nothing to worry about, the rest are guilty by association."

"I do if the Council finds out about it, Emmit!...They'll insist I release 'em,...at least, the other three!...Every one of McGuire's henchmen should be jerked from the streets of Dallas, they are bullyin' shop-owners and other business men into paying, what they call protection insurance, and in the form of twenty-five dollars a week!...I call that extortion, Emmit, and my hands are tied to stop it! The shopkeepers are afraid to bring charges against 'em, for fear they'll be beat up,...or worse!"

"What would you like me to do, Roderick?...As you know, since the Reconstruction was abolished, Government policy has been to pretty much allow City Government to rule itself."

"To tell you th' truth, Emmit, I don't know what I want you to do,... But Mister Mabry is tryin' to take on McCleary's Syndicate singlehanded,... and if he lives, I believe he eventually will!...If he lives?...He needs help, Emmit, and as of now I'm going to give 'im what little help I can!...If he gets in trouble, I'm gonna do what it takes to bail 'im out of it,...but it's not gonna be enough!"

"Can he do it?...This fellow, Mabry,...are you sure he can take them down?"

Dempsey sighed again. "I believe that, yes, Sir,...but then again I don't really know, anything can happen! I do know that as of right now between the two of them, McGuire is down to a minimum of seven or eight men, th' rest are in our custody!...But now, Judge McAllester has set the boy's trial, and hanging, by th' way, for this coming Thursday,...if they can find th' boy?"

"Where is he?"

"I have 'im,...I promised Mabry I'd keep 'Im safe while he got proof of his innocence. Emmit, it is my belief this boy is being railroaded just like Ringerman, and I will not turn him over to McGuire's Court!...It's also my hope that Mabry can can get his hands on McGuire's books, and that will be proof enough for me to go against th' Council completely!"

"It could also be proof enough to make this a Federal case."

"That's what I'm hoping, Judge. I've tried talkin' to folks about comin' forward, but they're too afraid to say anything about McGuire, or the extorted money! The only thing they do complain about is th' prostitution, young girls are soliciting in shop doorways and along the boardwalks, right out in th' open,…and if their clothing was open any more in front, they'd be breakin' public nudity laws!"

"I know," Smiled Emmit. "I've seen them. Some of them can't be out of their teens yet."

"Well, sir, Dallas is earning a bad reputation in all this, and I'm here to tell you it's makin' me mad as hell!"

"Roderick, I know how you must feel, I feel the same,…but as yet there have been no Federal crimes committed,…none that I know about, and until our new President gets some new laws on the books, that's pretty much how it is. I'm going to Washington next month for the first legislative session, and I will add my two cents worth."

"Yeah, well, thanks a lot, Emmit,…but it's gonna be a little late to help out right now!"

"Roderick, here's something I will do for you,…a little unorthodox, maybe,…but I will issue a bench warrant for the men in your custody, including that young man. You bring them here to the Courthouse and I'll lock them up till this is settled. They can't hold a trial if that boy is in Federal custody!"

"Can I get that warrant right now, Sir,…I'll have the prisoners here in an hour?"

"Give me five minutes, Roderick!...By the way, while you're here. United States Marshal, Griggs has been reassigned,…how would you like to replace him on my staff?" He got up and retrieved a paper from the large file-cabinet. "You think on that, Roderick,…I'll need to know sometime tomorrow." He sat down and began writing.

*   *   *

It was mid-afternoon when Marshal Dempsey walked into the Livery barn to see the old Hostler pitching fresh hay into one of the stalls.

"Howdy-do, Marshal!" Called out Gus as he came to greet him. "Come fer yer horse, did ye?"

"No," He grinned then shook the lanky man's bony hand. "I ain't rode my horse in so long, I might ought a just sell 'im, Gus." He saw Seth walking toward him then from the rear of the barn. "Naw,…I came to see

Mister Mabry there, Gus, excuse me." He walked to meet Seth and shook his hand.

"Good to see ya, Marshal." Grinned Seth, and shook the lawman's hand firmly.

"Seth."

"What brings you callin'?"

"Nothin' in particular," He sighed. "Just tryin' to stay abreast of things. Had any more trouble?"

Seth shook his head. "Not since last night, any activity from McGuire's bunch in town?"

Dempsey shook his head. "None of 'em's been seen all day, guess he's keepin' 'em close....There has been a development, though,...guess you heard I arrested four McGuire men myself last night?"

"Mister Tulane told me this mornin', and I want a thank you for it,... makes what I got a do a lot easier."

"Well, I came to tell you somethin' that might upset ya!...I moved th' lot of 'em over to th' Courthouse today, your son, too!"

"Why?' Queried Seth, his eye narrowing suspiciously.

"To keep 'im safe, Seth. I had a talk with th' Federal Judge this mornin' and he issued warrants for Greg, and th' four men,...otherwise, I would have no choice but to release them to Judge McAllester. Your son's trial had alreadybeen set for this Thursday!...Hell, I barely got back to my office when th' Town Council showed up, McAllester, too!...Believe me, Seth, Greg wouldn't have a chance in that Courtroom."

"And what about now?"

"No trial now,...Emmit Castle is a Federal Judge, Seth, a strict, law-abiding man. Nobody will try to lay a hand on Greg there. Neither th' Judge, or myself have any doubt as to your son's innocence,...he'll be released to you once we have th' proof we need to arrest McGuire!"

"I'll have to trust you on that, I guess!" Said Seth tightly. "But I will hold you to it!"

"I know you will." Nodded Dempsey as he looked back toward the open doors. "What's your plan now," He queried then looked back at him as he spoke. "It appears McGuire won't chance sending any more men to find you?"

"I'm callin' on 'im tonight, Marshal!...Am I gonna have any trouble with you about that?"

Dempsey met Seth's eyes for a long moment, seeing a determination mirrored in them that he could not remember ever seeing in a man before then he shook his head. "No, Sir," He sighed. "But I would hope you'll go for those log-books first and let us do our jobs!...Once we have his records,

Castle will issue warrants for their arrest, him and McCleary both!...They'll hang for sure, Seth!"

"It won't be th' same, Marshal," He sighed. "And Like I said before,... no promises there!...My son was viciously murdered, and Yancy McGuire murdered 'im!...So, no promises,...and as of now I'm holdin' you responsible for Greg's safety, Sir,...that's just th' way I am!...And by th' way, that weren't meant to be no threat, Marshal."

"I didn't take it as one, Seth,...but so far you haven't killed anybody, and I'd like to keep it that way!"

Seth nodded. "I would, too,...I ain't even pulled a gun on a man since before th' war." He sighed then. "An eye for an eye, Marshal,...I will not be wronged!...That's my law, Sir, and I'm bound by it,...but if you want a stop it, then take that Silva character back there and make 'im tell you th' truth of it!...He won't admit nothin' to me because he thinks I killed Butcher,... and he ain't afraid a dyin'!...But he damn sure knows everything you need to know!...You might want a check your posters for th' rest of 'em, too, especially th' gunfighter,...name's Charlie Devlin!"

Dempsey nodded. "I'll check th' posters again, however I don't recall seein' a Charlie Devlin on any of 'em....And as for Silva, if you couldn't make 'im talk by shooting 'im, he wouldn't talk to us, neither!...No, those men are better off here for th' time bein'.,...but think over what I said, will you,...help me get those books?"

"We'll see, Marshal."

"That's all I ask, Seth....I will have a talk with Mister Silva, this Devlin character, too,...maybe tonight. What time do you plan to go callin'?"

"Midnight, shortly after."

"I'll see if I can find out what they're up to before then,...I'll be back sometime after dark....In th' meantime, though, I think it's best you stay out of sight yourself."

"I plan on it." He nodded.

"Okay then, I'll be goin'." He shook Seth's hand again. "You need anything, Derrick Tinsley is across th' way at Rankin's wagon yard." He turned and walked away, shaking Gus's hand again in passing.

Gus watched him leave then reached to push his floppy old hat up and scratch his head before looking back at Seth and walking toward him.

"What do you think, old timer,...you hear th' conversation?"

"Some, yeah." He nodded. "He's a good man, yes'iree,...knowed 'im since th' war ended. Always friendly, he is!"

"Well, I hope your right!" Sighed Seth. "I purely do. What about this Judge Castle,...he a good man, too?"

"Never met 'im,…but he come here long b'fore th' war, he did!…Honest man, he is, too."

Nodding, he patted Gus on the shoulder and went back toward the rear of the barn, thanking Gus as he left.

"What did he say?" Queried Hicks, who had been watching from the barn's darker interior.

"Said he took Greg to th' Courthouse, got 'im locked up over there…. What do you know about this Judge Castle, Jordan,…can he be trusted?"

"I think so, yes, sir!…Word is, he saved a lot a folk's land from th' Carpetbaggers after th' war! Everybody likes 'im,…plenty tough, too, killed a man in his own Courtroom over in Denton a couple years ago. Men was trying to break a outlaw out a jail. Durin' th' trial, too,…can you believe that?"

"I guess so," He sighed. "I can believe most anything about this place!… But that's good to know, Jordan, thanks….You mind goin' for vittles now,… maybe take th' plates back to th' cantina with you?"

"You want anything special tonight?"

"We'll eat what they eat, stew, chili, anything."

"Be back in a spell then."

"Be careful, son, the Marshal seems to think McGuire won't be sendin' any more men lookin',…but you never can tell!"

"I'll use th' alleys." He nodded.

"You got money, son?"

"Not a problem, I'll sign for it!"

Nodding, Seth watched him gather up last night's utensils then opened the rear door for him then watching as he worked his way along the corrals until he was out of sight….Sighing heavily, he closed and locked the door again before sitting down on a hay-bale again to meticulously roll and light a smoke, taking care to insure the match was out, by rolling it around in his mouth before dropping it.

He didn't quite know what to make of Dempsey's news?…Greg would have been safe where he was, he thought, so why take him to the Courthouse, unless it really did have to do with him holding on to the other four men. Maybe he was afraid that crooked Judge would find Greg there. If that happened, Dempsey would have no choice, but to let them have him, having been appointed to his office, and not elected to it. That being the case, Dempsey had probably done the right thing, he thought. The only thing wrong with it was that now, he was forced to trust this Judge Castle! Right now, though, he felt like the whole deck of cards was slowly being stacked against his getting to the truth, or getting to McGuire! Maybe Dempsey was right, at least for now,…if he took revenge on McGuire like he wanted to, it could hurt his chances of taking Greg home,...or of going home with him!

In essence, he thought, he was being forced to steal those ledgers!... He also knew that if the books were in a safe, he would need McGuire to open it! He sighed then, because within reason, he knew that if he made the Crime Boss open his safe, he would kill him afterward,...he was sure of that!...He would have to because nothing less would satisfy the debt owed! There was also the possibility that McGuire didn't keep any books, maybe McCleary kept the logs? Maybe he should just go to McCleary instead, at least first,...he could call on McGuire after?...But either way he would have men with guns to deal with, and he might not get away without killing somebody,...and he found no desire in that possibility at all. Killing McGuire would be collecting a debt owed, maybe even McCleary, but anyone else would be a bit much! There was only one man he wanted to see dead, Yancy McGuire!

He scraped a bare spot on the straw-covered planking and ground out the spent butt, and that's when he saw Deputy Hurd come through the double doors and stop to talk with old Gus and watched him intently, to be sure no one was following him.

Business at the stables had been steady all day long, with people coming for their horses, wagon and team, or dropping them off, and he had tried not to be seen for the most part,...so when Hurd came in, he was satisfied to sit and wait for him to come to the rear of the barn.

"Hello, Mister Mabry." Grinned the ex-deputy.

"Richard?" He nodded, shaking his hand.

"Guess you heard we took Greg to th' Courthouse?"

"Dempsey was just here." He nodded.

"Well, I'm here to help you now, Sir."

"You ever shoot a man before?"

"No, Sir,...never had to yet, but I'm not afraid to!"

"You side me, it could come to that!"

Hurd shrugged. "Got nothin' better to do I'm out a work!...Besides, if it's within th' law I will shoot, plain and simple!"

"Good,...then tell me about McCleary's place?"

"Ringermans?...What do you want a know about it?"

"I want a know th' layout, what's it look like inside?"

Sighing, Hurd sat down on a bale beside him. "First of all, it's a big place,...th' whole bottom floor is crammed with gambling tables, poker, roulette, dice, you name it, it's there!...As you walk in there's a long bar on the left."

"Where's th' stairs?"

"Straight in from the front doors, two flights of 'em. Th' second floor is nothin' but rooms where the dealers sleep,…and the girls. McCleary's office covers th' whole third floor, he lives there."

"Any back way to his office?"

"Only back way in, or out, is a downstairs rear door to th' alley. That's where th' gamblers go when they got a go pee,…in the alley, you know."

"No back stairs at all?"

"Used to be I think, at least to th' second floor,…but it may have been closed off. Why do you ask?"

"I need access to McCleary's office, and I was hopin' for a way in, without goin' through th' saloon."

"Oh, well then I think there might be,…if you can get it open? I was walkin' by the place once, the alley runnin' alongside th' building?…Anyway, I seen Yancy McGuire come out of a door in th' side of th' building,…at first, I thought he came out a th' wall itself!…Anyway that alley is pretty secured by a high fence and some thickets,…but th' door is there, I went to look for it afterward. If you don't know where to look, you won't find it neither,…it's damn near invisible!"

"That could be my way in." He nodded. "Maybe I'll find out tonight.… What do you know of McCleary's routine, you know, what he does in the saloon when he comes down,…anything?"

"He generally can be seen walkin' around th' gaming tables about midnight every night, guess he's checking out th' gamblers or somethin', I don't know. But as far as I know, he don't have no set routine."

"You go there often?"

"Not on what I earn!" He grinned. "But I been there a couple a times."

"Say,…if you had fifty dollars in your jeans,…how long would it take to lose it?"

"That would depend on my luck, I reckon,…maybe thirty minutes, an hour, I don't know,…where you goin' with this, Sir?"

"Don't know yet, Richard." He grinned. "But if you're willin', I might need you after all,…unless my plans change?" He sighed. "And here lately, they been doin' that!…But I'll let you know."

"Well, I'm willing!…Anything to help bring this bunch down!"

*   *   *

Allan McCleary grunted out his passion then rolled away from the sobbing teenaged girl to sit up on the side of the large bed. He would normally be well sated after sex with the woman-child,…but he was troubled! For the first time since coming to Dallas, Texas, he was afraid,…

not only of Seth Mabry, but of Jesse O'Riely. He knew that if the powerful Crime Boss didn't hear from him soon, or didn't receive the funds he asked for, he would be sending someone to replace him,…permanently! He knew all too well, the men he would be sending, too,…men that would make the deceased Butcher a school boy in comparison. Not in size, he thought drearily, remembering the brutality of the New York enforcers,…but in many other ways. These would be the same men he had once commanded!

Sighing heavily, he looked back at the girl's naked body for a moment, and knew she was silently crying in her pillow. "Dry your tears, Lass." He said calmly, causing her to jerk involuntarily. "Go on now, go get yourself cleaned up, girl,…and me bed, too, I like fresh, clean sheets to sleep on!"

He got up and pulled his pants on, then his shirt before stretching the red suspenders up his arms and onto his shoulders. He watched the girl get off the bed, her ripe young, and supple body moving provocatively as she went to pour water into a basin. He knew she must hate him, after all, he was raping her, forcing her to do his bidding,…but what the hell, he thought, and then grinned evilly.…Was that not what a woman was for,…a man's pleasure?"

Shrugging, he slipped on his oxford shoes and tied them then plodded off into his office to open the metal box and extract a fat cigar. He lit it before opening the iron door of the safe then sighing once again, stooped to retrieve the ledgers and place them on his desk before sitting down. Opening the top book, he mentally went over the entries of the past, almost three years worth, and what he now had in the safe was close to two million dollars, not counting the original one million Jesse had sent with him to Dallas. In all, there was three million dollars in the large iron safe behind him, a lot of it in Gold and Silver coins, but the bulk was in currency, which was only now beginning to regain it's full face value. Sighing again, he wondered if he shouldn't just go ahead and ship a crate load of currency to O'Riely by train,…or should he wait until this thing with Mabry was finished?"

He cursed and closed the ledger loudly then leaned back to stare at the ceiling while he smoked. Things were going very badly, he thought worriedly, and all because of one man. One man, who was singlehandedly able to take out eleven of his men without firing a shot,…not excluding Mister Silva, he thought sadly, he had liked the silent Mexican, and his unique ability to throw a knife. Who was this Mister Mabry anyway, he wondered?…One thing was sure, he would be coming for Yancy,…and maybe even him for ordering his son's death. He never expected a routine mugging to go so wrong, he had done the exact same thing in New York many times with no problems.

But this man, he thought, this man was not like every other man,... he was not afraid!...He sighed again then, thinking that in New York City, or even in Belgrade, he would have gone after a man like Mabry with every man in his command, and he would have found him!...But here,...here he had to be careful, else he would have the United States Army to contend with.

Jesse O'Riely had no idea, he thought. Texas was a whole different place, with a whole different breed of man,...Jesse had no idea of how to handle men like this!...He looked across at the tall Chime-clock then. His evening meal would be arriving soon, and he was starved. He put the cigar in his mouth and got to his feet then with a sigh, put away the ledgers before going to the bedroom door.

"Put your lacy robe on, me darlin', we will be eating shortly,...and I expect you to be at your prettiest tonight!"

*   *   *

Yancy McGuire sat at his desk and stared at the only four men he had left in his command. "You lads know I can be a generous man," He sighed then, and shrugged. "So I am going to say this only one time!...I believe that our Mister Mabry has it in his mind to kill me!...Possibly on this very night,...so,...the man, or men who stops him from succeeding, will find me most generous indeed,...if you get me meaning? But,...and hear me well!... He must be stopped without gunplay, Gentlemen, unless,...unless there be no other way!...Am I clear, lads?"

"You want 'im caught, not killed!" Voiced one of the men. "We got it, Boss,...so what's th' plan?"

Yancy got up and came around the desk. "The only way he can get to me, is through the front doors,...and that be where I want you men, all four of you. Sit at the tables, stand around and chat, I do not give a shit,...just stop the Son of a Bitch!"

"That'll be no problem, Mister McGuire," This from another man as he also shrugged. "But we don't know who we're lookin' for,...he could be anybody?"

"God Damn it, man!" He glared at them for a minute then angrily paced the floor a couple of times before facing them again. "Forgive me, Lads,...that be my dilemma as well!...But if I knew this man, I would be quite capable of stopping him me self!...But I do not know him, nor what he looks like!...I have never seen him!...Just keep your eyes open, watch everyone,...if he appears to be a stranger, stop and disarm him, if you feel he means no harm, leave him be,...that be as simple as I can make it!"

"Will you be here, or down on th' floor?"

"I will be at my usual table, at my usual time,…maybe before, I don't know! Now get out of here, lads, find your places,…and be ready. And remember!…No shooting unless I be threatened, we must be careful here,… now go!" He watched them leave and close the door then cursed and fished a thin cigar from his inside coat and lit it. Where might Mabry be holding his men, he wondered? If there was ever a time he needed them, it was now!…'I wish I had never left Ireland' he thought angrily,…'or New York City'!…At least there his enemies came at him head on, and didn't give a damn about the odds,…but not here! Mabry scared him,…he was more dangerous than any New York Assassin!

He paced the floor again as he smoked, his mind searching for anyone under his control, that could possibly afford him any help?…But with Gaylon Gentry gone, he couldn't think of anyone. Before this, men were forced to do his bidding, he owned them,…and they were afraid not to!…But Butcher was dead now, and the Merchants didn't fear him. If they could help him, they would refuse!

He would have a hundred men at his disposal in New York, even two hundred men!…But in Dallas, Texas, he had four between him and possibly death at the hands of a gunman! What was he to do?…Damn Allan anyway!…He was all snug in his secure house, with a pretty young Lass to screw,…and he was the man who gave the order to kill that young Mabry boy!…He only carried out the order….He held out his hands then and saw them shaking. He was never afraid of anything before this Mabry showed up!

If he only knew what the man looked like, he would not be afraid at all, he thought, but then his eyes fell on the round block of wood on the wall across the room from him,…and he quickly snaked his hand up behind his neck, grabbed the hilt of the long, sharp dagger and threw the knife at the block, some thirty feet away. The thin-bladed stiletto buried its self in the block of wood, and he nodded his satisfaction as he walked across the room to retrieve it. But he had thrown the knife too hard and he couldn't pull it from the wood.

Cursing again, he went on to his desk and opened the top drawer, took out an almost identical blade and stuck it back into the leather sheath behind his neck. 'Let that Son of a Bitch identify himself' he thought savagely, and then looked back at the protruding hilt of the dagger in the target. 'Let him come'!

"I be forgetting I be a killer me self, Mister Mabry," He said loudly. "So come and get me, man,…I will be waiting!" And with a satisfied smirk on his face, he turned to the wall behind his desk, moved a large painting aside and opened a small wooden door on the wall,...and still smiling, removed a ledger and a large stack of papers and placed them on his desk.

There was just enough time, he thought, before going downstairs. Once this was all over the delinquent Merchants would most certainly realize the error of their ways, and he would take great pleasure in seeing to that personally,...'because I will know who they are'! He untied the string from the stack of contracts and began sorting through them. There were liens, contracts for loans to farmers, Ranchers and Dairymen, owner deeds, and contracts on the thirty-odd whores working the floor, and on the streets. But he lay those all aside when he came to those contracts he held on the city's Merchants. He then opened the large ledger, containing the names and dollar amounts received for protection and began going down the list, checking the extorted protection payments they had made, and then began making a list of those that had of late, refused to pay their dues,...and there were quite a few!...And all because the Butcher was dead!

He grinned then,...after Mister Mabry was gone, he would pay special attention to these misguided Merchants!...A few broken bones and missing teeth would go a long way in showing them the errors of their ways!...Yes indeed. He would hire much tougher men as well, smarter men, and meaner! Sighing, he retied the papers then folded the list and put it in his shirt before getting up to put everything away again.

He straightened the painting over the wall safety-box and pulled his pocket watch. Five o'clock, he thought, enough time for a nap before their supper arrived. Allan's four men would be arriving by nine pm to help him, and all would be well! He looked at the block of wood again and smiled. What did he have to worry about anyway,...he was the absolute best there was with a knife. He had killed many of his enemies from the darkness of an alley, he thought with a wide grin. Yes, he was the best,...not even Silva could best him with a knife!...Yawning, he mashed out the cigar and went to the long ebony, cushioned settee against the wall and lay down.

CHAPTER TEN

Emmit Castle was the youngest man to ever pass the bar and ultimately becoming a sought-after aide and advisor in Washington DC. With an I.Q. of more than two hundred, and a close friend of General Grant, he became Grant's aide and advisor during the war, proving himself a great tactician. When the war ended, he came to Texas to practice his law,...and once U.S. Grant was elected President of the United States, was appointed a Federal Judgeship,...his job being to oversee the Reconstruction process in the large state. Emmit Castle was in his early twenties by then and married to his job, a career bachelor who did not get married until 1876, in the midst of a great Depression that was devastating the country.

He was worried today, however, and sat staring idly at the painting of the now ex-President Grant, and the American Flag that was stretched between Grant's portrait and that of Abraham Lincoln. Dallas was his town, and it was in trouble,...and because of the Government's polices, he was pretty much helpless to do anything about any of it! If only the citizens would band together and bring charges against McCleary and his bunch, he could bring in Captain Hayward and his Rangers to clean up the mess! But, he sighed, if, was the largest little word in his vocabulary of late.

He had not known, or realized until now that County Judge Horace McAllester was on McCleary's payroll, and it was very upsetting to him because he liked the tough, wiry Judge. He knew, however, that he would need to step into this problem at some point,...and he knew he would be breaking Government policy by interfering in local Government. But Dallas, Texas was his home, and if he allowed a New York Organized Crime Syndicate to continue operations here, sooner or later it would be impossible to stop it,...and it must be stopped before that happened!

Roderick Dempsey wanted to do something also, but couldn't because of the Town Council who, according to him was also in debt to McGuire.

He had not known about Sheriff Gentry either, he thought sadly, and he had liked him also! The way it stands now, he thought grimly, it was all resting on the shoulders of one determined man, an obvious gunfighter who's only ties to Dallas was his son's quite obvious murder at the hands of McGuire, and another accused of the crime. Mister Mabry was a man alone, but with an excess of guts!...And he needed help!

Suddenly making up his mind, he got up and left his office then walked down the hall to the Telegrapher's office and went inside.

*   *   *

Leaving the Telegraph office, he walked farther down the hall and knocked at another door.

"Enter!" Came the muffled voice, and when Castle opened the door. "Come in, Judge!" Exclaimed U.S. Marshal Cyrus Griggs. "What's the occasion, Sir?"

"You're ready to go, I see?" Grinned Emmit as he eyed the packed boxes.

"Yes, Sir" He sighed. "But not by choice, Emmit. Little Rock, Arkansas somehow don't strike my fancy none!...Never th' less, I'm leavin' by train tomorrow." He grinned then, a little confused. "What's going on?"

Emmit grinned solemnly at him and closed the door. "I just sent for Captain Hayward, Cyrus, and I may be in a world of trouble for it!...But something has to be done about McCleary and his bunch!"

"Well, I agree,...and that makes me even sorrier to be leavin'!...What do you need, Emmit?"

"I want a meeting with Horace McAllester, and I'd like you to fetch him for me,...arrest him if you have to!...In case you didn't know, Cyrus, he's in McCleary's hip pocket!"

Grigg's jaw tightened when he heard that. "When would you like to see 'im?"

"Today, right now, Cyrus!...Do you mind?"

"Pleasure's all mine, Emmit. Be back in half an hour!" He moved around Emmit and grabbed his hat and they walked out into the hallway together, but there the Judge stopped him again.

"I'd like to see Roderick Dempsey as well, Cyrus,...if you don't mind, please call on him first,...and tell him it's quite urgent!"

*   *   *

"Hey out there!" Came the loud, somewhat muffled voice. "Hey, Mabry, you out there,...I want a talk to ya!"

Seth got up from the bale of hay, as did Hurd and walked to the locked door of the feed-room.

"Mabry," Came the voice again. "If you're there, man,…let's talk!"

"Who wants to talk?" Returned Seth.

"Charley Devlin!...Come on, Man, get me out a here!"

Seth looked at Hurd then and gestured with his head. "Back away a step, son, and pull your pistol,…and when the Deputy was in position, looked down at the padlock. "Back away from th' door, Devlin,…and just so you'll know, if this is some kind a trick I'll kill you!" He took the key from his pocket and opened the lock then slid the chain out of the holes in the door and opened it.

"Come on out, Charlie Devlin." And when the gunman moved past him, he closed the door again and locked it. "Sit on a bale there, Charlie and talk!"

"Does your deal still stand?" Queried the gunman as he sat down.

"Depends on what you tell me?"

"Then you ask th' questions, man, I'll answer 'em,…then you can let me go! I don't give a shit if I never see you, or Dallas, Texas again!"

Seth moved in to sit down on the bale beside him. "Okay, I will!...Where does McGuire keep his books, he got a safe?"

"Naw, he ain't got a safe!" Denied Devlin, reaching up to scratch his nose. "He's got a hole in th' wall behind his desk,…keeps everything there, money, books, everything."

"And you say it ain't a safe?"

Devlin shook his head. "Got a door on it, but that's all,…and he's got a big picture coverin' it all!...I only been there once, Mabry, but I notice things."

"Any way to get there without goin' through th' saloon?"

"None that I ever saw!"

"Any idea what kind a books he keeps?"

"Don't know that, I never seen 'em,…but several of th' girls told me he had their contracts, and some deeds maybe, stuff like that!" He shrugged then. "I don't know!"

"How many men has he got?"

"I don't know now, maybe eleven, or twelve,…you got th' rest in there."

"All right," He peered narrowly at the gunman then. "Who killed my boy, Charley?"

"McGuire did it,…I overheard Silva tellin' Butcher all about it!"

Seth nodded then sighed deeply. "Charlie Devlin, I'll kill ya, if I ever see you again!" He nodded then and stood up,…then sighing, gestured with both outstretched hands and moved aside.

"Don't worry about that, Mabry!" Grinned Devlin as he got to his feet. "You won't see me again,...and don't take offense, man,...but I still think I can take you!"

"Anything's possible, Mister Devlin, I don't claim to be th' best!...Your horse here at th' stable?"

Devlin shook his head as he looked at each of them. "Left it at McGreggors, across town."

"Then take Mister Silva's horse, he won't be needin' it!...Saddle's on th' rail."

"Which one is it?"

"Black with a blazed face." He watched as Devlin nodded and slowly began backing away toward the stalls. "You can walk away from me, Charley, I ain't gonna shoot you!" He grinned then. "Course I can't say the same for old Gus up there, so you better get a move on!"

"What about my guns, Mabry?"

"You won't need 'em!...Don't come back to Dallas, Devlin, Marshal's checkin' his wanted posters for ya right now!" He heard the knock at the rear door then and opened it for Deputy Hicks to enter with their supper.

"Who's that saddlin' Silva's horse?" Queried Hicks as he put the bucket and plates down. "You lettin' Silva go?"

"That's Charlie Devlin!" Sighed Seth. "And there's been a change of plan, Jordan."

"What kind a change,...what did I miss?"

"We'll be goin' to McGuire's tonight after all,...and I'm gonna need your help,...and Corines! Richard, you'll need to stay here with th' prisoners!...Now come on, I'll tell you both th' plan while we eat, I'm hungry."

*   *   *

"Come in, Roderick!" Smiled Emmit. "And take that badge off your vest!"

"I thought I had till tomorrow to decide?" Frowned Dempsey as he reached up and removed the Town Marshal's badge.

"It is tomorrow, Roderick!" Returned Emmit as he opened a drawer and came to pin the U.S. Marshal's badge on his shirt. "I made the decision for you!...I need you now,...and so does Dallas, now raise your right hand,...I'm about to swear you in!"

Emmit had just finished the oath of office, and both had seated themselves when Marshal Griggs ushered Judge McAllester through the door and closed it.

"What is the meaning of this outrage, Emmit?" Stammered McAllester as he violently jerked his arm from Grigg's grip. "I protest this sort of treatment, Sir!"

Emmit had gotten to his feet as they came in. "And I protest yours, Sir!" He returned with sarcasm,…and then he smiled at Griggs. "Thank you very much, Marshal,…and now, I'd like to introduce your replacement to you, you know Roderick Dempsey, I believe?"

"Yes, I do." He smiled as Dempsey got to his feet. "Congratulations, Rod." He shook the New Marshal's hand and then they both sat down to watch Emmit and the County Judge.

"Emmit, I demand an explanation for this!" Voiced McAllester, and was beside himself with anger as he glared at them. "What's going on here?"

"I was hoping you would tell me, Horace?...You can talk freely here, your Boss isn't here!"

"My, what?"

"Come on now, Horace, I know you're in McGuire's pocket!...All I want to know is why, man?"

McAllester opened his mouth in protest, but only stared at Emmit for several seconds before finally releasing his pent-up breath in a large sigh and suddenly seemed to shrink in size as he looked at him. But then, almost wilting in sudden weakness, McAllester reached for the back of a chair and almost fell as he managed to sit down.

Emmit quickly went to a table against the back wall, brought the man a glass of water and watched him drink it. "Tell me what happened, Horace?" He took the glass and placed it on his desk.

Nodding feebly, McAllester looked at each one of them before speaking. "Three years ago, I was losing everything I had, Emmit!...The bank suddenly closed without a warning,…I had no money, my clients had no money!" He swallowed then and looked up at him. "You knew about it, I told you!" He looked down at the floor then. "Shortly after that, every bank in Dallas began foreclosing on their outstanding loans to regain lost funds….I was on the road to ruin, Emmit,…so was most everyone else!"

"But then, along came Allan McCleary with a boatload of money to lend!...The dollar had lost most all of it's value, at that point, so I had to borrow heavily,…but I borrowed enough to literally pay off what I owed, I was told I could repay the loan in installments as things got better,…and it was great, I was suddenly back on my feet again,…then a few months later, this Yancy McGuire came to me and said that if I would do them this one big favor, they would mark my bill paid in full!...Well, like a fool, I became greedy,…I agreed!...I witnessed and legalized the bill of sale for Ringerman's saloon!...A week after that, they all burned to death, Emmit!...I never dreamed the whole thing was forged, I believed the sale was legal,...I swear I did!"

He sighed heavily then reached a kerchief from his inside coat and blew his nose. "I haven't been able to sleep since!...But I lived with the fact, and when I asked for my paid receipt they wanted me to do one more thing first,...so I issued a warrant for one of Double-Trey's cowhands, charging him with arson and murder in the case of the Ringerman fire." McAllester began to sob then. "I hung an innocent man, Emmit!...I had no choice!"

Sighing, Emmit walked over and placed his hand on McAllester's shoulder. "Stop crying, Horace,...I know you're a good man! You should have come to me with this before it got out of hand....Now,...is there anything else?"

"After that happened," Sniffed the Judge. "McGuire came to my office with that man, Silva, and that Ogre, Butcher,...and he said that if I ever refused a request from him, or Allan McCleary, that he would introduce Silva and Butcher to my wife and daughters!" He began to sob again then. "Wh,...what else could I do, but comply?"

"I have no idea, Horace, but you should have come to me!...Will you testify to all of this?"

"I can't do that, Emmit, my family?"

"I wouldn't worry about that, Horace,...Butcher is dead now, and Mister Silva is in custody,...but never the less, I will move your wife and girls into my apartment, right here in the Courthouse. I have not used it since I was married anyway."

"You would do that?"

"You should have come to me sooner!" Said Emmit angrily. "You have no choice now, Horace, you will testify against these men, else I'll have no choice but to bring you up on charges as well. What you did was a crime, whether you were forced to do it or not!...Now, I want you to go sit at my desk, there's inkwell and a quill there, and paper. I want you to write down everything that has transpired between you and these two men, beginning with the first loan!...And then,...you can write out your resignation."

"My God, Emmit!...I've been a Judge since before the war!"

"You can be again, Horace, that's what elections are for!...Now go on, it will take you a while to put all this down, but I have all night!" He helped McAllester from his chair and over to his own, allowing him to be seated there. Once the distraught Judge began writing, he sighed and came back to face Griggs and Dempsey.

"I don't think anything will happen tonight," He began then sighed again. "I don't believe McGuire or McCleary are likely to know we have Horace in custody. But first thing tomorrow, Roderick, I'd like for you and your deputies to move his family in here,...I'll have a couple of men with a wagon meet you there."

"You got it, Judge." Nodded Dempsey.

"Now, while I'm on a roll, so to speak,...Roderick, your first official duty as U.S. Marshal will be to bring every member of that City Council in here to see me,...I have a few words for them as well!"

"You want a see 'em tonight, Emmit,...all of 'em?"

"Just as soon as you can get them here,...unless not all are beholden to McGuire?"

"Well,...there's only one I know of, that's not!"

"Mason Cooper?"

"That's th' one."

"Then bring me the rest of them!"

"I'll go along with him, Judge," Grinned Griggs. "My last official duty!"

*   *   *

Allan McCleary studied the faces of the five men as he lit his cigar. "Lads," He said, shaking out the match. "I called you in here because I believe this man, Mabry, will try and murder me friend, Yancy McGuire tonight!...You all know what has been taking place since Sunday past,...we are down to eight soldiers between us. The others have fallen to this Mister Mabry, whoever he is?...He managed somehow to kill the Butcher,...and I am sorry to say, most likely, Mister Silva as well,...and that tells me we are dealing with a very dangerous gunfighter,...an adversary the likes we are not used to, so be very careful, lads,...this man is not to be taken lightly!"

"Except for Mister Roachman here, I want you four lads to join Yancy McGuire's soldiers at his place tonight. We do not know how many men Mabry may have helping him, if any at all,...but I want the man caught and brought before me,...and I want him alive,...Do I make me self clear, lads?" And when they all agreed.

"Good!...Now, off with ye, lads, and good hunting!" They watched the four gunmen leave then Allan went to the bar and poured himself, and Roachman a glass of Irish whiskey and brought it back.

"Gerrard, me lad,...we are going to make an example of our Mister Mabry, when he is caught!...You are going to shoot him down, right in front of me saloon here,...right in the middle of Elm Street,...and it will be a fair fight, as allowed by law! And when it is over, it will have served to prove a point to all the little peons out there who think they can defy Allan McCleary without consequence. They will pay their dues after that, you can be sure,...and they will do so eagerly."

"Well, pardon me for sayin' this, Allan," Voiced Roachman. "But this might not be as easy as all that!...I can be arrested for killing Mabry, you know,...there's a law against such a thing, unless it's self defense!"

"Relax, Gerrard, we have a Judge on our side, we also have the best lawyer in Dallas on our side!...It will be in self-defense, lad!"

"And if Mabry refuses, or doesn't show?"

"We will catch Mister Mabry tonight, lad,...and he will be glad to fight you, he will be very glad!...Now drink up, then go down and have your supper." They clicked glasses and drank their toast and then, without a word the gunfighter left.

Sighing, McCleary went and poured himself another drink before walking around to his safe and removing the ledgers again,...and sipping at the fiery liquid, sat down and opened the top book to study the entries for a minute as he drank. Tossing off the drink, he took another bottle from his desk drawer and poured himself another as he continued reading.

Maybe it would have been better if he had just allowed that Mabry cowboy to win and go home, he thought distastefully, hell,...it would have been better than all this! He should have known that his east coast tactics would not work here!..."God, where was the Blarney Stone when he needed it?...So much for Luck Of The Irish!"

He was not even sure that Roachman could kill Mabry, in fact, he wasn't sure of anything!...With all his power and confidence in himself, he was suddenly unsure of himself. How could one cowboy, a dirt farmer do this to him?...Allan McCleary was the most feared enforcer Boss in the whole of New York City,...and he was now a man afraid! Had he moved too fast in Dallas, in his bid for power?...No, he thought, he had not! He had worked his original plan to the letter,...he had gotten his Casino, and it was every bit as nice as those in New York, or the Bronx. He had bought himself a Judge, an Attorney, a Sheriff, and even a whole Town Council,...and every one forced to do his bidding!...No,...he did everything right, except for one thing,...he told Yancy to kill a young, overly lucky cowboy and now, his whole organization was in jeopardy of collapsing around his large, Irish ears.

Jesse O'Riely was even upset with him, and it was not wise to have the Crime Boss mad at you,...he knew that fact, first-hand! Maybe he should just take his three million dollars and run with it?...But he knew O'Riely well enough not to be that stupid,...at least not yet. But he knew that if it came down to winning, or losing his war in Dallas tonight, and he was sure it would culminate this very night,...he would not hesitate!...But if Yancy were to be killed tonight and he, himself somehow survived,...he could have an out by blaming everything on him?...But Dear God,...what was he thinking? Yancy McGuire was his only friend, had been since childhood in Ireland,…they came to New York together!…No, he thought sadly,…he could not abandon him.

Angrily, he poured and drank another whiskey while he smoked the long cigar. He would come out of this on top, he decided, he was Allan McCleary, he had always come out on top, and he would this time as well! Once this thing with Mabry was settled, he would send Jesse a million dollars and then,…business as usual!

He took a deep breath then and tossed off the drink, his eyes on the bedroom door, and his mind on the fourteen year old, naked Nymph that waited for him there. Suddenly aroused, he pushed to his feet and followed his calling.

*   *   *

"Eight-thirty." Sighed Seth as he put away the watch.

"What time are we doin' this again?" Queried Hicks nervously, as he watched the activity in the stable. "I keep forgetting."

"Scared, Jordan?" Grinned Seth.

"A bit, yeah!…what we're gonna do is gutsy as hell, man,…ain't you scared at all?…We could get ourselves shot, ya know?"

"I'm always a bit nervous, son,…but you still got time to back out if you want….I can do this alone?"

"No, sir,…I'm committed to this now, and we're gonna pull it off, too!"

"Man in a buggy just drove in," Commented Deputy Hurd. "He's talking with Gus about somethin'." The statement caused Seth and Hicks to crane their heads and look also. "I think I know him, too!" Added Hurd. As he stood up

"Yeah," Breathed Hicks. "I've seen 'im before, too. Wonder what's goin' on?"

"That's Reverend Muenster, all th' way from Lewisville." Returned Hurd. "I'm gonna go see what's up?" He moved out of the shadows and walked toward Gus and the preacher, and when Gus saw him coming, he got the Reverend's attention and pointed at him.

"Reverend Muenster?" Smiled Hurd and held out his hand. "Richard Hurd, Sir,…what brings you all this way?"

"You're George and Marlene Hurd's boy, aren't you?"

"Yes, Sir, I am."

"Well, I came to see the Sheriff, Ricky, but there's no one there!…I even went to see the Marshal, but he ain't there, neither,…where is everybody?"

"Well, th' Sheriff is away right now, Reverend,…but I'm his Deputy, what can I do for you, Sir?"

"It's Rebecca, Ricky,...she's gone!...She was walking home from Church a week ago and she never got there. Sheriff Coffey and myself have looked everywhere in Lewisville,...we can't find her, Ricky!...So I thought I'd come here and look."

"Was there any witnesses,...did anybody see anything?"

"A Mexican was seen in the area, but that's all we know!...This is devastating to us, Ricky, I have got to find her, her mother has made herself sick with worry!"

"If Becky's in Dallas, I'll find her, sir, I promise....Now why don't you go on back home, it's not gonna be safe here for you!...Please, Mister Muenster, you have my word, I will look for Becky I promise,...now please, sir, you'll never find her on your own, anyway!"

The Reverend peered tearfully at him for a moment then nodded, turned and climbed back into his buggy and left.

"Ya think he'll go home, do ye?" Voiced Gus as he watched him.

"I hope he does!" Sighed Hurd and headed back to join Seth and Hicks,...and after relaying the Reverend's story to them, he sat down again in deep thought.

"I remember that little girl," Said Hicks. "They came to th' Sheriff's office a couple a years ago. She was a cute little thing, too!"

"I came to Dallas about then, myself." Sighed Hurd. "Anyway, when this is over, I'm gonna look for her."

"We all will, Ricky." Nodded Hicks.

*   *   *

"It's eight-thirty." Sighed Emmit as he came to sit beside Dempsey, and they were both watching the six Councilmen as they continued to write out their statements.

"Will you have them resign, too?" Queried Dempsey.

"No need for that." Sighed Emmit. "If I remember correctly, the town had a hard time finding anyone to even run for City Council!...No,...they're all good men, hell, they helped make Dallas a City,...and they'll still be good at their jobs."

Cecil Redman owned Main Hardware and Mercantile, and he looked up at them with a bleary expression then signed his name to the statement,...and five minutes later, all of them laid down their pencils.

"Are we to be arrested now, Emmit?" Asked Redman as he stood up.

"No, of course not!" Returned Emmit getting to his feet. "Not unless you refuse testimony if called on? Each and every one of you, have been a significant factor in the growth of Dallas, Texas and I know you will continue to be a factor. But I will say that as of now, the decisions you make will need to be run by me before it can be passed into ordinance. Also,… should McGuire, or McCleary come to you for a favor before we can finish this business, you must go along with them as usual, agree to anything they say,…and then come to me with it. They will never know of your refusal!… And don't worry,…none of you are in any sort of trouble,…but what you must do right now is exactly what you normally do,…don't change a thing!… Take care of your business and family, because tonight is the beginning of a new day for Dallas. Texas Rangers will be here in two days, and by the time they leave, we will have our clean city back,…and Gentlemen, let this be a lesson to never let this sort of thing happen again."

"Oh, and one more thing.…I have gone way out on a very shaky limb today,…I have interfered with local Government without Federal Governmental authorization! And because of that, the Marshal and myself just could need your support when this is all over. But either way, my friends,…the bottom line will be a Syndicate-free Dallas!…Mister McCleary, and McGuire will no longer be a threat, you have my solemn oath on that!"

"You have ours as well, Emmit!" Said Redman with feeling. "Thank you,…now if it's all right, I'd like to go close up,…all of us would?"

"By all means, Cecil,…and thank you all for your honesty." He sat back down, and they both watched a dejected City Council file out into the hallway.

"Hopefully we are on our way, Roderick." Sighed Emmit. "I'm only sorry I let it go this far!"

"You gonna issue warrants for McLeary and Company now?…We still need their books to put 'em away."

"I'll have to do that when Hayward and his Rangers arrive, Roderick. We can't afford to jump too far ahead of things because unfortunately, civil rights apply to them also.…Besides,…I need to wire Washington of my activities here,…and I dread it,…I don't know if I can plead my case well enough to get an approval."

"You will!…But I got a tell you, Sir,…Seth Mabry ain't gonna wait!…In fact, I look for all hell to break loose tonight!"

"And you know this, how?"

"My gut, Judge,…I can feel it!…That, and because he as much as told me so."

"Then get out there and go to work, Marshal, you've a free hand now,… and I did not say that, you understand!…But if our Gunfighter friend is fired on, give him the support he needs. Just do your best to keep the peace.… If Mister Mabry succeeds, Roderick,…there will be no Governmental repercussions on my part!…And that sounds selfish, I know,…but if this

doesn't work, I could be facing serious penalties for my part in all of this!...
Especially if it fails!"

"Believe me, Emmit, I understand!" He got to his feet as he spoke.
"All right then....First thing tomorrow, I'll bring in McAllester's family as
planned, and...."

"Unless it won't be necessary by then." Interrupted Emmit.

"Right!" He nodded. "But I'd better go anyway, I've had my two
deputies watching Mabry since Sunday, and I'd best check on them. If I
can keep th' man in sight long enough, we might settle this thing without
anybody dying!" He reached and shook Emmit's hand then.

"Thanks, Emmit,...I'll do my best!"

"You always did, Roderick!"

Dempsey quickly left, pulling the door shut behind him as he stepped
into the hallway and pausing there for a minute to run his hand over the
Federal Marshal's badge,...and he grinned widely before continuing his way
to the Courthouse doors. He had just had his shackles removed,...he could
now do the job that was expected of him. True, he would still have to report
to Emmit Castle, but he would pretty much be free to uphold the law now,
and that was what he had always wanted.

He went through the Courthouse doors and down the steps to the street
and almost immediately, began shouldering his way through pedestrians and
dodging street traffic,...and wishing at the same time that he knew what
Seth Mabry had in mind to do tonight?...Whatever it was, he felt almost
certain it would result in McGuire's death, unless he was there to stop it!...
He found himself hoping that Mabry would go for the ledgers first, instead
of McGuire,...but that was a long-shot, Seth Mabry was not a man to be
denied his eye for an eye!

*   *   *

Hearing the noise behind them, Jake Tulane, already sitting on his knees
in the darkness, pulled his pistol and cocked it as he whirled.

"Hold it, Jake!" Said Dempsey quickly. "Don't shoot me." He chuckled
as he slowly came forward to join them. "You was pretty damn quick on th'
draw there, Jake, I didn't know that about you?"

"Yeah, well, we weren't expecting you, Boss!" Breathed Tulane while
holstering the weapon.

"Well you both scared hell out a me!" Voiced Derrick.

"Anything goin' on over there?" Queried Dempsey as he hunkered down
between them.

"Business as usual, as far as I can tell." Returned Jake. "Somebody resembling a preacher was there a while back,…don't know what it was about, but it brought Ricky Hurd out a hidin' to talk with 'im."

"What about Mabry?"

"Haven't seen him at all lately,…he might not even be there."

"He's there all right," Breathed Dempsey. "And he's gonna take on McGuire tonight, he told me so."

"What do we do?"

"Well,…th' shackles are off now, Jake, you're free to do your jobs,…so watch 'im!…If he gets in trouble, bail 'im out!"

"What do you mean, our shackles are off, Marshal?"

"Just what I said,…Now, give me that Deputy's badge!"

"Am I fired, Marshal?" He asked as he shakily took off the star.

"Nope!" Said Dempsey as he accepted it. "You can pin this one on,…you're now the acting Town Marshal!"

"What,…how come,…you didn't quit, did you?"

"Nope again,…I am now a United States Marshal,…got sworn in today by Emmit Castle."

"Well, hot damn!" Blurted Derrick Tinsley. "Congratulations, Marshal, oh,…and you, too Jake,…I mean Marshal."

"'Thanks Derrick,…you got any fault with workin' for Jake here?"

"None a toll, no, sir!"

"Is acting Marshal a good thing, Marshal?" Queried Jake as he pinned on the new badge.

"For tonight, it is,…once I talk with Emmit Castle, it'll be official!…Castle had Redman and th' Council members in his office today, made 'em fess up to being on McGuire's payroll. Your hands won't be tied anymore, neither,…and I'll still be around to help you out if you need me!"

"Then you'll still be th' Boss?"

"Nope, you are, Jake,…but I'll likely still give you orders from time to time."

"Good,…Cause I'm apt to fuck up a time or two!"

"Everybody does!…Now, come mornin',…unless something happens tonight to change it,…I want you two to meet me at your office, we got a job to do for Judge Castle….Now, Jake,…if Mabry leaves them stables stay close on 'im, ya hear, and be careful, man,…McGuire's men are seasoned gunmen!"

CHAPTER ELEVEN

Yancy McGuire opened his eyes and sat up on the settee then yawning, looked around him at the furnishings before getting to his feet. He could hear the faint noise from the usually crowded saloon two floors down and thinking that before now, it had always made him smile, because it was making him money. But tonight even the off-key piano was playing on his nerves.

He managed a smile then as he reached a thin cigar from his vest and lit it before looking at his watch. 'Nine thirty', he thought,…and he knew that Allan's four men would already be downstairs by now. Putting away the watch, he sighed as he stared at the block of wood across the room,…and the visible hilt of the dagger gave his confidence the added boost he needed to smile broadly. He was actually looking forward to meeting Mister Mabry, he decided, but then remembered that Allan wanted the man alive,…and although he had never disobeyed one of his best friend's orders, he was sure he might disobey this one! He wanted Mabry dead,…and he would kill him the same way he killed his son,…with his knife!

Still grinning, he went to his desk and poured himself a whiskey and as he drank it, was thinking that Mabry would probably not show himself before midnight,…and maybe not until the wee hours of the morning. But he would be waiting, of that he was certain! Allan would be mad when he killed him, he knew, but once things were back to normal again he would get over it!…Besides, defending one's self in his own establishment did not constitute a Federal Crime!…It would be business as usual."

He poured more liquor in his glass and walked across to the large window overlooking the saloon's much larger floor and moved the heavy drape aside. Almost every table was occupied, and the scarcely dressed young women were doing their jobs of securing drinks and soliciting their bedroom clients. Closer to the front wall, he saw the eight gunmen and was satisfied that he had it all covered….With that much fire power, Mister Mabry was in trouble!...All he had to do now was wait. He looked past his men and studied the dark, undraped front windows overlooking the boardwalk, and wondered if Mabry might be watching the saloon from the street?

Sighing, he sipped at the drink as his eyes took in the poker tables, and all but a couple of those were full, causing him to wish he had more gaming tables, high limit tables like Allan had. What was he thinking anyway, insisting that the brothel have only penny-ante poker,…and how in the hell did that Mabry kid win five thousand dollars at one of them, damn his cowboy hide?...It was him that started their troubles, him and his God damn luck!

He angrily dropped the drape and paced the floor a time or two, feeling impatience beginning to work on him….He had never been a patient man, he thought, never had to be,…things moved too fast in New York City to be patient! Shaking his head, he went to the desk and placed the glass down, walked around to his chair and donned his jacket then opened the top-middle drawer and removed the short, single barreled Derringer and worked it up his sleeve before walking across the room to blow out two of the kerosene lamps,…and leaving a single lamp burning he left his office to go downstairs.

*   *   *

Seth Mabry took out his watch and checked the time then reached for the well-used pair of cowhand's chaps and worked them onto his legs,…and at the same time shaking his head. Gus must have had these things laying around that tack-room for years, he thought, the chaps hadn't been oiled down in at least that long! They were quite stiff,…and the floppy old hat, too. He fitted the hat on his head and peered at the two deputies while running his hand over the week's growth of graying beard.

"What do you think," He queried then gestured outward with his hands. "Will I pass for an old cowhand?"

"Works for me!" Grinned Deputy Hurd.

"Me, too, Seth," Nodded Hicks,…"Everything but your gun. Cowhands don't usually wear a gun on their side, it's usually somewhere between there and their butt!"

"That's true!" He nodded. "Thanks Jordan." He bent then and picked up the older pistol from the hay-bale, took his own from the holster then reached behind his back to pull the tail of his shirt out before hiding the gun inside his belt. "I think we're ready!" He nodded, dropping the older gun in the holster. "What about it, men, you ready to do this?"

"Right now?" Blurted Hicks. "I thought we were goin' at midnight?"

"That's what McGuire thinks, too, Jordan. He knows I'm coming,...but he won't be expectin' me this early!"

"Then I'm ready!" He breathed.

"Good man!...Mister Hurd, you know what you got a do, so give us a half hour then follow us. Just make sure you're in that alley under McGuire's office window,...and I don't know which one I'll be droppin' them books from, so stay alert!...Once you get 'em don't waste any time, come on back here....if somethin' happens to me, take 'em to th' Marshal!"

"I'll be there!"

"Keep that door key in your pocket, too,...old Gus just might want a use his shotgun on our guests!...Let's go, Jordan!"

*   *   *

Once in the alley beside the Brothel, Seth stopped just short of stepping up to the boardwalk, readjusted the holstered gun slightly behind his hip, then readjusted the old chaps before looking back at Hick's dark features. "You know what we got a do, son,...now, who am I?"

"You're Will Burton, an old family friend,...you practically raised me!"

"Where do I work?"

"Th' Double Trey, of course,...I brought you to town to meet Corine, remember?"

"I do now,...McGuire might think somethin's out a place when he sees you, so we better tell 'im you been out at Double Trey since Saturday,...and you have no idea what has happened in town!"

"Or where Sheriff Gentry is,...I know, Seth,...I'm ready!"

Nodding, Seth reached behind him to check the gun in his belt then adjusted the bandana around his neck and stepped up to the semi-busy boardwalk, and together walked slowly toward the swinging doors. Suddenly, Hicks stopped to look through one of the windows.

"He's ready for us, Seth!" Whispered Hicks. He's got at least six gunmen along the inside wall here."

"But they don't know me, now let's go!"

Hicks pushed open the swinging doors and laughed loudly as he stood aside to let Seth come in, and both of them began nodding and pointing at things of interest, talking about anything and everything as they moved to one of the tables and sat down, both still laughing like they'd just shared a funny joke.

"That's Yancy McGuire against th' far wall." He laughed.' That's his regular table, by th' way."

Seth shook his head as he laughed loudly, his eyes taking in the well-dressed Irishman in a sliding glance. "He's gettin' up!" He laughed, reaching to slap Hicks on the shoulder.

Hicks got up as McGuire approached the table and shook his hand. "How are you, Mister McGuire?"

"Fine, lad,…just fine,…and it is you, I am happy to see!"

"You are,…why's that, sir?"

"I be wanting to see the good Sheriff Gentry, lad,…but he is nowhere to be found!...Would you not know where to find him?"

"He spends his nights at home, Mister McGuire,…we just came by th' office, and he's not there,…there was nobody there, in fact!"

"Do ye not know what has happened, lad?"

Hick's face grew serious then, and he shook his head. "No,…wh,…has somethin' happened,…is th' Sheriff okay?"

"I'm sure I do not know, lad,…I was asking you!"

Hick's mouth fell open, and his eyes grew larger as he had to sit down. "Me?...But I've been out at Double Trey since Saturday!" He lied then suddenly got to his feet again. "Maybe somethin' happened to him, sir,… maybe I'd better go find 'im?"

"No, no, no, lad,…I am sure he must have had business somewhere…. there be nothing to worry about, I'm sure! But tell me, lad, what might you be doing way out at Double Trey?"

"Oh,…I went to see Will, here, he works out there!...Practically raised me when I was a kid."

McGuire peered down at Seth's grinning, bewhiskered face then grinned. "I be Yancy McGuire, Sir!"

"What?...Oh!" He said quickly and got up to shake Yancy's hand. "William Longfellow Burton, at your service!" He leaned closer to McGuire then. "Hell of a nice joint ye got here, never seen so much pussy in one place before,…all of 'em nekid, too!"

"Will!" Blurted Hicks and grabbed his arm.

"Well they are,…look at 'em, boy!"

"Will,…this is a whorehouse, that's th' way they dress!"

Seth looked at him. "Ye don't say?" He laughed with sarcasm then. "Hell, I knowed somethin' was wrong, boy, ain't no busybodies swarmin' th' place!...Now, you watch yourself, boy, I weren't born yesterd'y,…I know it's a Cathouse!"

"He ain't never been to a real brothel, Mister McGuire." Grinned Hicks, and then shrugged his shoulders. "But I might never get 'im to leave now."

"Now you listen to me, boy!" Came Seth sternly. "A cathouse, is a cathouse, in Mexico, here, everywhere, and I damn sure know my way around one!...Smart aleck!"

"Now, now, Gentlemen!" Grinned McGuire, who then looked toward the wall and shook his head, signaling the men there to relax. "If Mister Burton here has the money, he can move right in, lad, there be plenty of room!"

"Yeah," Said Seth with a grin. "You heard th' man, Jordie,...now where's Corine?"

Hicks shrugged at McGuire again. "That's why we're here, sir,...I told 'im about Corine, I mean, Baby."

"Yeah,...I like big knockers!" Laughed Seth.

McGuire laughed, too. "Then you will not be disappointed, sir. I will find her for you! Deputy Hicks, lad, if you should think of where our good Sheriff might be, please let me know?"

"Yes, sir!"

"Then enjoy yourselves, lads!" He turned away then, and after speaking to one of the girls, went back to his table and sat down again to watch the door.

"ME, LADS?" Grimaced Seth. "What kind a talk is that?...You did real good, son." He nodded, and waving his arm again he looked around in time to see the transparently-clad girl walking by and quickly reached out to run his hand over her soft be-hind, bringing a startled shriek of surprise from her,...then he gestured wildly with his hands again, as if Hicks was warning him to behave.

"Here she comes, Seth, settle down old timer!" And grinning, they watched the extremely attractive young woman walk briskly toward them, her almost perfectly proportioned body swaying provocatively as she maneuvered her slender naked self around the tables,...the loose, transparent gown moving with the swaying of full, overly ripened breasts.

"You know how to pick 'em, son!" Said Seth as Hicks stood and greeted her with a kiss.

"You look good, Baby." Grinned Hicks as he seated her next to Seth, and then placed his hands on both her shoulders as he leaned down close to her ear. "Don't let on, Corine, and don't look surprised. We need your help, honey!...You told me once you'd give anything to be out a this place for good,...if that's true, move over next to Seth there and put your arm around him,...and Baby, laugh like you're thrilled to death!...Come on, Corine,... this is for real!"

She stared at Seth with a puzzled look on her face then suddenly released the breath she was holding and laughed loudly as she scooted her chair closer to him. Tears were in her eyes as she put her arm around his neck and leaned closer.

"I want a thank you, Mister," She sniffed. "But you can't help me, nobody can! Yancy McGuire owns me, bought and paid for."

"Honey?" Said Seth sternly. "You ain't no horse to be bought and sold like one!...So I'm tellin' you right now,...you help me get to his office, I'll tear up that contract and your Mister Yancy will never bother you again!"

"But,...there's guards there,...you can't!"

"You take me up to your room, I can,...will you do that?"

"Of course," She nodded tearfully. "That's what I do!...You're his daddy, ain't you?...I mean, that was your son that was killed Saturday night?"

"Yeah," He nodded grimly. "It was!...Tommy was my oldest."

"One of the street girls told me she saw Yancy and that sick little Mexican follow him and his brother outside that night, said they pushed them into the alley by the Casino!"

"Thanks, Corine,...now, will you help me?" And when she nodded, he kissed her and helped her up, with her hanging all over him. Looking down at Hicks, He winked then whooped loudly, grabbed a handful of her shapely backside and allowed her to steer him quickly toward the stairs where a burly man exited his chair to bar the way.

"Johnny," She smiled sweetly. Meet Mister,...what is your name, sweetie?" She giggled loudly then.

"William Longfellow Burton, Sir, at your service!" He nodded briskly.

"Well, Mister Longfellow, that'll be five dollars in gold, or ten in currency for th' room,...in advance!...You can pay Baby when you're done!"

"Worth ever penny, I bet'cha!...Just look at these knockers?"

"I'll need your gun, too, old timer!" Chuckled the guard as he took the money.

"My what?...oooh, yeah, my gun!" He began to feel nervously around on his hip, turning one way then another before finally finding the holster and fumbling for the weapon.

"Hold still, old man!" Laughed Johnny. "I'll get it!" He pulled the old pistol from the holster and stuck it in his belt. "Have fun, Baby!" He grinned then shook his head.

"I'll want that dad-gum shooter back, young feller!" Corine tugged on him then and he grinned. "Got a go!" They climbed the stairs together then paused while he shook the other guard's hand in passing, but he was thinking that he had not been able to see this man from the saloon's floor and that was to his liking, he thought as they went on down to her room and slipped inside.

"What are you going to do?" She breathed as she placed her back against the door. "This is scaring me to death!"

"I'm gonna steal his books, Sweetheart,...and maybe your contract."

"Oh, God,...you're crazy!...He'll kill us both for this!" She whimpered.

"Well, let's hope not, okay?" He pulled his watch and looked at the time, but then moved her away and opened the door a crack when they heard another girl's laughter,...and watched as she showed a client into her room.

He closed the door then and smiled at her. "Now listen, Corine,...we'll wait a couple a minutes then I want you to go out and tell that guard that I passed out in here,...tell 'im you want him to get rid of me."

"Oh, God,...please don't do this, you don't know him, he'll kill us!"

"Listen to me, sweetheart,...after tonight, Yancy McGuire will never hurt anybody else again, I promise!...Okay?" He saw her nod then checked his watch again,...and after another minute had passed, he opened the door.

"Do it right, Corine,...and be careful!...Stay in the dark and when you get close enough, call him." She nodded again and he let her out then quickly tugged the holster back in place and tied it down, pulled the pistol from the small of his back and stepped behind the door.

It was easy to put the muscular man's lights out and between the two of them, had him hogtied, gagged and in the closet in only three minutes.

"What now?" She whimpered. "Ohhh, God, he's going to catch you, I just know it!"

"Just keep this door shut!" He whispered. "And don't worry about that, you hear me?...Just wait here for me. I'm gonna need that valise over there, too, is that okay?" And when she nodded, he grabbed the bag and slipped out of the room. He made his way along the unlighted hallway and after checking the area of the stairs, climbed them quickly to the next level,...and staying close to the wall moved slowly toward the only visible door on the floor.

He reached for the knob, but paused long enough to move out and peer over the railing at the whorehouse floor below, and grinned slightly when he saw the fidgeting Deputy Hicks still at the table....Backing up to the door again, he turned the knob and went inside. The one lamp dimly illuminated the office, introducing him to the plushest, largest one room he had ever seen,...and he took a minute to take it all in. There were paintings on every wall, polished tables with matching chairs, and a couple even adorned with bottles of whiskey and glasses. Even the floor was of polished hardwood,... and it was adorned with a very large hand-woven Navaho Indian Rug. He spotted the desk then, and the large western painting on the wall behind it,...and that was where he headed.

Coming to the wall, he moved the painting aside and opened the hidden door, placed the valise on the floor and quickly emptied the hideaway. Working quickly then, he strapped the bag shut and carried it to the nearest window, raised it and dropped the valise to the alley's floor before checking his watch again,...ten minutes had passed, so he put it away and walked across the office to the bedroom door and opened it. That room was very large also, and one wall consisted of a very impressive display of guns of every caliber and make, both rifle and sidearm,...and the collection covered the whole of the wall behind the bed.

Sighing, he began opening the doors of several closets and seeing nothing he could use, was about to leave when he spotted the large trunk at the foot of the double bed and opened it. After checking his watch again, he grabbed the coil of rope and hurried back to the window then holding one end of it, tossed the coil through the window and began looking for some place to tie it off.

*   *   *

Corine's heart was in her throat as she watched the faintly-lit hallway through the slightly open door. She knew he had told her to keep it closed, but had been so worried she couldn't help herself,...she had to watch for him. She also knew her allotted time with a client was quickly coming to a close, and was terrified by the time she saw him returning.

"I was so scared!" She confessed as she let him in. "We have to go now, the guards will come to throw you out if we don't!"

"One of 'em won't!" He grinned then readjusted the holster behind him, and hid the pistol behind his back again. He pulled the tail of his shirt all the way out for the disheveled look.

"Now, honey when we get downstairs, wait till we're gone then get th' hell out a this place, can you do that?" And when she nodded. "Go to Jenson's Livery barn on main street!...If you meet up with Deputy Hicks go with him, but get out a here! And, Corine, try not to be seen,...Deputy Hurd is at th' Livery waitin' for us. Tell 'im I'm okay and I'll be along later....Oh, yeah,...better put some clothes on!"

"I will, but you go downstairs ahead of me, I can't go with you!" She saw his expression then and touched his arm. "They don't expect me to come down with you,...private time, you know,...after sex?"

"Okay," He nodded. "Can you get out a here,...there a back door up here?"

"No,...it's heavily locked!...I'll come down in a few minutes. I can slip out the back way!"

"You'll have to leave, Corine!" He whispered anxiously. "Once they find our friend in there,..."

"God, I know, Mister,...now go, will you?" She sniffed.

"Thanks, Lady." He pulled her close and kissed her then slipped out and back down the hallway, and almost to the stairs, he looked back and could see the dim light from the partially open door,...and knew she was watching.

Deputy Hicks was on his third expensive shot of liquor, trying to make each glass last as long as he dared, and having also turned down a dozen or so solicitations from insistent prostitutes while he watched the stairs,... he was so intent, that he did not see Yancy McGuire approaching his table again.

"Are ye nervous, lad?" Queried the Crime Boss, suddenly stopping at the table. "I assure you, your friend is all right!"

Hicks jerked when he spoke. "What?...Oh, Yes, sir, I know that!...I'm just worried about th' Sheriff now." He shrugged then grinned sheepishly.. "I was kind a hopin' Will would hurry up!"

"Ahhh, yes,...I am some worried me self." He pulled his watch then. "Your Mister Burton's time is up now, he should be along."

"Hey, you're right," Grinned Jordan. "There he is now!...We'll be goin' now, Mister McGuire, I want a look for Sheriff Gentry,...this sure ain't like him!"

"I agree, lad, it is not!...You will keep me informed, will you not?"

"As soon as I find 'im, Yes, Sir!" They both watched then as Seth redeemed his gun and started toward them.

McGuire grinned and shook his head at Seth's disheveled state of attire. "It does appear he had his fun, Lad." He chuckled and still grinning, turned and threaded his way back to his table again.

Sick to his stomach, Hicks sighed his relief and got up to meet Seth,... and under the guise of reluctance on Seth's part, hustled him out to the boardwalk and back to the alley where Seth stopped him.

"You okay, boy?"

"Hell no,...I feel like pukin'!" He gasped.

"Good," Grinned Seth. "make your way to th' rear of th' building now, Corine could be comin' out that back door any time, wait on her, see she gets to th' Livery."

"Didn't you get scared at all in there?" Gasped Hicks. "I felt like a mouse in a den of cats!...Scared th' crap out a me!"

"Sure I did, Jordan, I ain't a hero!...It was somethin' that had to be done,...and there was no other way to do it. Now get a move on, they see Corine leavin', she'll need some help"

"What are you gonna do?"

"I'm gonna have me a talk with Mister McGuire,…if he shows up?"

"If he shows up,…where?"

"His office, Jordan,…I'm gonna wait on 'im there."

"Seth, you ain't killed anybody yet, do you really have to do this?"

"Oh, yeah," He gritted. "An eye for an eye, Jordan, that's my way!... Now off with ya." He sighed heavily and watched Hicks disappear in the darkness and once he was gone, quickly stuffed his shirt back into his pants and removed the very uncomfortable chaps, and dropping them there in the alley readjusted the gun belt.

Moving back to the corner of the building, he waited his chance and stepped up to the boardwalk then after waving off a soliciting young woman with tired eyes, leaned to look through the window. McGuire was still at his table, and grinning he walked on down the walkway.

Two minutes later, he was in the debris strewn alley on the brothel's opposite side, and it took several long seconds in the dark, having to wave his hands above his head to contact the dangling rope,…and after looking back toward the lighted street he jumped and grabbed it, tested his weight then hand over hand, slowly walked up the side wall to the third story window and climbed inside.

*   *   *

With gun drawn, Deputy Hurd opened the barn's rear door, but put it away when Hicks stepped into the semi-darkness of the livery. "Who's this?" He queried as Hicks Ushered Corine in ahead of him.

"Her name's Corine, Rick,…I told you about her." He turned to her then and urged her to sit down on a hay bale. "You get th' files, Rick?"

"Files,…oh, th' books, yeah, I did!" He nodded at the valise. "Where's Seth, didn't he come with you?"

"No," Sighed Hicks. "He went back to kill McGuire,…I couldn't stop 'im!"

"Good God, man,…he's gonna get his self killed!"

"Maybe,…come on, Rick!...We knew what he was here for,…and we knew what he was gonna do!...Both of us together couldn't a stopped 'im!"

"You're right about that, I guess." Sighed Hurd. "But th' Marshal might,…maybe we ought a take this stuff to him, tell 'im what's goin' down?"

"He said we should wait for him here!" Stammered Corine. "He said he would be here,…and I believe him." She stared at the valise then. "Is my contract in there, you think?"

"I'm sure it is," Nodded Hurd. "But it's evidence against McGuire. Seth said if he didn't make it, we're to give it to th' Marshal!...So we best not touch it!"

"Something may have already happened to him!" Sighed Hicks. "McGuire has eight gunnies waitin' for him."

"Then let's take this stuff to th' Marshal?" Argued Hurd. "Th' prisoners, too!"

"And what about me?" Voiced Corine. "I've got no place to go,...I can't go back now, they'll kill me!"

"Oh, you ain't goin' back there, Corine!" Grinned Hicks. "You're never goin' back!...If Seth don't kill th' Son of a Bitch,...there's enough evidence in that bag to hang 'im!"

"What about your folks, Corine?" Asked Hurd. "They still live her, don't they?"

"I don't know,...and I don't care,...I'll never darken their door again!... Daddy sold me to McGuire for two hundred dollars, even signed a contract with him, saying I was no longer his daughter!...They could die tomorrow and I wouldn't care!"

"Then you're gonna stay with us, Corine." Nodded Hicks. "You're safe here."

"What do you think, Jordan," Insisted Hurd. Let's take this stuff to th' Marshal?"

"Let's give Seth a little time before we do something like that, Rick,... let's wait a couple a hours before we make up our minds!"

CHAPTER TWELVE

Walking around the dimly lit office, Seth peered closely at every painting, and was filled with awe at their beauty,…and at the same time, wondered where the Bastard had gotten them?…Likely murdered somebody else for them, he thought,…and shaking his head, wondered why he had not just walked into the place and shot the son of a bitch two days ago?…Chances were good he'd have gotten away with it, too. But two days ago, he didn't know the Sheriff was a crook,…and he didn't want to blatantly break the law! Sighing, he walked to the long settee to run his fingers along the smooth mahogany finish, thinking that must have cost a pretty penny as well?

Coming to the door, he opened it a crack to peer out and seeing no one, closed it and continued around the wall. All the paintings had the appearance of being expensive. 'And what's this', he thought as he came to the round block of wood on the wall,…and reached to try and pull the knife out, and when he could not, backed up a step or two to stare at it. The dagger had been thrown hard, he thought, and likely from across the room to have that much thrust.

Mister McGuire was a knife man as well, he mused. He not only used one to brutally murder young men, he can also throw one and by the looks of it, with accuracy. He grinned then, actually pleased at the discovery,… he'd planned on killing him with a knife anyway,…and he wanted him to fight back!…He believed in giving a man a chance, but only one,…and that was one more than he gave Tommy!

There was also the possibility that he was tougher than the first two,… course, Mister Butcher had no option, but Silva did!…The Mexican should have tried harder, he thought. But such is the way with men who think they're better than other men, Silva thought he couldn't be beaten, he'd gotten so used to men cowering from him that he believed nobody could best him. That was the way with most gunfighters, too, he thought, they all lived for the challenge,…and so did he,…once!

Continuing around the room, he thought of Marshal Dempsey and the request, that he get the books and allow the law to hang McGuire. Well, he did that,…but he couldn't wait for the law to hang him, it would take too long,…and he wanted Mister Yancy McGuire to see him coming, to think about what he had done to deserve dying this way. He wanted him to suffer like Tommy had, and know that he couldn't stop what was happening to him!…He wanted to look Tommy's murderer in the eyes as he cut the life out of him!…An eye for an eye, Mister McGuire!…'that's all that will satisfy me'.

He thought of Laura then, alone and scared to death that he would also be killed, and he might very well be, he thought,…but he wouldn't die alone! She'd at least have Greg back,…she would be okay! He sighed heavily then,…she didn't deserve this, Tommy or Greg didn't deserve this!…But he was the way he was, the way he has always been, he couldn't stand being wronged, not by any man,…and if he was, he would get pay-back! He had no choice,…it had become his way. Laura knew this about him even before they were married, and she accepted him the way he was….He couldn't change what he believed in!

Sighing again, he went to the large drape-covered window and moved it aside for a look downstairs. He could still see the eight armed men along the front wall, and at least half the poker tables were in use, but there was no angle in which to see McGuire where he was sitting. He dropped the drape and checked his watch. A little past ten o'clock, he thought. He had at least two hours to wait, maybe longer and shaking his head he walked to the desk, grabbed an easy chair and pulled it across the floor to place it against the wall beside the door,…and with another look around the room, he peered at the block of wood again and the hilt of the dagger then sighing once again, sat down to wait.

*   *   *

Yancy McGuire was sweating profusely from the heat being generated in the large room. Even with all the ground-floor windows raised, it was hot,…and the heat from all the lanterns didn't help the situation. He thought about all of this as he wiped his face and neck with the white, lacy bandana,…and he knew, too, that the more liquor he consumed, the worse it was going to get. His patience was wearing thin as it was and his eyes ached from staring so hard at every cowboy that entered the place. That, and the fact that virtually every man in the room, as well as those just entering were all strangers to him,…and that fact was tiring him mentally.

He knew that until this had happened, he had figured that all he needed to know, or to recognize about the brothel's clientele was the color of their gold,...to him they had no face to remember. But now he realized that was a mistake!

He also intently watched the eight men he had stationed in the large, but now less than half-filled room. Trade was winding down earlier than usual he realized,...and if Mabry was going to show at all, it certainly should have been at the peak of business, of which usually did not occur until two or three in the morning!

Angrily, he got to his feet and lit another cigar as he scanned the smoky room. Even the girls were lined up against the long bar, having no men to solicit other than those already turning them down,...or the few remaining gamblers. Sighing, he slowly walked among the tables, stopping now and then to speak to someone, or to watch a hand of penny-ante,...and then finally made his way across the room to speak with his enforcers, seeing the man called Callum get up as he approached them.

"I don't know what to tell ya, Boss," He shrugged. "They just ain't nobody in here that looks suspicious enough to be Mabry!...To us, anyway. We'll do what you want a do, but without knowin' what this man looks like,...I don't know!"

"Neither do I, Mister Callum!" He sighed. "But the man is out there somewhere and he want's to kill me!"

"Then maybe you should get out a th' winder, Boss?"

"No, lad,...our, Mister Mabry wants to look me in the eyes when he does it,...He would not shoot me from the dark." He sighed again and looked back at the room. "He has been lucky so far, because no one knows him or what he does look like!...No, lad, we are dealing with a professional gunfighter, me thinks. He thinks like an assassin, he does.....A man after me own heart!" He grinned. "Literally!"

"Pardon me, Boss," Voiced Callum, reaching up to rub his bristled chin. "What's this, Assassin thing,...what is it?"

"Just another word for paid killer!...An assassin is someone who kills without being seen, Mister Callum,...like a thief in the night, so to speak. You don't know he is there until it is too late!" He took a drag from his cigar then and smiled at him.

"Of course I could be wrong, Mister Callum, and he is just a cowboy,...a very lucky cowboy!...At any rate, keep your eyes open, all of you!...Starting now, stop every man that comes in and disarm him." He pulled his watch again then sighed heavily. "It is after eleven, lads,...I am going upstairs with me headache.....If you find the man bring him to me!"

"You got it, Boss!" Nodded Callum, and all eight of them shuffled themselves closer to the entrance.

McGuire watched them for a minute then with a last scan of the smoky room, headed for the stairs,…and after speaking with the guard there, climbed them to the second floor and immediately stopped there when he failed to see the other guard.

"Walter?" He called out loudly. "Where the hell are ye, lad?" Frustrated, he walked back to the railing and called down, then waited for the guard to come up.

"Did Walter come down downstairs, John?"

John 's eyes flicked to the empty chair. "I don't know, Boss,…he could have, I guess,…I left to go piss a while back?"

Yancy sighed then nodded. "Well go check the girl's rooms for me, lad, I have a headache!…I'm going to lie down."

"Don't worry, Boss, I'll find 'im!"

"Good lad!" He sighed then climbed the stairs to his office.

"Two blooming hours!" He sighed as he opened the door,…and he knew he had drank too much. But his nerves and expectations had gotten the better of him. He took the kerchief from his lapel pocket again and wiped at his eyes while closing the heavy door,…but then he paused as a chill suddenly ran up his spine and swallowing, slowly turned to face the dimly-lit room. His breath caught in his throat then as he saw the twisted painting,… and he instantly knew it had been purposely left that way.

He began walking toward the desk and at that moment, he knew a dreaded fear such as he had never felt before,…and it was not because of Seth Mabry, although he knew instantly that Mabry had been here!…No, he knew his fear was of the Syndicate, Jesse O'Riely would never forgive carelessness like this!…And there would not be a thing Allan could do to save him. Breathlessly, and with his ears fluttering from the dread, he crossed the room and went to the wall, uttering an audible moan when he saw the empty hideaway. He was shaking violently when he turned back to face the room again only to suddenly go weak in the legs when he saw the large, cushioned arm-chair turning around,…and then uttered a loud gasp when he saw Seth in it.

Seth stared at him as he got to his feet. He had in fact almost been of a mind to go along with the Marshal's request, and actually would have left through the open window had McGuire waited longer to come upstairs. But seeing the man flooded him with hatred again, and he knew there was no way he could walk away from his justice due. His hate was a living thing in his heart as he reached and slid Silva's razor-edged dagger from inside his vest,…and clutching the blade in his right hand, lowered his arm to his side.

"You would be Mister Mabry!" Breathed Yancy. "How,…how did you get in here, lad?" He saw the taut rope then, and looked toward the open window. "I see." He nodded.

"No you don't, ass hole,…you don't see at all!" Said Seth tightly. "I walked in here right under your fuckin' nose!" He grated hatefully.

McGuire took a deep breath and let it out slowly. "You kill me guard, did ye?"

Seth shook his head. "Weren't mad at him,…but he will have a headache."

"How did you get up here,…and where are me books?"

"Well,…your books are with Marshal Dempsey by now,…and as for as how I got in,…I like big knockers!"

"Corine!" Nodded Yancy. "I should have known!"

"No, Sir,…you shouldn't a murdered my son!"

"I am not armed, lad," Breathed McGuire, slowly raising his hands away from his body. "Would ye shoot an unarmed man, sir?"

"I weren't born yesterday, McGuire,…and keep your hands right there!" He nodded his head at the block of wood on the far wall. "I've been admiring your handiwork." He grinned. "You're damn good with a frog-sticker!…Where was you when you threw that thing?"

McGuire nodded his head at the far wall. "The settee."

"God damn!" Gasped Seth. "That's got a be thirty feet across there!" He grinned wider then. "But I know you're a knife man, you took my boy's life with it!…And now, I'm gonna take yours th' same way you son of a Bitch!…You butchered my son,…you looked him right in his young, scared eyes and stabbed him to death!…And now, you red-headed Bastard, you have two choices. Shake that derringer out a your sleeve and shoot me, or use that knife you're so fuckin' proud of!…Either way, you're a dead man cause I'm gonna cut your stinkin' heart out!"

"Why,…why did you take my books?" Queried McGuire as he ever so slowly continued raising his hands toward the hidden blade concealed at his neck. "Me books were of no use to you."

"Marshal wanted 'em!…Now, Mister Puke, I ain't never took this much time to kill a man before, but I'm lettin' you take all th' time you need to reach for that hideout knife,…why?…Because I want you to know it's comin',…and I want you to know you can't stop it so come on Mister Crime Boss, I'm doin' a hell of a lot more for you, than you done for my son,…I'm lettin' you defend yourself!…But I won't wait forever!"

He continued to watch McGuire and his anger continued to build. He slowly worked the stiletto around in his hand, so that the long blade was against his forearm's inner side, with the hilt upside down in his hand, his forefinger beneath the hilt for leverage. He waited then as the seconds ticked away, all the while watching McGuire's right hand move closer to his head, when suddenly he reacheded for the blade.

McGuire snaked the dagger from its sheath in a fraction of a second, and as he was arcing his arm downward to throw, Seth slung Silva's stiletto underhanded, and the long throwing-knife embeded itself to the hilt in the Crime Boss's right shoulder. McGuire yelled in surprised pain, releasing his knife to flop uselessly across the room as he quickly clutched at the one in his shoulder.

"I know you're a knife man, you took my boy's life with it!...
And now, I'm gonna take yours th' same way!"

Seth grimly watched the enforcer stagger backward against the wall, knocking the large painting completely from the wall as he caught himself,…and still yelling loudly, tried desperately to pull the blade from his shoulder as he fearfully watched Seth walking toward the desk. He was nearing total hysteria when he saw Seth pull the long bladed hunting knife from his belt and come around the desk.

"NOOO!" Shrieked Yancy as Seth grabbed his throat in a strong left hand and slammed him back hard against the wall. "Please don't?" He yelled then screamed as Seth forced the hunting knife's wide blade slowly and deliberately into his other shoulder up to the hilt, only to savagely jerk it free again, slinging blood in an erratic pattern on the wall and floor.

Grinning, he backed away a step as McGuire sobbed in pain and leaned against the wall on weakening legs. He suddenly lashed out at him again, round-housing the knife in a swinging arc, the sharp blade slicing a swath across McGuire's chest, cutting clothing and all as it slashed a deep furrow in his upper torso, bringing yet another agonizing scream from his gasping lips as he sank to his knees against the wall and began to cry.

Hate for the man was spreading in his feverish mind as he squatted in front of him to grab his thick, red hair and lift his head, forcing McGuire to look at him. He held the wide-bladed knife up in front of his fear-crazed eyes. "I'm gonna cut your fuckin' throat now, you miserable shit!" But as he said it, he was suddenly jerked from his stupor when the office door burst open, and dropping the knife, quickly got to his feet, his hand snaking the gun deftly from the holster as he stood.

"Mabry, stop!" Shouted the Marshal quickly. "It's me, Dempsey!"

Blinking his eyes wildly, Seth barely caught himself before firing on the Marshal and breathing heavily, shakily lowered the hammer on the pistol and holstered it as he slowly regained his composure.

Dempsey holstered his own weapon as he straitened. "You just scared ten years off my life, Seth!" He breathed.

"Get out a here, Marshal,…this scum murdered my son and he's gonna pay for it!"

"Your right, Seth, he is,…he's gonna hang for it!…For that, and a lot of other things!"

"Thought your hands were tied?" He breathed then bent to pick up his knife.

"Not any more,…now come on man, get on out here, let th' law take over,…please? You ain't killed anybody yet, don't start now!"

Nodding, Seth sighed then glared down at the bleeding Yancy McGuire for a hate-filled second before leaning to wipe the knife clean on the man's expensive trousers,...and nodding again, put it away and came back around the desk.

Dempsey sent Jake Tulane and Tinsley to get the stricken man to his feet and move him to the settee before laying him down. "Go get Doc Mitchell, Jake, tell 'im to hurry,...McGuire needs a hospital and a surgeon!... Derrick, you try and stop some a that bleedin'!"

"How'd you know I was here?" Queried Seth, still watching McGuire.

"Weren't hard, I just didn't know when exactly!...Hicks and th' girl brought me th' books, I told you that was all I needed!...We got here as soon as we could! The men downstairs gave up without a fight,...all but one. He managed to escape, likely went to warn McCleary!"

"You goin' for him now?"

"Not tonight, and neither are you, not without a warrant,...and I'll have that in th' mornin'! It's over, Mister Mabry, you have avenged your sons, both of 'em."

"It ain't over till he'd dead!" Gritted Seth, looking back at the settee. "It might never be over for me, anyway, Dempsey,...Tommy ain't comin' back!...And Marshal,...if that man don't hang for it, I will be back!"

"I know, man, and I am sorry,...but th' law applies to you and him both,...and murder is against the law....At least, it is now!"

"Well somehow that don't seem to get me all tingly inside, Dempsey!"

"I can understand that, too, Seth."

"What about them little girls downstairs, you tell them 'em they can go home yet?"

"That Corine girl is with 'em now, Seth,...they know they're free to go,...and they have all agreed to testify in court against McGuire and McCleary!"

"I hate it for 'em." Sighed Seth. "The stuffed shirts in this town'll never let 'em live this down!...They won't even care whose fault it was."

"Unfortunately, you're right about that!"

Nodding, Seth breathed deeply. "What about th' men at th' stables, you got them, too?"

"Already in jail,...Hurd and Mister Hicks took 'em to th' Courthouse for me." He chuckled then. "Jailer prob'ly gave 'em a tongue-lashing for wakin' 'im up this late!...But that's what th' Judge would want."

"Marshal,...if you got any influence with that Mayor, or Town Council,...Mister Hicks will make th' town a good Sheriff!"

"I'll look into it,...but I'm afraid Mayor Richards is not th' Mayor anymore!...Judge Castle brought 'em all in, Town Council, too."

"Clean-sweep!" He grinned. "I guess things are lookin' up!"

"It's time!" Nodded Dempsey.

"What about Greg,...he okay?"

"He's doin' fine,...worried about you, is all!...Don't worry, he'll be released to your custody in a day or so,...as soon as the Judge gets all th' statements."

Seth nodded. "You need me anymore tonight,...I'm suddenly tired as hell?"

"Where'll you be?"

"Got a room at th' Dollar,...and I'll want a see Greg tomorrow!"

"Come by th' office, I'll walk you over."

Nodding, Seth started to turn away, but paused and looked back at Dempsey. "I want a be there when you serve th' warrant on McCleary!"

"Why?...The case is cut and dried, Seth. Corine told me one of the girls saw McGuire and Silva follow your sons out that night,...and that girl will testify, I'll see to that!"

"Tommy won his money at Ringerman's, Marshal,...that's McCleary's place and McGuire was his man. To my way of thinkin', McCleary made th' decision to kill my son!"

"Yeah,...okay!" Sighed Dempsey. "We'll go see your son, then serve th' warrant!...Although th' Judge wants to wait for th' Rangers, he sent for 'em yesterday."

"Wait too long, McCleary'll be gone! He knows by now what went down here....Wouldn't surprise me none he ain't cleanin' out his safe right now!"

*   *   *

Allan McCleary had never had any trouble sleeping and so, after his love session with the teenaged girl, had fallen asleep as she curled up in the tangled sheets and sobbed. So, why was he awake now, he wondered, but then remembered the dream and shuddered,...suddenly very glad it was only a dream!...However, he knew that it could very well become reality,...Jesse O'Riely could send assassins after him at any time!

He sat up on the side of the bed, and was sweating from the room's heat,...and yawning, picked his discarded pants and shirt from the floor. Pulling the trousers over his legs he got up and finished dressing before going into his large office,...but then cursed when he peered at the large Chime-clock, thinking of Yancy McGuire and wondering if they had caught the gunfighter? But then again, he thought, it was just after midnight and could be hours yet before he heard anything.

It was times like these that he wished he had his New York Death Squad with him they would have found this mysterious gunfighter and done away with him already! How could a simple mugging incident turn out to be so wrong?...He should never have told Yancy to do away with that boy! He went to his desk and plucked a fat cigar from the box and lit it then poured a drink from the open bottle of Irish- Whiskey and drank it. Feeling somewhat better as the fiery liquor burned its way into his stomach,...he grunted and worked the cigar between his teeth.

Maybe he was just tired of this business, he thought, but then again,... it was all he had ever known. Even as a child in Ireland, he'd been at war with one faction or another,...though too young to fight he had grown up on blood, and murder!...He'd never known anything else, never knew there was anything else! Maybe, however, he would be better off trying to be an honest and respectable business man?...But the truth of the matter was obvious,...he loved the power he wielded over other men! But of late, he sighed,...that power was in danger of being revoked, and he had a solitary, lone Gunfighter to thank for it!...Who the hell was this Mabry character anyway, he wondered,...an assassin? Hell he worked like one! He had taken out their soldiers one at a time!

Maybe he should start planning an escape route should the unthinkable happen?...Yes, he thought as he eyed the large, empty trunk against the wall,...preparation was the success of any venture. He went to the trunk and dragged it behind his desk, opened it and then emptied the desk's contents before he opened the large safe, transferring everything into the trunk before closing the thick door. But what should he do with it now, he wondered?...It was much too heavy for one man.

Of course, the below-ground wine cellar, he thought, remembering that he had had it built after acquiring the place, and only him and Yancy knew of it's existence. Just the place, he thought wryly. He could stow the trunk there, and even hide there himself if need be!...Yes, as soon as he had men to help him, he would move the heavy trunk to the cellar. If things did fall apart he could hide out there a few days then slip away one night after they had stopped looking for him....Not even Jesse's assassins would find him there!

He was on his third drink when he finally decided it would be better to stow the trunk in the cellar anyway, just in case! Sighing, he went to move the drape aside enough to peer down at the casino's main floor, seeing business as usual. The girls were working the tables, and the men were gambling,...nothing was amiss. He even spotted Mister Roachman trying his luck at the dice and then sighed, thinking he should have turned him loose on Mabry at the onset,...maybe the situation would not have gotten this far?

Dropping the drape, he walked across the wide expanse of his office and back into his bedroom, picked up his white and brown oxford shoes and socks, and then returned to the settee in his office to sit and put them on. Standing, he pulled the suspenders up over his shoulders, grabbed his light dress jacket and went out into the hallway as he pulled it on. Then sighing, went down the two flights of stairs to the casino floor where he stopped to talk with the stairwell guard.

"Hi, Boss?" Grinned the guard, quickly getting to his feet.

"Leo,…I need you to find Barney. I have a large trunk in my office that I want brought down, can you do that, lad?"

"You bet, Boss,…where you want us to put it?"

"In the kitchen for now,…we'll move it again later." He watched the bouncer hurry toward the bar then crossed the floor to where Roachman was just rolling the dice down the length of the table.

"Any luck, Gerrard?"

The gunman peered at him then shook his head. "Breakin' even!"

Nodding, Allan scanned the large room before looking back at him. "Anything I should know about, lad?...Any word from Yancy?"

"You'd know that before I would, Allan….But I wouldn't worry none, he's got eight men!...Besides, that gunfighter can't be that good,…they'll get 'im!...And if he shows up here, I'll get 'im,…so relax!"

"Then why is Milburn back?" He blurted, watching Callum come through the swinging doors.

"Don't know." Replied Roachman, also watching the man. "Let's find out." He quickly began working his way around the gaming tables toward the door, with McCleary on his heels and when Callum spotted them, he changed his course to meet them.

"What are ye doing here, lad?" Queried Allan. "Have they got Mabry?"

"Not hardly, Boss," He panted. "Th' Marshal's got all seven of our men in custody, though!...I managed to get out durin' th' rukus!...They could be right behind me, too!"

"Now, just hold on a minute!" Interrupted Allan. "Are ye saying the Marshal arrested all our men?" And when Callum nodded. "Did he show you a warrant?"

"I wouldn't know about that, Boss,…I just knowed I weren't about to pull down on no lawman!...Maybe you ought a clear on out a here!"

"Have they got Yancy, lad?"

"I'd say so, they was headin' for th' stairs."

"Then it is safe to assume our Marshal has a warrant!...Milburn, start clearing the place out, tell them we are closing,…go on man, do it now!" He quickly went to the cashier's cage then.

"George, lad,…cash out all the chips, then close up and go home!…We are closing early tonight." He went back to Roachman then.

"What's on your mind, Allan?"

"We are through here, Gerrard," He sighed. "I will be arrested shortly unless I can prevent it!…Now we will be getting out of sight for a while, so if you will be so kind, tell the bartender to close up and go home, will you, lad?"

"Why don't we just wait for 'em right here?" Argued the gunman.

McCleary sighed again. "Lad,…there be a time for everything!…Never fight on another man's terms!…We will fight on our own and of our own choosing, now come on, lad, do it!" And when the gunman nodded and left, he grabbed the arm of one of his waitresses.

"Mable, darlin', we are closing, tell the girls to go to their rooms,…and stay there!…Do you understand?"

"Yes, sir!" She placed her tray on a table and began telling the other girls what he said and they all hurriedly climbed the stairs to their rooms.

"What's up, Boss?' Asked one of the dealers as he circled the tables.

"We're closing, lad,…tell the other dealers,…tell them to go home, and quickly!"

Thirty long minutes later, they were barring the large double doors, leaving him, Roachman, Milburn, and the two bouncers being all that were left on the casino's main floor. Allan sent the bouncers to extinguish all the lamps along the walls while milburn lowered the chandeliers and did the same until at last, the only light that was left was the lone lamp that lit up the hallway to the kitchen.

Allan led the way across the floor and past the stairs then down the hall, taking the lamp from its hook as they entered the kitchen. "Leo, me lad,…You and Barney grab me trunk and follow us." He went to the rear of the pantry where he enlisted Callum's help in pushing the large, wooden utility-rack sideways along the wall, and then inserted a large key into what appeared to be a solid wall.

"When did you do this?" Chuckled Roachman as part of the wall swung inward. "I didn't even see a door there!"

"That be the idea, lad, watch your step, now." He held the lamp in front of him and led the way down the narrow steps and into the quite chilly interior of a fair-sized cellar. He stepped aside to let them move past him with the trunk, and once they placed it down.

"There be more lanterns on the walls, lads,…light them please?" He climbed the steps again, pushed the door back in place and locked it then grabbed an iron ring on the wall above him and backed his way back down the steps as he pulled the length of rope through a hole in the wall,…and they could all hear the heavy utility rack as it was pulled back into place.

"There be a stove down here for cooking, lads." He said as he came to place the lamp on a discarded table. "And we have supplies and firewood enough for a few days….There be air vents between the inner, and outer walls all around us that go to the roof,…the air will come in through the screened vents along the ceiling there. We can do our cooking at night so the smoke will not be noticed. We are safe here, Gentlemen, once the good Marshal finds the casino empty, he will stop looking for us,…then we will slip away unnoticed!"

"You knew this was coming, didn't you, Allan?" Came Roachman.

"A man must be prepared, Lad,…but no,…this is not actually me escape route in fact, it was just an afterthought tonight. Ye see,…I had planned to stock this special room with the best, most expensive imported wines in the world when I had it built,…but became too busy to do so!" He sighed and looked at all of them then.

"Now listen to me, lads….Tonight,…or maybe tomorrow morning, the good Marshal Dempsey will be coming to serve an arrest warrant for me and all of you!…He also wants me books,…but will not find neither!…They will search the premises several times over the next day or two, and then they will conclude that we are gone and stop looking….You men have been loyal employees, but I do not expect you to share in my fate against your will!… But what I must do is insist you stay here until the search be over. At which point, I will allow you to go your own way. But for now, lads,…we must all wait!"

CHAPTER THIRTEEN

"How you feelin', son?" Asked Seth as he entered the cell, but then grinned widely. "Heyyy,...your face is recognizable now!"

Greg got off the bunk and came to hug him. "I was worried about you, Daddy!"

"I'm okay, Son." He steered him back to the bunk and sat down with him. "They treatin' you all right in here?"

"Yes, sir,...Doc Mitchell has been here just about every day, Judge Castle, too! How's mama, Daddy, you think she's all right,...I'm worried about her, too?"

Seth sighed. "I'm sure she is, son, I ain't been home since Sunday....She's likely worried stiff about us, too,...but Trey's there with 'er, she'll be okay."

"I been meanin' to ask," He choked suddenly at the lump in his throat. "Have you,...have you seen to Tommy, Daddy,...I mean, is he,...?"

"Trey brought Tommy home, son,...we buried him Sunday."

"Oh, God, Daddy!" He sobbed. "I'm so sorry!...I tried to get him to leave that night,...but he wanted to win you ten thousand dollars first?"

"I know, son, Dempsey told me....Did he do it?"

"I think he did,...I know he had a lot of chips in front of 'im, the hundred dollar ones!...Guess they took it all back, though,...except for what they found on me."

"They found chips on you?"

"No, sir, cash money!...Tommy never went to that cashier, but once that I know of,...and that was to get the money he wanted me to hold for 'im!... But I guess he could have had some money on the table, I don't know!"

"Well, I wouldn't worry about that now, son."

"Judge Castle was here today and said The man that killed Tommy is in custody,...is it true?"

"That's true, son!" Said Dempsey from the open cell door. "And your father and me are on our way to serve a warrant on Mister McCleary right now!"

"Will you get Tommy's money back, sir?" He sniffed. "I don't want him to have died for nothing?"

"I will make that effort, Greg, you have my word!"

"Got a go now, son." Sighed Seth as he reached to run his hand through Greg's untidy hair. "We'll be goin' home in a day or so."

"I won't have to stand trial?"

"Why?" Said Dempsey loudly. "You didn't do anything,…and since you slept through it all, you won't even have to testify!"

"I'll be back this afternoon, son, okay?...We have to go now."

"Yeah,…I love you, Daddy." He hugged Seth again.

"I love you, too, son." He whispered. "I'll be back!" He got up and blinked away his tears then nodded at Dempsey and followed him out.

Once on the busy street, they crossed to the boardwalk and started the several block-walk to Ringerman's Casino.

"I envy you, Seth, you know that?" Sighed Dempsey.

"How's that?"

You got a family that loves you, man, and you obviously feel th' same way. That's somethin' I never had!"

Seth glanced at Dempsey's profile as they walked and then grinned. "We got any help today, Marshal?" He queried as they worked their way along the crowded walkway.

"The usual suspects, me, Marshal Tulane and deputy, Mister Hicks and Hurd, they'll meet us there. And you were right again, I think,…we might be a little late!"

"And how's that?"

"Jake told me th' place was closed up!"

"Don't surprise me none." Sighed Seth. "If he's gone, so's them books!"

"He'll still be my headache, never the less!" Sighed Dempsey. "I'll just have to track 'im down,…me, or the Rangers."

"Hey, that's right!" Grinned Seth. "You're a United States Marshal now,…I saw th' badge last night!...When did that happen?"

"Castle swore me in yesterday."

"And Jake's th' Town Marshal?"

"Jake Tulane is Town Marshal,…but he ain't been sworn in yet."

"He will be."

Tulane and the three deputies saw them coming along the boardwalk and worked their way through the onlookers toward them.

"Place is locked up tighter'n a jug, Marshal!" Remarked Tulane as they met. "What do we do?"

"Warrant gives us th' right to go in, Jake….Bust it open!"

"You got it!" He grinned and all four of them turned back through the curious mob with them following.

The doors were wide open by the time they climbed up to the casino's boardwalk and went inside, Jake having kicked the doors hard enough to shatter the glass as they flew inward.

"Damn place looks deserted all right." Commenteded Dempsey and gave the interior the once-over. "Mister Hurd, you and Mister Hicks look it over down here, confiscate all money and weapons you find,…and be thorough!" Jake,…you take the second floor, and Derrick,…you stay by th' door down here,…nobody comes inside!" Once Hicks and Deputy Hurd went about their search, both him and Seth followed Tulane up the stairs then continued on up to McCleary's office.

"Open up, McCleary, I got a search warrant, and a warrant for your arrest!" And when he didn't get a response, he backed up a step and kicked the door, sending it slamming into the inner wall as it flew open,…and with drawn guns, they entered McCleary's immaculate office and living quarters.

"Some place!" Breathed Dempsey as they walked out into the room. "Look at all that art work, got a be worth a fortune!"

"Like McGuire's place." Nodded Seth as he went on to the large desk. "Safe's empty, too!" He commented as Dempsey walked around the desk to go through the drawers.

"Bastard took everything!" Sighed the Marshal, but at that moment both were startled by a noise that caused them to quickly look toward the bedroom door.

"Somebody's in there!" Breathed Seth as he cocked his pistol.

Dempsey nodded and they both moved slowly across the room to stop at the closed door, Seth at one side with gun drawn, and Dempsey to try the door, finding it locked.

"This is United States Marshal, Roderick Dempsey,…come on out a there!…You don't open th' door, we'll kick it down!"

"Leave me alone!" Came the muffled, high-pitched wail, causing them both to look questioningly at each other.

"Ma'am,…ain't nobody gonna hurt you, now please come out, we are lawmen?" There was several long moments of silence then before she responded.

"Um,…okay." Came the faint voice as she opened the heavy door, and they were both speechless at sight of the young woman. She stood before them in only a bed-sheet and most of that was trailing the floor behind her.

"What's your name, sweetheart?" Soothed Dempsey as they both put away their weapons.

"Re,...Rebecca Muenster." She sobbed weakly, but then began to cry brokenly. "He,...he hurt me!" She wailed...."don't let him hurt me any more?"

"Ahhh, honey," Calmed Seth. "Ain't nobody gonna ever hurt you again!"

"You, pa,...Promise?" She sobbed.

"You got our word, honey," Said Dempsey. "How old are you, sweetie?"

"Fa,...fourteen, my last birthday." She sniffed. "My,...my daddy is a preacher!"

"Of course,...The Reverend Muenster,...over in Lewisville, that him?"

"Yes, sir!"

"Where's your clothes, baby?"

"He,...He wouldn't let me have any,...I don't know!"

"Well, you come on out here and sit down, honey, we'll find you some clothes to wear." He nodded at Seth as he led her out to the office. "Come on, sugar, keep th' sheet tight around you now....Seth," He called back. "Look around in there, will you, I'm gonna send Mister Tulane out for some clothes!" He sat her down then went out to the third floor railing and was about to call down for the deputy, but instead found himself counting the thirteen girls.

"Jake!" He shouted. "Hey,...Jake Tulane!" And when the new Marshal looked up, gestured for him to come upstairs and went back inside to wait for him, but instead, found hisself growing very angry as he watched the cowering child on the settee. Damn a man that would take advantage of a kid this way, he thought,...then turned back as Tulane rushed through the open door.

"What is it, Marshal, you okay?" Gasped Tulane,...but then he saw the girl and looked questioningly at Dempsey.

"She was in McCleary's bedroom, Jake," He gritted. "He was raping her, no tellin' for how long!"

Son of a Bitch!" Stammered Tulane as Deputy Hurd came into the room behind him.

"My, God," He gasped, stopping in his tracks. "Becky,...good Lord, is that you?"

"Don't look at me, Ricky!" She sobbed then began crying again.

"You know this girl, son?" Queried Dempsey.

"Yes, sir!...Her father was here lookin' for her two nights ago,...said some Mexican took her!...Marshal, I know her and her folks real well."

"That Mexican had to be Silva!" Nodded Dempsey. "Son of a Bitch stole her for McCleary!...Okay, she's gonna need some clothes to wear, Rick,...

why don't you go get her some, okay?...Try th' dress shop, tell Mildred I sent you!...And you'll need everything that a fourteen year old girl would wear, you can guess at her height and weight. She'll need shoes and socks, too!... And do not tell that old Gossip what happened here!"

"No, sir, I won't,...but,...which dress shop, there's more than a dozen?"

"There's only one by th' Sheriff's office, Mister Hurd!"

"Oh, yeah, Mildred's?" Nodded Hurd and quickly left,...and grinning in spite of his anger, Dempsey turned back to Tulane.

"Where'd you find the other girls?'

"In their rooms on th' second floor." Nodded Jake. "A couple ain't any older than this one, neither!"

"They dressed fairly decent?"

"Yes, sir they look okay, they weren't exactly whores, more like waitresses,...hungry, too, they been locked in their rooms since last night."

"Then go back down and get Hicks to help you walk 'em over to see Judge Castle, he'll need their statements and where they live,...and tell 'im they need food."

"What about this one?"

"This one is goin' home, now go ahead, Jake,...and see that crowd minds its manners, these girls had no choice in what they did!...They've been through enough." When the Marshal was gone, he sighed and went to squat in front of Rebecca.

"Mister Hurd, Ricky, I mean,...well, he's gone to get you some clothes. Are you okay now, Darlin'?"

"Don't call me that!" She shrieked. "He called me that!" She cried brokenly then. "I just want to go home?"

"I know, honey,...and I'm sorry, okay, I won't call you that again!...You can go home, too, just as soon as you see a doctor, I'll have Ricky drive you is that okay?"

"Yes, sir." She sniffed. "But,...will my daddy be mad at me for sinning?"

Tears came to the seasoned lawman's eyes as she said this and he knew that it must be hard being the child of a preacher, especially a daughter. "No, he won't be mad at you,...because none of this was your fault....I'm sure he loves you too much to be mad."

She cried brokenly again. "But,...but God don't!" She wailed. "I want my mother!"

He blinked at his blurred eyes and got to his feet. "You'll be home soon, honey."

"Is daddy gonna whip me?" She cried. "I ain't a virgin no more,...I got the devil in me now!...I don't want a go to hell!" She wailed even harder then. "I just want a go home,...please?"

"As soon as Ricky gets back with your clothes, sweetheart, I promise. Now I've got work to do, will you be okay by yourself for a bit?" And when she nodded, he sighed and got to his feet to survey the room's contents again before going to the far wall and angrily removing the paintings, taking them down one at a time and stacking them atop each other on the desk and once he was finished, counted twelve of the works of art. Sighing once again, he came back to the bedroom to find Seth going through one of the several closets.

"That poor child is scared out of her mind about going home!" He blurted as Seth turned around. "She's so sure her folks won't forgive her."

I heard." Nodded Seth then shook his head. "Bein' th' daughter of a Preacher has got a be tough!...But you never know, Marshal, God fearin' folks have strange ways about 'em,...especially Preachers."

"Yeah," He breathed, looking around at the large room and the two large western paintings on the wall above the bed. "Look at all this stuff, man,...none of these paintings was cheap!" He saw the painting of a lewdly displayed woman then and shook his head. "I'd love to blow this Bastard's balls off!" He grated then sighed and turned back at Seth.

"You find anything important in here?"

"Nothin' to incriminate 'im!" Sighed Seth. "Man did wear expensive duds....Also found a secret door in that second closet there, and some stairs leadin' down to th' alley,...probably th' one Mister Hurd told me about."

"When was he up here?"

"Weren't,...said he was passin' the alley one night and spotted McGuire coming out that way. Said th' door was like part a th' buildin', had to look hard to find it."

"Escape route?" Sighed Dempsey. "They leave that way, you think?"

"Don't think so, door was barred from this side. I figure they likely got out through that alley door downstairs, Greg said it was always open for th' gamblers to go piss." He shrugged then. "Either that or they're still here somewhere."

"Then maybe we need to look for more secret doors, or more rooms we don't know about?"

"Wouldn't be a bad idea," Sighed Seth. "But this room checks out!...I did find a cabinet full a guns over there, seems both of these old boys was collectors, McGuire had a wall covered with 'em!"

"I seen 'em," Nodded Dempsey. "I've got just the place for 'em, too!... Okay,...so, we'll check out that office real good for hidden rooms, and then work down from there,...sound okay?"

Ricky Hurd was back by the time they finished with McCleary's office, and after the girl was properly dressed, Dempsey told the Deputy to take her to see the Doctor and explain her circumstances.

"And Mister Hurd, if Doc says she's okay buy her a hot meal then go rent you a buckboard and take her home. Get th' wagon at Jenson's, tell Gus it's on my bill."

"Yes, sir,…you ready, Becky?" He took her hand and left the office.

"Seth," He sighed as he watched them leave. "Guess I'm ready for the second floor, if you are?"

After a thorough search of the rooms and walls on the second floor, they were just coming down to the Casino floor when Tulane and Hicks returned,…and all four of them began another extensive search of the large room, but to no avail.

"What now, Marshal?" Queried Hicks as they gathered in the center of the Casino's ground floor. "We've looked everywhere,…there's just no secret rooms or trap doors."

"It does appear you're right!" Sighed Dempsey. "They're gone, must a left sometime last night….DAMN IT!...I shouldn't a waited for that warrant!" He shrugged at Seth then. "Sorry, man?"

"Yeah, me, too!" He nodded.

"Mister Hicks," Continued Dempsey. "How about th' girls workin' th' streets at McGuire's place,…they been rounded up?"

"Don't know, Jake had Derrick look for 'em last night,…maybe they got scared and left,…but I'll ask 'em."

"Then I guess we're through here!" Returned Dempsey, looking back at the stairs. "Jake,…find Derrick and send 'im for a carpenter,…I want these doors nailed up! While he's gone, you and Jordan go back up to McCleary's office,…there's a cabinet full of guns in the bedroom, I want them and all th' paintings taken over to my new office at the Courthouse, Marshal Griggs vacated it yesterday. You'll find more of th' same at McGuire's office, too, I want it all! Derrick can help when he gets back." Sighing again, he watched Jake leave to find the Deputy then turned back to watch Hicks and Jordan climbing the stairs.

"Guess I'd best report to th' Judge now, Seth." He shrugged as he looked at him. "You comin'?"

"Not just now," He answered, looking at the stairs also. "Maybe I'll just hang around here,…at least till they're through upstairs."

"What are you thinkin'?"

"I don't rightly know. Guess I ain't convinced he's gone!" He sighed heavily then. "Hell,…I'm prob'ly wrong, Dempsey!...Anyway, I'm gonna think on it some."

"Well, be it far from me to doubt you,…you been ahead a me all the way so far!"

"Not ahead of you, Marshal,…I was just madder than you!"

"See you at th' Courthouse, then." He nodded.

"Yes, sir, in a couple a hours, I guess." He watched the lawman leave then sat down at one of the tables to roll and light a smoke as he scanned the room's large interior again. He knew McCleary was a clever man, criminal minds usually were,…and the man was obviously a career criminal! He was smart enough to build an emergency escape route should he need one,…so why didn't he use it? Maybe he had more than one? Sighing, he blew smoke at the ceiling, thinking that he had forgotten to ask Dempsey if they had questioned folks on the street,…if McCleary did leave, somebody was bound to have seen something?…But there was also the nagging feeling in his gut that told him the man was still here somewhere. He would never have taken the chance that he'd be seen leaving, too many folks hated him!…So where was he hiding, they had searched everywhere and by all appearances, the Casino was vacant!…Maybe they did leave through the back alley?…Maybe they were gone from the Casino, but still in town somewhere?…He would need to run that by Dempsey, he thought as he smoked.

*   *   *

"I'll never get a binding conviction of McCleary without his books, Roderick.…Sure, I can put him in jail with the testimonies we have,…but I want him to hang for the crimes he has committed,…If we can find him! He deserves to hang,…he's a murderer!…The worst kind, too!" He said as he paced the hardwood floor. "These men ruin people's lives, enslaves them and now?…Now we can't find one of them!"

"We'll keep lookin', Judge,…Seth seems to think he hasn't left at all."

"Does he know where he is?"

"No, sir,…But he thinks he's still at the Casino."

"Well, did you search the place?"

"Twice!" He nodded.

Emmit peered at him for a moment his hand on his chin. "Just who is this Mister Seth Mabry, Roderick,…what is he,…an ex-lawman,…or an outlaw?…The way you talk about the man, he thinks like a veteran lawman?" He sighed then and came to a stop in front of Dempsey.

"Forget that, Roderick, it doesn't matter. We owe the man a lot,…if not for him we wouldn't have come this far, in fact,…I would not even be involved!"

"Yes, Sir,...but to be honest,...I don't know who he is, and what's even stranger,...I'm sure I know him from somewhere!" He shrugged then. "Every time I see 'im it almost comes to me, but then it's gone again!...But I do believe this,...his name ain't always been Mabry!"

"No matter, Roderick,...in my experience, I have come to accept the fact that half the men in this great country of ours is not using his God Given name!"

"I like him, whoever he is, Emmit!...He's as honest a man as I ever met,...and you're right,...if he wasn't a lawman, he'd make a damn good one!"

"I like him, too,...and that son of his appears to be honest and trustworthy as well. Too bad about his other boy, though,...that must be hard to live with."

"I can't imagine!" Sighed Dempsey. "But I'll tell you somethin', Emmit,...if I can't find McCleary in town anywhere, Seth Mabry will track him down, and when he finds him he'll kill 'im!...He knows McCleary gave the order to kill his son!"

"And so do we, Roderick!" Sighed Castle. "And Mabry strikes me as a man confident in his abilities, too,...and that tells me that he's a seasoned gunfighter as well."

"He can use a knife, too," Chuckled Dempsey. "He was in the process of drawing and quartering McGuire when I stopped him!...Had th' man cryin' like a baby."

"I know," He said, going to his desk and taking a knife from the drawer. I was at the hospital while you served your warrant. The surgeons worked on Mister McGuire for two hours to save his life!...But he'll be fit for the gallows!...They also gave me this,...Doctor Roland said he removed it from McGuire's right shoulder!" He brought it to Dempsey as he spoke. "Now you said Mabry was using his hunting knife on him,...So, how did this get in the man's shoulder?"

"Well," Sighed Dempsey. "It wasn't McGuire's, I found his across th' room on th' floor, and another one lodged in a block of wood on th' wall.....No, sir,...Jake told me Silva carried a bone-handled dagger like this,...and if that's th' case, Emmit,...Seth beat Mister knife man to th' draw!"

He threw that thing at him?"

"It appears he did, and while McGuire was trying to throw his!"

"Well," Sighed Emmit. "Mister Mabry never ceases to amaze me!...Oh, well...I have good news now, Roderick!...I recently received a wire from the Department of Justice,...and I have now been authorized to do whatever is necessary to bring stability back to Dallas!"

"Well, congratulations, Emmit, that's one worry off your mind!...That mean you don't need th' Rangers now?"

Maybe not,...but it's too late to stop them. Hayward wired me they'd be here on the five o'clock train tomorrow....But it's good I suppose, they can help you dig McCleary out of his rat-hole!...If you don't find him by then."

"Hopefully I will!...Judge,...when this is over,...after you've gone through all the bills of sales and contracts on McGuire's and McCleary's Prostitutes,...I would like permission to bring charges against those parents who sold McGuire their children. These were innocent, loving and vulnerable young women most of 'em,...and they were sold into slavery by their own folks!"

"Roderick,...you do not need my permission for that, it's the law!"

"Thanks, Emmit." They heard the knock then and both looked toward the door.

"It's open!" Said Castle, and they both watched the three deputies and Seth Mabry walk into the office. "Come in, Gentlemen,...take a seat."

"Excuse me, Judge," Came Seth. "But if you don't mind, I just came by to see Greg?"

"Of course, Mister Mabry, but I would like a word with you first,...if you don't mind?...So please have a seat?" He turned back to Dempsey then.

"I thought there were four deputies, Roderick?"

"Mister Hurd is on an errand for me, Judge."

"Very well," He said, looking back at them. "Which one of you is Mister Hicks?"

"I'm Jordan Hicks, Your Honor." Said Hicks and stood up again.

"Mister Hicks,...As you know the job of Sheriff is open now, and you also know that a Sheriff has to be elected to the post. However, we are in strange times now and that being the case, I am the deciding electoral vote, at least for this election!...Now, you have been highly recommended for the job, so I have only one question for you....Can you fill Gaylon Gentry's position, sir,...the right way?"

"I'd sure like to try, Your Honor.' He grinned. "Mister Gentry was a damn good Sheriff,...till all this happened!...Does this mean I have the job?"

"It does,...now, if you'll take a chair in the hall out there, I'll swear you in after a bit?"

"Yes, Sir,...but Judge,...if it's okay, I'd like Richard Hurd to stay on, too?"

"It is,...and the budget will call for two more deputies besides, should you need them."

"Thank you, sir." He turned and left the room.

Mister Tulane,…Roderick tells me you have been serving as acting Marshal for a day or two now, so,…I had a lengthy talk with Mister Redman and the other Councilmen a couple of hours ago, and they have all unanimously agreed that you would make an excellent Town Marshal. Would you want that permanent position, sir?"

"No, Sir,…not if I'm gonna be stopped from doin' my job!"

"You will not be hindered, sir!…I will be overseeing the Town Council's decision making for a while now. They were all good men before McCleary got his hooks into them. You, sir, will have my full support, and theirs as well."

"Then, yes, sir, I accept!"

"Good!…How about you, Mister Tindall,…you want the Deputy's position?"

"Sure, yes, sir!"

"Then wait in the hall please, both of you." He watched them leave then smiled at Seth.

"No, Sir," Grinned Seth, "None a that for me thanks!"

"If I thought you would, I would offer, sir." Nodded Emmit as he came on to shake Seth's hand. "First, Sir,…you have my deepest sympathy, and regrets for the death of your son,…that must be a devastating thing to live with,…and this may sound selfish and unfeeling to you,…but, if this had not happened Dallas would have eventually become a den of corruption,…it was on the downhill side!…But now," He said, releasing Seth's hand.

"Now I can help finish what needs to be done here!…So, tomorrow morning, I am going to release your son to you and you can take him home.…He won't even need to testify!"

Seth peered up at him for a moment then sighing, looked down at his boots for another few before looking up again. "Judge Castle, I appreciate that a lot,…I really do,…and under different circumstances, there would be nothin' I'd rather do!" He looked across the room at Dempsey, then back at the Judge. "I can't go home without justice bein' served, Your Honor.…Like I told th' Marshal there,…I believe strongly in an eye for an eye, Sir! I will not be wronged by any man,…If I am, I will have justice. I'm sorry, Judge,… but that's my way!" He sighed then while Emmit only stared at him.

"I want a see McCleary caught!" He continued."And I wanta see 'em both hang for killin' my son, and Sir,…I don't mean this as a threat of any kind,…but if you can't find McCleary,…if th' Marshal can't find McCleary,…I will!" Shrugging, he looked back at the floor again.

"Well," Blurted Emmit, turning to shake his head at Dempsey, who only shrugged in return. "That, Mister Mabry is straight and to the point, I must say!…But now, I have to tell you the way I am!…You see, Seth,…I am the law in Texas,...I'm also the Judge, jury, and executioner if I choose to be. I believe in the law, Sir,...and I will enforce it with all my energy and power! It's true, however, that my hands, like Roderick's there, were tied before you came to town,...all because of one of those laws!...But they are not tied anymore and Justice will be served,...you have my word!...Take your son and go home, Seth Mabry,...let Roderick and myself finish your job for you?"

Seth reluctantly shook his head before looking up again. "I can't, Judge!...But I will promise you one thing,...I won't get in your way!...I'll let th' Marshal here do his job, because I believe he's a capable man,...And you have my word, too, Sir!...If he can't do it,...I will!...I won't have any choice.... When they killed my son, they killed a part of me,...and my wife. We'll never be th' same again....I can't leave now, Judge!"

"You, Sir, are a stubborn man!" Nodded Castle. "Reminds me of myself!...And for that reason I'm going to agree to let you stay involved in this,...for the time being!...But only, and I say this with conviction,...only if you will wear a Marshal's badge and follow Roderick's lead!...Otherwise, you could be arrested for obstruction of Justice and I emphasize, could be!...And that, Seth, is not a threat, either! So what will it be, sir,...a Marshal's badge, or home?"

Seth stared at Castle through narrowed eyes, feeling himself on the verge of an overwhelming anger,...but then forced the feeling out of his mind before he said something that might wind him up in jail, and instead. "You've sure got a way of pissin' a man off, Judge!" He shook his head then, knowing the Judge was right, knew it because he knew himself,...he would kill McCleary if he found him!

"That I do, Seth!" He chuckled. "What's it gonna be?"

"I can't fight th' law, Sir,...I won't fight th' law,...so I guess that's why I'm gonna agree to your terms,...I only came here to prove my son's innocence, and I done that!...But, Sir,...I know that I will never be able to live till I see Justice done!,,,And I fully intend to do that! So I'll wear your badge, Your Honor,...and I'll follow th' Marshal's lead,...as far as I can!... And that's the only promise you get!"

"Fair enough, Seth!" Grinned Emmit. "And I'll tell you something now....You can piss a man off as well, Sir, because you are stubborn!...But you are also a very good man, Mister Mabry,...and I might add, one I would not want mad at me!...And that being said,...Thank you?...Now, would you consider telling us who you really are, just for curiosity's sake?...Because we both think you may have been a lawman at one time,...and the reason I say this, Sir, is because you have the deductive powers of a lawman,...and a dedication Like I have not seen in a while."

Seth had to grin then. "Judge, I don't mind at all telling you who I am. Name's Seth Mabry, and no, sir,...I ain't never been a lawman!"

"Again, fair enough!...Roderick here swears he knows you from somewhere, but can't remember where....That right, Roderick?"

"Yes, Sir, it is!...But if I did know you, Seth,...it was before th' war,... or maybe during, I don't know. There's just somethin' familiar about you, man,...and please don't be offended."

"I'm far from that, Marshal,...I just feel sorry for th' man you think I am!"

They all laughed over that, and then Emmit pulled out a drawer and removed the Deputy United States Marshal's badge. "Stand up, Seth Mabry and be sworn in!"

*　　　　　*　　　　　*

Allan McCleary sat against the brick wall of the underground cellar, his head resting against the cool bricks behind him as he idly watched the four men arguing over the card game they were playing atop the upturned beer keg,...and all the while wondering what he was doing hiding from someone, anyway?...He was Allan McCleary, he had never in his whole life ran away from anyone, or anything?...Yet, here he was, cowering like a weak-kneed common criminal hiding from the law!...He might be a criminal in the eyes of the law, but he was sure not a common thief!...He was a Crime Boss,... he was from the toughest city in the world,...people did his bidding, not the other way around! No Policeman had ever stood in his way, and lived!...And here he was, not even in the company of his own kind, hiding like some kid caught stealing candy,...and all because of one man, one piss-ant of a man no different than a hundred others that he had stepped on, then laughed about it!

He had grown to hate Mabry with a passion, and his desire to see him dead was fast becoming unbearable. He knew within reason that Yancy was dead, and he had always believed that Yancy could take out any man, had proven it a hundred times!...Yet, his best friend was dead, killed by a cowboy from Texas, not some rival gang's Crime Boss,...a Texas Gunfighter!...That should not have been possible, he thought angrily....In Ireland, or even in New York City, this killing would be returned two-fold, the retaliation would be swift and deadly!...But he could not avenge Yancy from the cold floor of a root-cellar! He should be up there in his own establishment waiting for Mabry,...and the law!...He was above both of them, he was stronger than the law!...He was stronger than Mabry, too,...and far deadlier!

He sighed then,…because deep inside, he knew that he would never be the Allan McCleary of before,…not until he killed Mabry, or at least saw him die. He would also be lying to himself if he thought he could just pick up and leave Dallas, without first avenging Yancy.

He sat and watched the penny-ante poker game, his eyes focusing on the black-clad figure of Gerrard Roachman, thinking that he already had the means to avenge Yancy McGuire. Mister Roachman was as deadly a gunfighter as any man in the country, even Mister, fucking Mabry!…There had to be a way to prove that, he thought,…and at the same time, save face,…and his reputation?…And at the same time, avenge Yancy and leave Dallas unmolested!…Yes, he thought wryly, he liked that idea a lot,…and he would do it, he thought, an idea already forming in his calculating mind,… besides,…Mister Roachman needed to earn his keep anyway!…So, how was he going to do it?…He grinned then and reached his last cigar from his vest and lit it,…then shaking out the match, grunted to his feet and walked over to the keg to get their attention.

"I have come to a decision, lads." He sighed. "The five of us together would not be able to safely leave Dallas undetected, we have no horses,… and the good Marshal will be watching the stables. Besides,…you three lads have done nothing to break the law! So tonight,…I want you three men to leave,…you be on your own. Go home, or leave Dallas, whatever you wish. The law be after me, not you!…Besides, Mister Roachman and myself will stand a better chance of escaping alone!…I have two hundred dollars for each of you in me pocket,…and I do thank you for your loyalty.…Is this acceptable to ye, lads?"

The three men thought about this for a moment, and finally all three agreed that it would be better than being shot trying to escape capture, or hung if they were caught with McCleary!

Sighing, McCleary took the bills from his pocket and paid them. "Now,…as soon as it is dark, you will go through this door," He walked to the wall, inserted a key and pulled the almost invisible door outward to show them yet another set of steps. "There be another door at the top of these steps, and on the other side, another door to the alley outside. The outside door be locked by a length of wood from the inside!…You will leave one at a time, and a minute or so apart,…and if you use the alleys, you will go undetected. You have been good soldiers, lads,…and I thank you!"

"Thanks, Boss." Nodded Milburn as he put the money away.

McCleary nodded, and then with his eyes, gestured Roachman aside.

"What's goin' on, Allan?" Queried the gunman as he joined him.

"Me friend,…for one, I be not happy with being forced to run away from the likes of a dirt-poor, and would-be gunfighter, the likes of this

Mabry! I am not used to running from any man!...We will leave,...but we will do it with the dignity I deserve, and without fear of being shot down in the street,...if you be willing to practice your chosen trade, that is?"

"You want me to kill Mabry, I already agreed to that!"

"That you did, Lad,...and right out there in front of this Casino!...But you will do it with the good Marshal, the Federal Judge, and scores of people looking on!...Only then, will we leave!...And we will do so unmolested. Now, here is what we do."

*   *   *

"Mama's gonna have a heart attack when she sees that badge on you!" Laughed Greg. "She'll think you found it or something."

"I expect so," He nodded. "It's temporary though, just till we find McCleary,...she won't even see it!...I just hope she hasn't made herself sick by now, not knowin' what's happened to us." He sighed heavily then. "So I'll tell ya what, son,...the Judge said he would release you tomorrow, so,...I'll bring your horse with me in the mornin' and you can go on home, okay?... That way, you can ease her mind some, and tell her I'll be home soon. ...You feel up to ridin' that far?"

"Yes, sir, I'm fine, but,...I really don't think I should leave you here!... Maybe I'll stay for another day or two and we can go home together?"

"What would help me th' most is for you to go, Son, we'll be huntin' for McCleary everywhere,...and I don't want a be worried about you!"

"Then come home with me tomorrow, Daddy,...Mama needs to know we're both okay."

"I know she does,...but if McCleary gets away, I'll..."

"You can come right back if you want to!" Interrupted Greg. "Come on, just for a day,...it'll ease her mind?...Besides, what if he's already out there on the road somewhere, waitin'?"

Shaking his head stubbornly he stared at the cell-bars for a minute then slowly realized he was right, that as much as he wanted to catch McCleary his self, he knew that Dempsey could do it just as well....As long as the man died, whether by hanging, or by him, the debt would be paid! He nodded then, and grinning looked down at himself.

"Okay, Son," He sighed. "I've just about wore my duds out anyway, brushin' 'em so much!...We'll go home tomorrow."

"Heyyy!" Chuckled Dempsey as he suddenly appeared at the cell-door. "I'm glad to hear that, Seth!"

Startled, Seth jerked his head around as he spoke. "Well, don't get too excited, Marshal, I'm comin' back!...And how is it that you seem to always be there when I'm in here?"

"My specialty," He grinned. "Besides, I'll have McCleary in custody by then,...I hope!" He was still grinning as he came on into the cell. "You're lookin' fit, Greg,...you feelin' better, Son?"

"I feel fine, Marshal, I really do!"

"That's good." He said and looked at Seth. "The reason I'm here, Seth, is that we're about to expand our search for McCleary in a four block radius around Ringerman's. I thought you might want a join us?"

"I want to!" Nodded Seth and got to his feet. "I'll pick you up tomorrow, son,...say, about ten?"

"Reckon I'll be here, Daddy." He nodded, and then looked up at Dempsey. "Look after him for me, okay, Marshal,...he ain't never wore a gun before, and he sort a has a mean temper!"

Dempsey cocked his head a little and still grinning, flicked a glance at Seth. "I know all about his temper, young Mabry,...he'll be okay!...Oh, your lunch will be here directly, by th' way."

"Thanks, I'm hungry."

"Get some rest, son." Smiled Seth. "Got a go now!"

"You comin' back tonight?"

"Don't know,...but I'll be here tomorrow for sure!" He reached down and ran his hand through Greg's thick head of hair, smiled again then followed Dempsey out and down the hall.

"I guess you never told your family you was a gunfighter?" Grinned Dempsey as they walked down the courthouse steps.

"I ain't wore a gun since sixty-five, Marshal," He sighed, "And only a time or two since before th' war broke out,...carried nothin' but a Henry Rifle while workin' cows,...found that sufficient!...And I ain't a gunfighter!"

"Not anymore, you ain't!" He looked at Seth and they both grinned widely.

"The man I was, is dead, man,...let's just leave it that way, okay?"

"Suits me," He grinned. "But just between you and me, I will remember you, sooner or later,...I always do."

"Then what?"

"Then nothin'!...I'll be able to sleep again!...Don't worry about it, my friend, besides,...I already checked all th' wanted posters I could dig up. Part of th' job, you know!"

"Yes, sir,...I expected that already!...Where do we start lookin'?"

"Back rooms, store rooms, attics, cellars, anywhere a man could hide,... or two men. We still ain't rounded up th' one that got away at McGuires!...

One thing's for sure,…unless he forces somebody, nobody's gonna hide 'im, not after what he's done to 'em."

"What about th' gunfighter, th' one you told me about?"

"That's right, I forgot about him!…He may, or may not still be with 'im, I don't know, I ain't even got a good description of th' man."

"What was his name?"

"Roachman, I think,…Yeah, Gerrard Roachman, you heard of 'im?"

"Don't get around that much!"

"Well, I ain't got a poster on him, neither, at least, not by that name,… but he'd be a man to watch!…Okay, there's Jake and th' others,…now, we'll put two men on Main Street, one over on Commerce, and you and me here on Elm,…we still got six or seven hours of daylight left!"

*   *   *

"What time's it getting' to be, Boss?" Queried Milburn. "This place is startin' to make me feel trapped!…You think they're still up there lookin' for us?"

"That be hard to say, Lad." Sighed McCleary. "But we are all better off right here until time for you to leave,…going outside now might get us seen by someone, they be a lot of people on the streets there, ye know." He pulled the gold pocket-watch and checked the time. "It be only five o'clock, lads,… be patient!" He turned to Roachman then. "What time does it get dark here, lad?"

Roachman looked up at him and shrugged. "Damn if I know, Allan,… eight, maybe,…eight thirty, never gave it much thought!"

"We have another four or five hours to wait, lads!" He said loudly. "Be patient." He smiled at Roachman then. "Where might you be from, lad?"

Roachman peered up at him, not quite understanding why he would want to know that, but then shrugged. "Me,…I'm from Alabama,… little place called Selma!…Ain't been there since before th' war, though." He grinned. "Killed th' man Mama was sleepin' with,…shot th' fucker's pecker off!"

"Holy Mary, Lad!" Gasped McCleary. "That be an awful thing to do!" He grinned widely then. "Did your father know, lad?"

"Ain't got a clue, Allan,…left out that same day!…I liked doin' it, though."

"Of that, I am sure, lad!" He laughed. "I like it as well!"

*   *   *

Mason Cooper was leaning on the end of the long bar with a glass of the previous owner's Brandy when he saw Seth enter and grinning, watched as he worked his way toward him. He also noticed that, as a rancher with a family, he seemed to be well at ease in a saloon.

"As I live and breathe." He said as he shook Seth's outstretched hand.

"Mason." Nodded Seth then placed his elbows on the counter-top to lean on it tiredly.

"When you didn't make it back Monday night, I thought you might have run into trouble or something?" Sighed Cooper. "But then I heard old Gus tell me you out-gunned Silva,...is he in custody?"

Seth looked at him and nodded. "All except McCleary,...can't seem ti find 'im."

"That's what I hear, too,...You think he left town?"

"I really don't know, Mister Cooper, maybe he has. But my gut tells me he's still somewhere in that saloon,...waitin' for his chance to get away clean!"

"It's a big enough place all right," Nodded Cooper. "You thought about the roof?"

"I don't think so,...I will mention it to Dempsey, though,...I'm takin' my boy home tomorrow,...and I came by to see what I owed you?"

"Where you staying tonight?...Your room's still vacant up there, and you look like you could use a good night's sleep!...We'll discuss what you owe me in the morning."

"I believe you're right, Mason, I think I could use it!"

"I know I am."

Seth turned around to lean his back against the bar. "You're crowded tonight, I see,...must a helped, closin' down th' competition?"

"Yes it did!" Mused Cooper. "I've noticed that the air is fresher, too. Even got a few Double-Trey cowboys in tonight, they all but stopped coming to town after the Ringerman fire,...went over to Fort Worth instead, I guess!"

"Yeah, well,...th' more I hear about all this, th' more I'm glad I don't live closer'n I do!"

"I understand." Grinned Cooper. "How about a shot of very good Brandy before you go up, Seth?...It'll help you rest."

CHAPTER FOURTEEN

Allan McCleary let the last of the three men out into the alley then closed the door and barred it again in the inky darkness of the crawl-space before making his way back to the lighted cellar.

"Well," He sighed as he nodded at Roachman. "That be it, lad,...now for the next step in our preparation. Come, I will need you to watch for trouble." He immediately climbed the steps, inserted the large key and opened the door into the kitchen,...and after waiting a moment to listen for noises, grabbed the rack and grunting, managed to slide the heavy utensil-rack back out of the way,...and then both of them felt their way across the room to peer down the hallway before going out.

A faint light was filtering in through the several windows facing the street, and after walking into the large room, they stopped for a minute or two to look the room over, making sure no guard had been posted inside.

"Stay here, Gerrard." He whispered. "I shan't be long." He quickly climbed the two flights of stairs and slipped into his office,...and knowing exactly where to go, grabbed the two large valises and emptied their contents onto the bed before closing them and going back into his office to feel his way to his desk. Dropping one of the bags, he felt around until he contacted the box of cigars, stuffed them all in his coat pocket then went back downstairs.

"Anything amiss?" He whispered as he made the bottom step.

"What?"

"Did you see anything, lad?"

"Nothin' but people stopping to look through the windows,...you get what you wanted?"

"Yes, I did,...let's go back now!"

Once back in the cellar, he locked the door again while Roachman watched him, then came down to the large trunk, dropped the two bags beside it and sank to his knees to open it.

"That's one hell of a lot a money there, Allan!" Breathed the gunman, showing his greed as he came to look closer. "How much?"

"Almost three million dollars, lad,...And one Million dollars will be yours when we are safely away from Dallas!"

"Now that's what I call damn generous of you, Allan,...what am I gonna have to do for it?"

McCleary smiled up at him as he began transferring the thick bundles of cash, and bags of coins to the valise "Believe me, lad, I have several reasons for doing this! The most important one is to keep you from wanting to murder me and take it all,...the second is that you will never be able to spend that much money, therefore you will not need mine!...And lastly,... we are going to be partners, you and me!...We are going to find us another town, maybe in Tennessee,...anyway,...we are going to start over!...But do not worry, there will be very dangerous people looking for us,...of the kind that will never stop!...You will need to be prepared, lad,...because you are the only one that can stop them,...and by doing so, you receive half of what we earn."

"A hell of a deal,...but somethin' tells me you ain't talkin' about the law here?"

"Oh, yes,...the law be included,...but you would be right,...I be speaking of those I be working for, you see,...until now, I, too had a Boss!... Jesse O'Riely is a very powerful Crime Boss in New York City and he has many men, such as yourself under his command,...and he will send these men to find me!...And one day, Gerrard,...they will,...and that, me lad, be when you will earn your half of our partnership!" He closed the valise and buckled the straps around the bulging bag, then pulled the second one closer and began filling it and lastly, placed his ledgers on top of the money and closed it.

"But!" He continued, getting to his feet to smile at him. "This man, Mabry, damn his soul, must be made an example of. He alone has managed to destroy me!...I had everything here, it was perfect,...Dallas, Texas belonged to me, Allan McCleary!"

"You need to take a breath, Allan," Cautioned Roachman. "Too much hate makes a man careless, besides,...no man can do all of that alone!...It's true, he might have started it, but he had help!...So lighten up, or you'll bust a gut,...your Mister Mabry will be dead tomorrow!...Then your job will be to get us, and that money away from here with a whole skin. Are you positive your plan is gonna work,...that's th' big question I have?"

"Of course it will work, Lad,…It has been used hundreds of times in the old Country,…In New York City as well!…Do not worry, it will work!…Cecil Redman is one of the most respected people in the city,…his wife be head of the Committee for Women's rights, It will work, lad!"

"We're still taking a big risk!" Sighed Roachman. "Too many things can go wrong with somethin' like this. Wouldn't it be better all around to just leave,…hell, they'd never miss us?"

"You be forgetting one very important thing, lad!" Returned McCleary, placing his hands on his hips to peer at him. "Mister Mabry wants me dead and he has proven that he will not stop coming until I am!…Everything be a risk, lad,…that be what makes success so sweet!"

Roachman sighed and looked down at his boots. "Allan,…I got a say this goes against my better judgment!…I'm a man likes things cut and dried, so to speak.…But then again, a million dollars is a hell of a lot a money,…so, where am I gonna find this, Redman?"

"Redman's hardware is almost directly behind us, lad,…on Main Street!…We enjoy the same alleyway in back. You will leave through the Casino's rear door at about six tomorrow morning, that be the time they will open the store. You will bring them back here,…nothing be simpler!"

Roachman stared at him then nodded as his eyes flicked back to the two bulging valises on the floor. His thoughts were that Allan McCleary had, in fact lost his mind,…however, he was still a ruthless and calculating individual who, he figured was also a very dangerous man in his own right!…And a million dollars was a tremendous amount of money, even though the currency was still not back to it's full face value. He looked at the still smiling McCleary then brought a hand to his chin to rub it as he turned to pace the floor a couple of times.

This was not a risk that he wanted to take, he thought,…because he knew the odds were stacked against them. The law, and half the town would be in the street tomorrow to witness Mabry's death,…and their chance of escape would depend on how much those people respected the woman!… He did not like it at all, he mused. But he had no real choice in the matter, and that was what scared him. His horse was at McGreggor's Livery,… and should he decide to just shoot McCleary, he would still have to carry the valises to the stable. No,…he had no choice but to go along with him, he thought,…even though he knew that if he stayed with the Irishman, it would likely get him killed!…McCleary was a greedy man himself,…and just might not have any intention of giving him the million dollars once he killed Mabry.…But,…McCleary really had no choice in that matter, either.

"I do hope you're right, Allan!" He sighed as he turned back toward him. And at that moment, made up his mind to kill the Crime Boss somewhere between Dallas and where they were going. "I guess we can pull it off!"

"Good lad!...Now, we had best get some rest while we can, tomorrow will be a tiring day!"

*   *   *

"Morning, Seth!" Smiled Mason Cooper as he left the stairs and came to his table. "Sleep well?"

"Like a rock!" Nodded Seth. "That hot bath last night done me in."

"It always does." Grinned Cooper. "Pull a chair around and sit,...have some coffee."

"Sounds good!" He sat down as Cooper called to Leon for another cup. "I want a thank you for th' change a clothes, too,...I feel like a new man!"

"Not a problem,...a cowboy left the clothes and a good coat in one of the rooms some months back,...about your size, too, it seems." He nodded his thanks when Leon brought the cup then poured the strong coffee.

"Place is sure different this time of day." Commented Seth as he accepted the coffee. "Real peaceful like."

"My favorite time of day," Commented Cooper. "We don't open for business till around ten anyway. When you leaving for home?"

"Judge Castle is officially releasin' Greg at ten o'clock this mornin',...so I figure on leavin' right after that,...right after I get me a bait of breakfast, that is!...I still got a get our horses, too, so, I'll be cuttin' it pretty close!...By th' way, how much do I owe you, Sir?"

"Seth,...you don't owe me one dime,...you have more than paid that bill!"

"I'm much obliged then." He grinned, taking another swallow of the coffee.

"You are very welcome!...But did I hear you say, you were coming back?"

"In a couple of days, yeah." He nodded. "I want a find McCleary,... man's got a lot to pay for!"

"That he does!" He poured Seth more coffee as he spoke. "Maybe they'll find him while you're gone?"

"That'll work, too!...But I intend to watch 'em both hang!"

"Amen to that!...There's already a different atmosphere in town. I can almost feel the relief in the streets."

"I'll feel relief when them two are danglin' from a rope!"

"What if McCleary's not in Dallas anymore, Seth,...what if he's already gone?"

"Then my job is cut out for me!" Said Seth with conviction. "I'll have to track 'im down, Mason,…and if I do,… I'll kill 'im!"

"Then I wouldn't care to be him!" Grinned Cooper.

Seth sighed and placed his cup down. "Sorry, Mister Cooper," He grinned. "Sounds like I'm makin' myself out to be some kind a vicious killer or somethin',…well, I'm not, sir, I'm far from it!…I just happen to believe that when I'm owed, I have to collect!…That's th' way I am and I'm too damn old to change!…An eye for an eye," He shrugged then. "My Mother used to read the bible a lot,…and that passage sort a stuck with me, I guess. But it means, that when a man is wronged he should seek justice!" He shrugged again then. "That's what I do!"

"Nobody in Dallas can blame you for that, Seth." Sighed Cooper. "A man's family is everything,…I lost mine a long time ago, so I know what it feels like."

Seth drained his cup and got up. "Mister Cooper you have my thanks." He reached and shook the man's hand. "I appreciate th' coffee, Sir,…and th' duds!"

"So long, Seth?' He grinned. "If you're ever in town, come see me."

*   *   *

Jake Tulane walked into the diner as Seth was eating and seeing him, came on to the table. "Mornin', Seth?" He grinned, pulling out a chair to sit down.

"Mornin', Marshal,…and congratulations, by th' way?"

"Thanks, Seth, I'm still hopin' I'm deservin' of it!"

"You are,…gonna expand your search today?"

"It appears so,…guess we'll do what Marshal Dempsey wants. Personally I think he's long gone!"

"Can I get you some breakfast, Sir?" Asked the waitress, and after he ordered she briskly walked away to get his coffee.

"You come by th' Sheriff's office, Jake?" Inquired Seth as she left.

"No, I didn't,…Jordan's meetin' me here in a bit for breakfast, though, what do you need?"

"I need to pick up Tommy's gun and belt, my old Walker gun, too!"

"No need, I've got those over at my office now. Marshal Dempsey cleaned out Gentry's desk a couple days ago.…I'll meet you there after breakfast, if you like?"

"That'll work, Jake, thanks,…I'll have to get our horses anyway."

"Yeah,…I heard you was takin' Greg home today. I sure hate to see you go, man,…you made things happen around here!"

"Oh, I'm comin' back, Jake,…I want a see this Bastard caught, and both of 'em hanged,…my bill ain't paid till I do!"

"I understand, Seth, I really do!…And you know what,…I'd like to have known your other son, too!"

Seth cleared his throat and nodded. "If you met Greg, you met him,… they were just alike,…inseparable!"

"I sure am sorry for your loss, Mister Mabry."

"Thanks, Jake." He drained his cup then wiped his mouth on the table linen. "Here comes your breakfast, son, so I'll be goin'. See you at your office, say,…in a couple a hours?" He got to his feet as he spoke, reached a coin from his pocket and dropped it on the table.

"Yes sir!" Nodded Tulane and then smiled as the girl placed his breakfast in front of him.

"Mornin', Jordan,…or rather, Sheriff," He grinned, shaking Hick's hand. "Jake's waitin' for ya."

"Yes, sir!…I hear you're leavin' today, Seth,…you comin back?"

"In a day or two, yeah,…I'm just takin' Greg home."

"I'll see you then." He nodded.

"Yeah, see ya, Jordan." He nodded and walked on down the boardwalk. It was a good mile to Jenson's Livery, and most of it without a boardwalk making it a somewhat hot walk, but he was able to push the worries of the past day or two out of his mind and enjoy his stroll along the wide street,… of which, he noted, was quite crowded with wagons and horsemen, most of them cowboys from the Double Trey, and surrounding ranches, he thought as he studied them.

He watched the unsmiling faces in the creaking wagons and wondered how bad the people riding in them were having it?…But if it was very bad, the children did not reflect it, they were laughing and waving at everyone they passed. He smiled at them and waved back, but it only reminded him of his sons at that age,…they were always happy and go-lucky, too.

It took almost an hour to walk the distance to Jenson's, and he caught the old man with a pitchfork shoveling hay into one of the stalls.

"Heyy," Cackled Gus as he walked in. "Ain't seen you in a day or two?"

"How are ya, old timer?"

"Toll'able,…say," He said, coming a little closer to look at the street. "You ain't told nobody whut I did, did ya,…you know,…Butcher?"

"Your secret's safe with me, Gus," He grinned, placing a hand on the old man's bony shoulder. "As long as you don't do it again,…comprende?"

"I sure do," He cackled. "Whut's on yer mind?"

"I come for my horse, old timer,…my son's, too!"

"Oh, yeah,…you leavin' town, are ye?"

"For a day or two." He nodded.

"Uh-huh,…well I turned everthing out to th' corral yesterdy, which one's are they?"

"My Buckskin,…and a Dappled gray mare."

"I know 'em!... be right back,…ya want 'em saddled?"

He nodded. "Both of 'em."

"Yes'iree,…say, you look tuckered, have a seat there, I'll get 'em ready."

"Believe I will, Gus,…that was a long walk!" Grinning, he walked to a bale of hay and sat down to lean against the wall of the tack-room while he rolled and lit a cigarette, wetting the dead match in his mouth before dropping it.

He inhaled the relaxant as he pulled his watch, noting that he still had over an hour before picking up Greg. Then, on hearing the horse and buggy enter the barn he looked up and grinned as Deputy Hurd stopped the team.

"Get your girl home okay, Richard?"

"Sure did," He grinned. "I'm a hero now!" He looked down then, and shook his head. "I'm real worried about her, though," He sighed as he looked at him again. "She ain't a little girl anymore,…she might not get over this, Seth!"

"Her folks give her time, she will,…a little love and understandin' works wonders."

"I hope so….Well, what have I missed,…you get McCleary?"

Seth shook his head. "Bastard's hidin' out somewhere! Dempsey boarded th' place up!"

"I'd sure like to draw a bead on th' Bastard!" He sighed. "What then, they lookin' for him?"

"Yeah, still lookin'!" He sighed.

"I thought you'd be with 'em?"

"I'm takin' Greg home today,…be back in a day or so!...By th' way, you got a new boss while you was gone,…Jordan was made Sheriff yesterday."

"Then I still have a job?"

"You are still a Deputy." He grinned.

"Then I'd best go give 'em a hand!" He jumped to the ground and looked at the team. "Will you tell Gus I had to go?" And when Seth said he would, he turned and hurried out through the open double-doors while he shook his head and sat back down to finish his smoke.

*   *   *

"Will ten dollars cover our bill, old timer?" Queried Seth as Gus led the horses over to him.

"Nope,…but twelve dollars would!…Yes'iree!

"I think you're double-dealin' me here,…but twelve it is." Grinned Seth. He paid the old man and shook his slender hand. "Thanks, Gus,…you been a real help th' last few days!" He took the reins from him and pulled himself into the saddle, nodded down at the old man and reined the Buckskin out through the double-doors,…and leading the gray horse, headed back toward town.

Main street was a bustle of traffic, wagons filled with freight, farmers with their families in large creaking wagons returning home with supplies, pedestrians constantly crossing the wide thoroughfare. He urged the Buckskin past, and sometimes around this traffic on his way toward the center of town and at the same time intently watching every window and scanning the boardwalks and roofs for any possible sighting of McCleary. But he knew it wouldn't be that easy! Dempsey's job was cut out for him, he thought,…because as much as he hated to admit it, McCleary was a very clever man.

Turning down a side street, he rode out on Elm to finally dismount at the hitch-rail in front of the Marshal's office,…and after a long look up and down the busy street, went inside.

"Mornin' again, Seth." Grinned Tulane as he stood up."

"Jake?" He nodded. "Them my guns there?"

"Well, one of 'em. I'm not sure about your son's gun, you can take a look at the one here?"

"Tom's was ivory handled, Jake,…that looks like it on th' wall behind you."

"I wondered about that one?" He lifted the holstered gun from the peg and placed it on the desk. "Don't see many a these old percussion pistols anymore." He grinned, picking both up and giving them to him. "Don't remember ever firin' one, neither."

"That was my very first gun, Jake!" He sighed. "Well, first revolver anyway."

"Sentimental value then?" He nodded.

"Somethin' like that." He nodded. "To tell ya th' truth, though," He patted the one on his hip. "I like this one a lot better!"

"Well, I'm sorry, Seth,…but I couldn't find any powder and shot for it!"

"Didn't leave none,…got all that in my saddlebags!…Thanks, Jake." He shouldered the weapons and turned toward the door.

"If it's okay with you, Seth,…I'll ride to th' Courthouse with ya?…I need to rejoin th' search anyway. Marshal Dempsey's waitin' on me there."

The ride to the Courthouse took them past Ringerman's Casino, and they both strained their eyes at the darkened windows in passing.

"You still believe he's in there, don't you?"

"I think he was!" Sighed Seth, still looking. "Likely left last night in th' dark!...I would have."

"Well, if he stays in Dallas, we'll find him!" Returned Tulane, his voice filled with conviction.

They rode up in front of the Courthouse and dismounted just as Dempsey pushed through the doors and came down the steps toward them.

"Seth," He smiled, coming on down to shake his hand, and then Jake's.

"Any search results yet, Marshal?"

"Not yet,...Deputies Hurd and Tinsley are over on Main, they'll check out every building from here to th' Texas Road, and come back down Commerce. Jake and me will take Elm Street here as soon as we see you off!...It won't be long, th' Judge has gone for Greg now!"

*   *   *

Allan McCleary pushed his watch back into his vest pocket and stared across the small floor at his captives. He was suddenly having second thoughts about what he was doing,...but he also knew it was too late to change his plans. The time for that would have been before Roachman brought them here. He sighed heavily,...to let them go now would mean disaster all around, because they would surely go to Marshal Dempsey, first thing! Sighing once again, he got up and went to squat in front of the gagged and bound Cecil Redman and his wife Maggie,...and the couple's eyes were wide with fear!

"Mister Redman, me lad,...I apologize to you, sir for what I must do, and so you will know,...I do not have a choice in the matter now!...So,...you will now listen to me, very intently!...And then you will do exactly as I say,...because if you do not, sir,...I will be forced to kill your beloved wife!" He smiled at the expression of utter hysteria on Redman's reddening face as he desperately tried to argue around the gag in his mouth.

"No, no, no, Lad...I said you must listen!...There will be no debate, no argument! Do what I say and you will save both your lives,...do you agree, lad?" And when Redman nodded.

"Good, lad!...It is now eight forty-five in the morning,...and in a few minutes, I will untie your hands and remove the gag. Once I do that, you will go to McGreggor's Livery Barn where you will rent a team and a buckboard wagon. You will drive it back here and tie it off in front of the saddle-shop next door!...Do you understand that part, lad?" And after Redman nodded again.

"It should be nine thirty by the time you get back here,…so, after you tie the wagon, I want you to go to the Courthouse and find that Marshal Dempsey,…no one else, mind you!…Now, this is important, Cecil!…You tell Marshal Dempsey that I want that Gunfighter, Mabry in the middle of the street out there,…right out front there,…and he will have only fifteen minutes to do so. Tell him if he does not, I will kill your Darlin' Maggie here!…If he takes sixteen minutes, it will be too late!…Do we understand each other, lad?" He got to his feet then bent to grab the storekeeper's arm and help him to his feet.

"Are ye sure you understand now, lad?…And remember, sir,…if you tell anyone other than the Marshal about this,…well, you know!" He smiled and looked at Roachman then. "Gerrard, me lad, please take our dear friend out to the alley door and release him?"

*   *   *

"Seth?" Sighed Dempsey as they waited. "I'd like you to give some thought to stayin' home when you get there. I know we've been over this before,…but there's been so damn much violation of th' law around here that I sure wouldn't want any of it to roll over on you, man!…You done more for this town in three days, than any of us have been able to do in three years!"

"You know I can't do that!" Shrugged Seth. "I couldn't if I wanted to,… which I don't. So why are we havin' this talk again?"

"Because th' Texas Rangers will be here today, and they'll be goin' over this case with a fine-tooth comb!"

"Don't fret that, Marshal, weren't no Texas Rangers before th' war….I ain't no outlaw,…I just aim to see justice done, pure and simple!"

Nodding, Dempsey pulled his watch. "Almost ten." He sighed, looking up toward the shaded Courthouse doors. "And here they are!" They all watched Castle escort Greg down the steps, as did a couple dozen bystanders in the street,…and they had just stepped down into the street when they all heard the Marshal's name being called out, then turned to watch the crowd move aside, and a hysterical Cecil Redman running toward them.

"That's Cecil Redman!" Said Emmit as he rushed out to intercept the Councilman, but Redman pushed past him and came on to Dempsey.

"Help me, Marshal," He panted as he grabbed Dempsey's arm. "Please, he'll kill her?"

"Hold on here, Cecil!" Yelled Dempsey. "Slow down,…who's gonna kill who?"

"Maggie,…my wife, he said he'd kill her?"

"Mister Redman I can't help you, if you don't settle down!...Who said he was gonna kill Maggie?"

"McCleary!" Sobbed Redman. "He's got Maggie, Marshal!"

"Okay," Said Dempsey and took Redman by the shoulders. "Where are they?"

"Ringerman's!" He gasped. "But you can't go rushing down there,... he wants somebody named Mabry!...I don't know anybody named Mabry!"

"I do!" He gritted, turning to look at Seth's stone-cold expression. "What does he want exactly?"

"He wants this Mabry in the middle of the street down there in fifteen minutes, or,...or he'll kill Maggie!"

Seth turned to grip Greg's shoulder. "Stay here, son." He said tightly, and then quickly swung astride the Buckskin.

"No way, Daddy!" Greg took the gray's reins and mounted as Seth jerked the horse around and spurred it to a hard run toward Ringerman's Casino, with Greg, and Jake Tulane on his heels,...leaving Castle, Dempsey, Redman, and the crowd of onlookers running after them on foot.

He slid the Buckskin to a stop at the gun shop's hitch-rail, almost directly across the street from the Casino then dismounted to watch as the Crime Boss, his left hand full of the woman's long hair, forced her up out of the alley and onto the boardwalk. Her arms were bound behind her back, and a rag was stuffed in her mouth.

Seth gave the reins to Greg and reached down to remove the loop from the pistol's hammer.

"Daddy, be careful, he's a killer!" Urged Greg and by then, Castle, Dempsey and the crowd arrived, with Dempsey and the Judge coming on to stand beside them.

Breathing hard Dempsey placed a hand on Seth's chest. "Hold on,...I'm gonna go talk to 'im!" He walked out into the street as McCleary put the knife to Maggie's throat.

"It is not you, I be wanting, Marshal!" Warned McCleary. "Come closer, and the lovely lady dies!"

"Don't be a fool, McCleary,...let th' woman go!"

"Well now, Marshal,...I be many things, lad, but never a fool!"

"Ain't no way in hell I'm gonna let you get away with this,...you know that! You got nowhere to run that I won't find you, man,...and if you hurt that woman, it's all over for ya!...Come on McCleary, be smart, man,...you ain't got a chance in hell of getting' out a Dallas alive, if you do this!"

"You have two minutes to bring me that gunfighter, Marshal," He returned hatefully. "I want that Son of a Bitch in the street, right where you be standing!" He looked the crowd over then before continuing.

"And do not think you can ambush me, lad, because it will not save this poor woman, I will slit her throat as I die!...You have less than two minutes, Marshal,...Bring me Mabry, right now!"

Sighing, Dempsey looked back at Seth and Judge Castle then with a last look at the determined McCleary, turned and walked back across the street.

"It's your decision, Judge." He sighed. "Because I won't send Seth out there to maybe die!" He shrugged then. "And there's no time to put a sniper in place."

"Sniper wouldn't save th' woman!" Gritted Seth, his face filled with hate for the man. "He'd kill 'er as he fell....This is my decision, so stay out a th' way!" He started forward as he spoke but stopped when Greg grabbed his arm.

"You ain't a gunfighter, daddy!" He gasped. "You can't go out there,... he's just waitin' to shoot you!"

"It's a long story, son." He said softly. "And he ain't got a gun." He removed Greg's hand and gestured at Dempsey. "Keep 'im back, Marshal." Once Dempsey pulled Greg back, he walked out into the street to face McCleary,...walking slowly until he was within a dozen feet of the boardwalk.

"I'm here, McCleary!" He said loudly. "Let 'er go!"

"You be Mabry, are ye?"

"That I am,...now let th' woman go, you piece a shit!"

"Oh, I can not do that, lad," He smiled. "And I must say, you do have a colorful way with vulgarity!...But no, I have grown quite fond of dear Maggie, I have!"

"Why,...wouldn't you rather use that knife on me?...Come on, man, you got th' edge, your knife is in your hand,...I'll have to reach for mine,...no contest!"

"Mister Mabry,...you be nothing but a pig farmer, a lowly cowboy with no upbringing!...You be nothing!...You have ruined everything for me!...You have murdered me best friend in all the world, a life-long friend, mind you!... And I will not leave Dallas until you pay for that!" He looked from Seth to the crowd of onlookers then.

"Listen to me, you ignorant, little people! I came here when you had nothing,...you were all begging for help like bums on the streets,...no one but me, Allan McCleary offered to help you!...I gave you the money to survive on, I put you back on your feet,...I did that, me and Yancy McGuire did that!...All we asked of you, was that you pay us back with a bit of respect!...Of which you did not,...and that is why you will always be little people. That is why you will watch today, and you will know what happens to those who disrespect Allan McCleary!...You allowed this unkempt sheepherder of a cowboy to destroy all that we stood for,…and now you will watch as he is executed!"

Seth listened, but couldn't believe the madness of the man,…he was insane! He was seething with anger and hatred for the arrogant Crime Boss by now,…and was weighing his chances of killing the man before he could kill the woman,…but he couldn't chance it. He took a deep breath then as McCleary turned his crazy eyes on him again,…then shrugged.

"Here I am!" He said tightly. "And I'm waitin'! So what now,…you expect me to just drop dead or somethin'?" He saw McCleary look toward the alley then and followed his stare,…and that's when a hush fell over the crowd as the black-clad Gerrard Roachman exited the alley to step up to the boardwalk,…and the gunfighter's eyes were boring into his as he slowly crossed the walkway and dropped back to the dirt of the street. He studied the gunman intently, feeling the old and almost forgotten stirrings in his consciousness,…the challenge,…and it was exciting!

"Yes," Returned McCleary then. "I do expect you to drop dead, you little man,…and you most certainly will!…But in doing so, you will then know and understand the superior power of Allan McCleary! I will not dirty me hands with the likes of you,…but me friend there will!"

Seth's eyes never left those of Gerrard Roachman while McCleary ranted, and when the Crime Boss was done, he nodded at the gunman. "I guess then, you'd be Mister Roachman!" He grated, squaring himself to face the gunfighter.

Roachman grinned as he nodded. "Name ring any bells for ya?"

"Nope,…never heard of ya!"

"Makes us even,…I never heard a Mabry, neither."

"Then why fight for this piece of garbage?"

"A million reasons, man." He shrugged. "All of 'em dollars!…But, while we're at it,…ain't you a mite old to be a gunfighter, Mabry,…what are you, sixty, sixty-five?…Makes me a little sorry to have to kill ya!"

"Don't be,…I'm like a good wine, I just get better with age!…What are you,…thirty,…less,…think you'll make sixty?" He smiled then when Roachman's eyes narrowed. "But, hey,…don't let that stop you, man, I was thirty once, I know how it is." He grinned widely then.

No longer smiling, and without hesitation, Roachman went for his gun,…and as smooth and fast as he was, had just cleared leather with the pistol when he grunted loudly, his breath suddenly forced from his lungs as he was hit.

Seth had been watching the gunman's eyes as they talked, and he knew he was facing a killer,…a man who was obviously as good with his gun as he looked to be. He saw the blink then, and as fast as he had ever been in his life, drew and fired, the slug striking Roachman in the chest and driving the air from his lungs in a gushing grunt as he was lifted by the impact and thrown backward to hit the ground hard,...and then he was still, his eyes staring lifeless at the sunlit sky.

It had all happened in a heartbeat and the instant after he fired, Seth turned the pistol on McCleary who, in total surprise and disbelief had dropped the knife wielding hand away from Maggie's unprotected throat, and fired again,...the slug jerking a gasping scream of agony from McCleary as it tore through his shoulder. Already off balance at being hit, his own momentum spun him around then backward into the Casino's large window, shattered glass flying inward with him as he fell through the opening. Maggie Redman had fallen to the boardwalk in a sobbing, screaming heap when McCleary released his grip on her hair,...and then there was chaos as Redman, and a score of bystanders rushed to her side.

The shots had been so close together, they sounded almost as one as they echoed sharply for an ear-shattering moment then just as quickly faded away in the distance. Seth watched as Dempsey rushed by him to leap to the boardwalk and climb through the window,...and then sighing heavily, holstered the pistol and walked back toward a wide-eyed Greg, and a smiling Emmit Castle.

Seth's eyes never left those of Gerrard Roachman while McCleary
ranted, and when the Crime Boss was done, he nodded at the
gunman. "I guess then, you'd be Mister Roachman!"

"How did you do that, Daddy?" blurted Greg with disbelief. "I never knew!...I never seen anything so fast, he never got off a shot!"

He put his arm around the boy's shoulder. "We'll talk about all that on th' way home, son." He looked back then as Dempsey half dragged the wounded Crime Boss out through the window.

"Thank you, Seth!" Smiled a satisfied Emmit Castle, as he also was watching the Marshal drag the ranting McCleary off the boardwalk and start across the street with him,...and still smiling, he turned to one of the onlookers.

"George,...go get Doctor Mitchell, will you, Sir,...and bring him to the Courthouse!" And after he was gone, he turned back to Seth. "Seth,...I don't know exactly who you are, sir,...but I really do not care! You have singlehandedly brought down a Crime Syndicate,...and you only killed one man doing it!...That is phenomenal to say the least!...You, Sir, have the gratitude of every man, woman and child in Dallas, Texas,...and I thank you for it!"

"No need!" Grinned Seth. "Th' debt's almost paid."

"It will be paid in full, sir, you have my word. Now, if you please, you and Greg go on back to the Courthouse while I attend to this mess here. I'll be along shortly,...paperwork, you know!"

"Hey, Marshal,...Judge!" Shouted Jake Tulane as him and another man half dragged, half carried the two large valises toward them. "Found these in th' alley yonder!" He panted as they dropped them at their feet.

Castle squatted and just happened to open the one containing McCleary's ledgers, and smiling up at Dempsey removed them and closed the bag again as he looked at Tulane. "Marshal, confiscate that buckboard over there, if you please, and bring it over here." And as Tulane left at a run, turned to stare hatefully at the still glaring face of McCleary for a second and then disgusted, nodded at Dempsey.

"Roderick, you can use that wagon, Jake is bringing. Get him to help you take McCleary and these bags to my office, I've already sent for a Doctor." He turned back to Seth then. "Seth, you and Greg go with them, please, I won't be long?" And gripping Seth's hand for a second, he nodded then immediately started across the wide street to comfort Cecil Redman and his wife.

*   *   *

Seth, Greg and Marshal Tulane were sitting in the hallway outside Emmit's office when the Judge and Doctor Mitchell hurried down the hall and entered, quickly closing the door behind them. None of them had spoken for a while, but the relief of finally ending the search for McCleary was evident on their faces.

"Daddy?" Queried Greg suddenly. "You okay?" He reached and put an arm across Seth's shoulders. "I'm damn proud of you, Daddy,...Tommy would have been, too!...We love you very much,...both of us!"

He looked at Greg and smiled. "That means a lot, son,...thanks."

Tulane listened to the conversation and when they were done, he cleared his throat."You still leavin' today, Seth?"

"By th' way it looks, I don't know!" He grinned at the Marshal. "Soon's th' Judge says it's okay, I guess....This waitin' is hard on a man."

"I've noticed you're not a man with much patience!" Grinned Tulane. "Guess they're patchin' McCleary up."

"I know, Jake." He sighed then pulled his watch. "Goin' on eleven already,...getting' hungry yet, son?"

"I'm always hungry, daddy, you know that!"

"Ya know what?" Stated Tulane. "So am I,...and I'd be honored to treat you both to lunch before you go, Seth....I know a place that cooks up a real good steak, so, what say,...my treat?"

"You're on, Marshal!" They looked up then as Dempsey pushed a scowling McCleary out of the office. He was shirtless, and had a sling around his neck and injured arm,...and was still cursing a blue-streak as they passed. Dempsey shook his head then pushed the ailing man on down the hall to knock on the outer office of the cell-block, and when the jailer opened the glass-topped door, pushed the Crime Boss inside and came back to join them in the hall.

"Emmit said he'd be right out, Seth." He grinned and sure enough, as he spoke the Judge opened his door and ushered Doc Mitchell out ahead of him.

"Thank you, Scott." He smiled. "Send me a bill, will you?"

"You know I will, Emmit." Mitchell shook his hand then nodded at Seth before leaving.

Emmit walked across the hall and smiled down at Seth before giving him a large leather pouch.

"What's this, Judge?"

"Well,...while Scott worked on McCleary, I counted out your son's winnings, Seth. Ten thousand dollars, was it not?"

"You don't have to do this, Judge!...I know enough about th' law to know all a that money is evidence."

"Oh, it is,...all but ten thousand dollars of it!...And you are wrong, sir,...I do have to do it! Just think of it as a reward from a grateful Dallas!"

He sighed then and stared back at his office door before looking back at them.

"There has to be several million dollars in them satchels in there, extorted money, all of it!...And I have a Prosecutor, Mister Ralph Phillips,... he'll be coming over shortly to go over those ledgers and count the money of which, by the way,...will all be returned to the folks this Scoundrel has robbed in the last three years!"

"Then, we're free to go home, now?"

"Of course, Seth Mabry,...and thank you again, Sir!" He shook Seth's hand as he spoke, and then Greg's. "Son,...it has been my pleasure to meet you."

Seth reached up and removed the Marshal's badge from his vest and held it out to him. "Then you'll be wanting this back."

"No, Sir, I won't,...you have been sworn in! From this day forward, you, sir, are an honorary United States Marshal, with all the privileges of one!... You keep it, Seth, you earned it!...You'll never again be able to say you were never a lawman."

"It appears, I won't!" He nodded and got up, as did Greg and Tulane, to watch as he pinned the badge on again. "Thanks, Judge." He grinned. "Now,...when's th' trial?"

Emmit laughed. "You are one persistent man, Seth!...But I'll tell you,...I will set the trial for thirty days from today, how's that?"

"I'll see you then!" He grinned and turned to leave.

"I'll walk out with you." Laughed Dempsey.

"Me, too," Mimicked Tulane. "We're goin' for steaks."

Once outside, Seth, Greg and Tulane mounted their horses then Seth leaned down to shake Dempsey's hand again. "Be a seein' you, Marshal,... you're a damn good man!"

Dempsey took his hand and walked in closer, pulling Seth lower onto his saddle. "So are you,...Mister Dancer!"

Seth released his hand and stiffened for a second and then, after glancing at Greg and Tulane, dismounted to peer into Dempsey's serious expression. "When did you remember?"

"When you drew on Roachman." He grinned.

"What did that have to do with anything?"

Dempsey raised a hand and gripped Seth's arm. "It had everything to do with it,...it was th' key to th' whole thing!...He grinned even wider, also raising to peer over the saddle at Greg and Tulane.

"Let me explain, Seth....In fifty-eight, I was a deputy Sheriff in Nacogdoches, Texas. In fact, I was there when that gunman called you out!... That was in fifty-eight, wasn't it?"

Seth nodded. "About then, I guess." "His name was Matt Hollister,... He'd been trailin' me for a month!" He sighed sadly then. "I came home to see my Mother,...but I was a little late."

"I know." Nodded Dempsey. "I saw you at th' grave."

"That still don't tell what gave me away!"

"It's simple,...when you draw your gun, you turn it on it's side to fire it. You're the only man I've ever seen do that!"

"I didn't realize I still did it." Sighed Seth. "I guess some old habits never die."

"Why did you shoot like that anyway?"

"It was my old Walker gun." He shrugged. "Th' percussion cap had a habit a jumpin' off th' next round when I fired it,...but by layin' th' gun on it's side,...it didn't!...So, what now, Marshal?"

"So, nothin'!...Now, I can sleep nights!" He shrugged. "Don't worry, my friend you're right,...th' fellow I knew, died a long time ago."

"Yes, sir, he did,...before th' war."

"Oh!' He said, reaching to pull the knife from the inside vest pocket. "This was found in McGuire's right shoulder,...you beat him to th' draw also, didn't you?"

"I wanted to kill 'im th' way he killed Tommy!"

"How'd you learn to throw one like that,...you had to be across th' room from him?"

"Practiced a lot as a kid, I like knives,...always did."

"I saw that old Pine tree in front of your mother's porch, sure was scarred up.,...that was your target, wasn't it?" And when Seth nodded. "I knew your Mother, Seth, Magdalina Dancer was a fine lady,...I was at her funeral, too!" He shook his head then.

"You know,...th' day you shot Hollister,...I chased you for every bit of ten miles. I wanted to bring you in,...make a name for myself!...But after watchin' you again today, I must a been crazy!"

"I wondered who that was?" Grinned Seth. "And I'm glad you didn't!...Thanks, Marshal,...I'm damn lucky to know you!...I'll see you in thirty days." He pulled himself into the saddle again and nodding, reined the Buckskin away from the hitch-rail, and the three of them rode off toward Main Street.

*   *   *

"Seth Joe-Bob Dancer!" Repeated Greg as they crossed the Trinity Bridge. "Why did you change your name like that,...I like Dancer?"

"There was a chance men would be lookin' for me,...and I didn't want a put your mother through that! Anyway, Mabry was your Grandmother's given name, before she married my father....It's a good, respectable name!"

"I still can't believe you were a gunfighter,...why didn't you ever tell us?"

"Didn't see any need,...I put all that behind me when I met your mother!" He shrugged then. "Till now, only she knew."

"Tommy was fast on the draw, too!" Grinned Greg. "Guess he came by it natural."

"I tried to teach you both how to defend yourselves." He sighed. "Guess I didn't do it good enough."

"It wouldn't have mattered, Daddy. There wasn't any way Tommy could have defended us against McGuire!...Besides, there was two of 'em. It was dark, and I know Tommy wasn't expectin' it, he was too worried about me!...I just hope he knows I would have stopped it, if I could?"

"He does!...Now come on, Mother's worried about us!" They prodded their horses to a gallop along the dusty road, each left to their own thoughts.

CHAPTER FIFTEEN

Laura Mabry sat on the long, L-shaped front porch and slowly rocked back and forth in her rocking chair, and her eyes were glued to the empty road all the way to the line of trees,…as they had been every day for five days. She had never been so worried about anything in her life. She was already devastated by the loss of one son, and so afraid she was losing another,… along with his father!

She was not all that worried about Seth, she knew what he was capable of,…but he was so bull-headed when it came to his beliefs of right and wrong! And if he should use that gun again, she didn't know what might happen? She did know that their lives would never be the same again with Thomas gone,…and had prayed nightly that their love would see them through. Tommy had been Seth's pride and joy, had always known that by the way he looked at him,…maybe because they were so much alike?

Seth had been everything she detested in a man when she met him, she recalled,…a common gunman, a killer!…He had even robbed the very stage she was on,…but she couldn't bring herself to hate him for that, couldn't even turn him in for it, even though she had recognized him right away! She grinned as she thought about that,…he had been so easy going and fun loving the day of the robbery,…and she'd been shocked when he stepped up, not two hours later to carry her bags to the hotel for her.

She often remembered that day, his handsome face, and easy smile,… and the way he walked, sort of a balanced swaying motion that seemed to emit confidence in himself. She guessed that was why she couldn't refuse him when he asked her on a picnic that same day,…and was why she was in love before they ever returned to her hotel.

She had been afraid a lot before they found their land, because she knew he might use his gun again at any given time, and would at the drop of a hat,…if he was wronged in any way? But he had not, not even during that dreadful war and then,...after the conflict, when he had come in one night and packed it away, she was the happiest she had ever been!...He had not worn it since,...until now, she sighed!...And that thought made her afraid all over again,...of what he might do?

She was reminiscing all of this for the thousandth time when she became aware of someone walking around the porch, but then smiled when Trey stopped to peer over the railing at her.

"Hope I didn't scare ya none, Miz. Mabry!"

"A little," She nodded. "I was a long way from here, Trey,...but that's all right."

"Yessum, I knowed you was,...and I sure don't like seein' you do that!... That's why I think it's time we went to Dallas,...I'm a mite worried about 'em myself!"

"Oh, Trey, do you think we should?"

"How else we gonna know they're okay, if we don't"...Besides,...they might need our help!"

"Then let's do it!...And thank you, Trey,...when can we go?"

"Well, not tonight, Ma'am. But first thing tomorrow, we're goin'!"

"Good,...I'll pack some food tonight for the trip. I'm so worried about them, you know."

"Yessum, I know,...so am I!...I just got through getting' th' buckboard all greased up and ready, brought th' team in, too!...We'll leave at first light."

"Thank you again, Trey." She smiled, getting up to straighten her apron. "I'll go in and fix supper now, it won't be long."

"Thanks, Ma'am,...I'll wait out here on th' porch."

It was almost dark by the time she was ready to set the table,...and she was excited at the prospect of going to see about her family, but reluctant as well. Not knowing what she would find when they got there was frightening,...Seth could be in jail, or worse!...And Greg,...she shuddered then, not wanting to even think about that. By the time she was lighting the coal-oil lamp on the table, she was doubting their decision to go,...and was just about to call Trey in to eat when he shouted at her. Dropping the tin of matches, she hurried through the house and out onto the porch in time to see the two riders galloping toward the house.

"Is that them, Trey,...it's so dark?"

"'Yessum, that's th' boss's Buckskin,...and that's Greg's dapple gray, it's them all right!"

"Thank, God!" She gasped and hurried down the steps to the grassless front yard, where they both were waiting when they rode up and dismounted. Without a word, she rushed, bawling to embrace Greg.

Sniffing, Seth wiped tears from his eyes as he watched them, then reached to shake Trey's hand firmly,...and then cleared his throat. "Many thanks, Trey,...I do appreciate you lookin' out for Laura this way."

"It was my pleasure, Boss,...but I'm shore glad to see you home, I was getting' worried about th' missus."

Laura released Greg then, and came into Seth's arms, still crying with happiness,...and they held each other for a time as Greg shook Trey's hand and talked with him.

After a few minutes, Seth held Laura away from him and kissed her and then, with both arms around her and Greg, steered them both up the steps and into the house, where she quickly pulled away and hurried toward the kitchen.

"You all sit down while I fix more supper!" She said as she left, and they followed her in to the table and sat down tiredly as she worked.

"Things go okay around here, Trey,...With th' ranch, I mean,...stock doin' well?"

"Yes, sir, I kept up with ever'thin'. But I did bring th' stock in closer to th' barn, got 'em in th' big pasture,...thought that was best, what with keepin' an eye on th' Missus, and all."

"You hadn't come home today," Grinned Laura from the stove. "We were coming to Dallas tomorrow to find you,...Trey already had the buckboard ready!"

"And what was you gonna do when you got there,...Dallas ain't just a town anymore, honey,...it's a hell of a big city?"

"We would have found you, that's what!" She smiled then as she placed more food on the table. "And that would be better than not knowing if you two were dead or alive."

"I know, honey," He smiled. "And I apologize for takin' so long!"

"Oh, sure you do,...now eat!...And then you can tell us everything that happened!"

They said Grace then began eating in silence,...and when they were done, the two men sat over coffee and a smoke while Seth related most of what had taken place in Dallas over the five days he was gone. He told them of Greg's beating, and the confession he was forced to sign, but purposely omitting his encounter with the Butcher, or his death at the hands of Gus Jenson. He told of his fight with Silva, and the Syndicate enforcers, and of how he helped Judge Castle and law enforcement by finding Tommy's killer,...and of how that helped bring down the crime ring.

When he finished, he smiled weakly at her pained expression. "I did what I had to do, honey,...and I'll do it again, everytime!"

"I know!" She sighed, looking worriedly at Greg's face. "I didn't see the discoloration till just now, Baby, are you okay?" She gasped.

"I'm fine, Mama." He soothed. "It's still sore in places, but it'll be all right, the color will go away."

"God, I hope so!" She looked blankly at Seth then. "Are you telling me everything,…do they know who you are?"

"Marshal Dempsey." He nodded. "And Greg now,…and I think it's time we let Trey know."

"I already know, Boss." Grinned Trey. "My daddy told me about you a long time ago."

"Don't make me sound so old, Trey!" He frowned. "So,…how long have you known?"

"Five days!" Answered Laura, suddenly looking at her plate. "I was so worried when you left, that I let it slip."

"That's good….I'm glad you know, Trey. But,…it stays here, okay?"

"You got it, Boss."

"I was afraid of what you might do when you got there, Seth." She sniffed.

"I understand, honey, it's okay. I was afraid of what I might do, myself,…and I nearly did a couple a times! In fact,…I probably would have, if not for th' Marshal!"

"Well, I'm just thankful you didn't kill anyone!" She saw the look on his face then. "You shot someone, didn't you?"

"I'm afraid so." He sighed. "But I told you about Silva,…I had no choice, he drew on me!...And I didn't kill 'im."

"Were there any more?"

He nodded. "Two,…but only one of 'em died, honey,…and there was no way around it!"

"Go on, Daddy," Laughed Greg. "Tell them about the gunfight, Mama will find out anyway?" He looked at his mother then and shrugged. "He had to, mama,…McCleary was gonna kill a woman if daddy didn't fight his gunfighter,…and you should a seen him, mama." He said excitedly. "It's unbelievable how fast Daddy is,…that man didn't get off a shot!"

She nodded weakly. "I know,…what about that poor woman, is she okay?"

"Yes, Ma'am,…after daddy shot the gunfighter, he shot McCleary in the shoulder."

"Everybody will know who you are now." She sniffed. "You know that!"

"I don't think th' Marshal will tell anyone, honey." Sighed Seth. "He's a damn good man."

"How did he find out,…did you tell him?"

"No,...seems he chased me once,...long before I met you. Said he knew my Mother before she died."

"Oh, Honey, did he tell you how she died?"

"No, and I didn't ask 'im,...th' memory was painful enough! Anyway,... I'll never forgive myself for not goin' home sooner!" He sighed. "What's done, is done!...There ain't no wanted posters on me, though,...so we're okay!"

"Then, that's the end of it?"

"It will be,...I'm goin' back in thirty days for th' trial, the hangin', too!"

"Not without us, you're not!" She said flatly. "I have to know my child didn't die in vain!...God!" She gasped. "That sounded awful, didn't it,...God forgive me?"

"We all feel that way, mama!" Soothed Greg. "Besides, Daddy's a United States Marshal now, he has to be there."

"Honorary Marshal, Son!" He sighed then hooked a thumb in his vest, pulling it aside to reveal the star on his shirt. "Sort a feels strange, too!"

"Seth Mabry,...something tells me, you're still not telling me everything!"

"Mama." Said Greg quickly. "McCleary was the Syndicate Crime Boss,...he was the man behind the whole thing with Tommy, Yancy McGuire was only the man that carried out the order!...Daddy singlehandedly brought down a New York Crime Syndicate, mama,...I heard the Federal Judge say so! They were nothing but a gang of killers and blackmailers,...and Daddy put 'em out of business!"

Laura placed both elbows on the table and dropped her face in her hands for a moment before looking up again. "Are there going to be people coming to kill you, now?"

"Nope!" Returned Seth calmly. "They're all either gone, or in jail waitin' trial!"

"Just the same," She sniffed. "From now on, when you leave this house, you'd better be wearing that gun, you hear me?...I will not see you dead because some New York Killer wants revenge,...or, or just because you don't want to wear a gun anymore. Now,...I know you took it off because of me,...but now, I want you to wear it for the same reason!"

"We'll all be armed, mama!" Returned Greg with a passion she had not seen before. "And I'll never take another drink, neither,...you won't have to worry anymore about that!"

"Thank you, Darling," She smiled, reaching to cradle his face in her hand. "And thank, God you're all right, both of you." She smiled at Seth as she spoke.

Seth cleared his throat to change the subject. "What are we behind on, Trey?"

"Well,...we still got hay to cut, Boss, we're gonna need it this winter!... And there's stock to move back to th' range,...other than that, we're in good shape."

"We'll get started on that first thing tomorrow,...I'd like to have that hay in th' barn before we go to Dallas."

"We will, Daddy." Grinned Greg. "I'll ready the blades, and grease the mower, while you two work the cattle tomorrow,...we'll get it done!"

*   *   *

"This was where they were hiding, all right!" Sighed Emmit as Captain Hayward, Marshal Dempsey, and himself came up out of the dank cellar and into the kitchen. "Damn ingenious, too, I might add!"

"Plans derived from twisted minds usually are, Emmit!" Nodded Hayward as he looked the large kitchen over. "What's gonna happen to th' place now,...auction-block?"

"It could come to that,...a saloon is about all it can be used for, except, maybe a hotel, and all these gaming tables must have cost a pretty penny!...Anyway," He sighed as they entered the large main room. "Devin Ringerman has a Nephew living in Gallop, New Mexico,...and by law, with the proof of Murder that I now have on McCleary, the place will revert back to him!...I've already sent him a wire to that effect. If he wants it, once the trial is over, I'll sign the deed back to him,...that's all I can do!"

"He might not even want it!" Declared Dempsey. "He didn't appear all that broken up at Ringerman's funeral,...to me, anyway!"

"I noticed that myself!" Agreed Emmit. "He can sell it, if he wants,... or give it back to the city. But I would like to see McGuire's place become a theater again,...Dallas needs some reprieve from this damn recession,... thank God, it's about over!...I received a wire from the Justice Department this morning, the Gold Standard is working,...or so they are saying."

"Still a long ways to go, though." Sighed Hayward. "You inventoried all this stuff yet?...Got a be two, three thousand dollars worth a liquor behind that bar."

"And bought with extorted money, Alex!" Returned Castle as they exited out to the boardwalk. "No, I have not inventoried yet,...but it will all be confiscated and resold....By the way, you still leaving today?"

"Got to, Emmit,...Mexican Border Raiders are at work again along th' Rio Grande,...it's gonna take every man I've got to round 'em up!...But if you're expectin' any trouble at that trial, I'll spare you a couple men?"

"Ahhh, no!...We have it covered, Alex. Captain Godwin at the Fort promised me a troop of cavalry for that if I think we need it,...we should be okay." He turned to the Mexican that had been patiently waiting on the boardwalk.

"Nail it up, Manwell,...and send me your bill!" And once the carpenter went to work, they went down the steps to the street and began dodging the traffic of an already busy day on their walk back to the Courthouse.

                    *   *   *

It had been three weeks since Hayward and his Rangers left, and it was business as usual for the relieved citizens of Dallas. Business was thriving again, people were spending their money once more,...and as the dollar grew stronger, were realizing more and more goods for their money's worth. Crime in town, as well as the county had come to almost a complete stop, allowing both, the new Marshal, and the new Sheriff some time to rest,... and to wonder what was happening? Of course there were still the usual drunks to put up for the night, family spats, and a few muggings, but otherwise the job was becoming a little boring and routine. Ricky Hurd had been assigned to night patrol, rattling doors along Main and Elm Streets after the town shut down at night. He was also assigned to the Depot at the onset of his shift, to watch who exited the trains on their arrival.

Sheriff Jordan Hicks spent his time at the office, or patrolling the county when the need arose, or when some farmer or rancher would come in and complain of missing cattle, or the theft of a hog, etcetera,...of which, most times would turn out to be nothing but false alarms leaving him mostly confused,...because he could not remember Sheriff Gentry having so much idle time on his hands. He had kept both him and Ricky busy most of the time, as well as Sam and Bert.

Marshal Tulane, and his Deputy had been spending their time in the city as well,...most times just patrolling the streets. Derrick Tinsley patrolled on horseback during the night, keeping an eye on those areas of town that tended to breed crime, such as the cantinas and the residential prostitution areas along the Trinity River. That area presented him with nightly muggings, fights with deadly weapons and drunken brawls,...and the jail at the Marshal's office was generally occupied by his shift's end. But all of this came under the definition of normalcy,...it was a constant thing, and something Tulane and his Deputy had already been used to.

Today, Jordan Hicks looked up from his papaerwork as Ricky Hurd opened the door and came in. "You're back in a hurry, Rick, somethin' happen at th' Depot?"

"You might say so, Jordan,...we got company, just like you thought we might!" He toed the chair around and sat down as he spoke. "Three fancy-dressed men got off th' train an hour ago,...so I followed 'em to th' Liberty Hotel. They're from New York City, okay, all three of 'em!"

"Who are they?"

"One of 'em's a lawyer," He took the paper from his shirt and looked at it. "A Lyle Greenburg. The other two have to be bodyguards or something, they're both big and rough looking!...One of 'em is a Jimmy McGrath, the other one,...as best as I could make out, is Brutas Feingold!...All three are wearin' some damn fancy duds!"

"Do me a favor, Ricky,...go tell Jake Tulane about this, he'll need to alert Marshal Dempsey and th' Judge,...and Ricky,...after you do that, go back and watch th' hotel,...they're probably up to no good!"

"I'll do that!" Nodded Hurd and quickly got up and left. Leaving a worried, and somewhat frightened Sheriff Hicks musing over the news.

What could a high-dollar Lawyer be doing in Dallas?...Had they somehow heard of McCleary's capture and impending trial this quick? No,...they couldn't have known what happened here, not this quick!...But why else would they be here, he wondered?...Unless this Greenburg was sent to try and get McGuire and McCleary off? But then again, they would have to have known about it!...But how? If they did know,...they could be here to lay claim to Syndicate property! He shook his head then and grinned,... either way, they're gonna be up Shit Creek, He thought. Judge Castle owns these Bastards property and all,...he is not about to let them slip away now!

No, he thought,...these three are up to no good,...and truth be known, were guilty of the same crimes as McCleary, and McGuire! He felt the beginning of gloom settling around him, and that feeling was telling him that the trouble was far from over yet, in fact,...the worst may yet be coming because it was obvious that McGrath and Feingold were enforcers, the likes of Butcher and Silva! The question was, however,...what were they really here for,...to protect Greenburg,...or to exact revenge? He sighed and got up to go peer through the window at the street.

Nothing was amiss there, he thought, people were shopping as usual,... and sighing again, he suddenly felt the impact of his new job's responsibility. He would need,...no, he had better be prepared for what might be coming!

*   *   *

"Well, I sure did not expect this, Marshal!" Sighed Emmit Castle as he paced the floor of his office. "But I will admit, I thought it was possible." He walked back to stop in front of Tulane then. "Marshal, I would appreciate knowing if, and when anyone might have wired New Your City in the past three weeks. There's a Telegraph office on Commerce, and another at the Depot,...and I have one, but no one here has access to it except myself, and Roderick,...will you have that checked out for me, please?...Because if someone did this, he is going to jail!"

"Th' Morning News has a Telegraph operator, too, Judge!"

"That's right, I completely forgot about that,...and that young Reporter, Grady Malone was here the day we jailed McCleary, I gave him an interview, an exclusive!...He would be my guess, Marshal." He sighed then. "But if he is the culprit, there isn't much I can do about it, I'm afraid....Freedom of the Press, you know!...That, from our new Commander in Chief!" He sighed again and patted Jake on the shoulder. "I appreciate the heads-up on this, Marshal, I will talk with Roderick as soon as he gets back, he will need to be prepared!...But check it out anyway to be sure. If it was Malone, get me a copy of that wire!"

"Yes, Sir, Judge." Sighed Tulane as he got up. "This is my town, Judge,...I want a be involved in this!"

"And you will!...But for now, take care of that for me, and have your Deputy keep an eye on them, especially the bodyguards, if that's what they are?...I will not have them bullying my witnesses!"

"Yes, Sir. Th' Sheriff has a man watchin' th' hotel right now, and my Deputy is at th' Depot....But I'll join Mister Hurd at th' hotel when I get through."

"That ought to do it, Marshal. Just keep me informed." His thoughts were a jumble of possible scenarios as Tulane left, and as he mulled over each one of them, continued pacing the floor until Dempsey arrived and he had relayed what Tulane had reported.

"What do you make of it, Emmit?" Queried Dempsey, who until now had been content to just listen and worry.

"Well,...I expect this Shyster Lawyer will pull some high-handed tactics to try and get his clients released, Roderick,...and if that is why he's here, he will be prepared! We'll just have to wait and see,...I have Marshal Tulane watching them as we speak,...and I believe Deputy Hurd is with him." He sighed then and leaned back in his chair.

"But that may not be why they are here at all, too!" He mused. "Mister Tulane is also checking the Telegraph offices. If they did not get a wire to the effect, they do not know what has happened here."

"They will, once they find Ringerman's boarded up!" Commented Dempsey.

"Yes, I'm sure of that!" Nodded Emmit. "And that being the case, we can expect a visit from Mister Greenburg at any time now, but I will handle him!...It's the two men with him, I'm wondering about, Roderick,...what are they here for?" The knock sounded at the door then, and they both looked at each other.

"Maybe we're about to find out!" Sighed Emmit, looking at the door again.

"Do come in!" He called out loudly then watched as the well-dressed man entered.

"Are you Judge Castle, Sir?" Smiled Lyle Greenburg after he had closed the door behind him.

"I am Emmit Castle, yes, sir?" He responded. "And you are?"

"My name is Lyle Greenburg, Sir." He said coming to hold out his hand. "Attorney at law."

Emmit shook his hand then. "And this is United States Marshal, Roderick Dempsey, sir!"

Greenburg shook Dempsey's hand then looked back at Emmit. "I represent a Client in New York City, Your Honor, but on arrival I found that his employee's place of business has been boarded up,...and needless to say, I am quite confused!...A passer-by informed us that Mister McCleary and his employee had been placed under arrest, and are now in your custody,... is that correct?"

"You are correct, Sir!" Responded Emmit. "Now, please have a seat, won't you?" And after Greenburg had sat down. "Now, just what can I do for you?"

"Well, Sir,...since I can not perform my duties as required,...I am naturally authorized to post bail for Mister McCleary, and McGuire,...and I would like to do so, if you please?"

"I am afraid that will be impossible, Mister Greenburg." He grinned. "Both have been remanded without bail, pending trial!"

"I see,...then I am here to represent them as Defense Attorney. I have not informed my Client of the situation,...but I am sure he would want that! May I see the charges against them now,...as well as the investigative reports, and eye-witness statements, if any."

"Mister Greenburg," Sighed Emmit. "There are more than fifty witnesses to the crimes of these two men, one of which is Mister Roderick Dempsey here,...and myself!...As for the names of any other,...I'm afraid that must be kept in my personal confidence. But please, sir, feel free to seat yourself at my desk,...because right here, and now is the only time you will see the charges against these men!"

He gestured to his desk, and as Greenburg moved to seat himself, he walked around his desk to open a thick folder and remove a stack of papers from it, placing them in front of the Lawyer.

"Your Clients are charged with Racketeering, Extortion, Kidnapping, Enslavement, Rape of a minor, Prostitution, Arson, Blackmail, and outright Murder, Mister Greenburg,...and there are actually more than fifty credible witnesses, who are set to testify to the charges!...And as far as seeing the witness copies, Sir, well that just will not happen!...I will not have you, or the Goons with you intimidating the good folks of this city with your New York Tactics and brutality!...They have had enough of that at the hands of these two men!"

He stared at the bewilderment in Greenburg's face for a moment then sighed. "I am sorry, Mister Greenburg,...but I have watched the corruption in my city for more than three years now, and until now have not been able to do anything about it!...And please, my anger is not directed at you, Sir, I don't even know you!. But McCleary, and McGuire represent a Syndicate Crime Organization, and your Client is the head of it,...he sent them here to do his dirty work!"

Greenburg gazed at him for a moment longer then cleared his throat. "I think, Your Honor, that you have me all wrong, Sir!"

"I admit that I may have come on too strong here, Mister Greenburg,... but I am mad, Sir,...and so is everyone in Dallas. That is why it would behest you, and the men with you to take that train back to New York City and tell your Crime Boss Client that this is Texas, not New York City!...Tell him we deal in Justice here, Mister Greenburg, not intimidation, and sir,...I have to say this before you open those pages. If I hear that you, or your two cronies are involved in these sort of tactics while in Dallas, in any way, I will bring you to trial as well!"

"With all due respect, Your Honor,...I do not know what business my New York Client is in,...I have heard rumors to the effect, mind you." He shrugged then. "But normally, I take no notice in rumors. But regardless to their charges, these men are entitled to representation,...and I can not put together a proper defense without being able to question the witnesses."

"You can question them in Court all you want, sir."

"Then, may I request a change of venue, Sir, my Clients will never receive a fair trial in this city, with you and everyone so set against them?"

Emmit leaned on the desk in front of Greenburg and sighed. "I would like to apologize to you, Mister Greenburg, both for my outspoken rudeness to a colleague, and for believing you were other than what you say you are. I do believe you have, or had no knowledge of what happened here beforehand. But, given that,...I also have to refuse your request for a venue change, and my reason is this,...it's a Federal Case, Mister Greenburg, and I am a Federal Judge. Therefore, be advised that I am forced to follow the law to the letter bias be damned!...Now, please, feel free to read over any and all transcript there before you."

"Thank you." Nodded Greenburg. "But I must say,...this, sir, is quite out of the ordinary,...and quite Discriminating!"

"That may very well be!" Returned Emmit. "But the trial is set for this coming Saturday, right here in this Courthouse and it will take place, and with myself presiding!...So now, Sir, with all due respect to a Colleague,...I am not in the least happy to make your acquaintance, so please,...since you obviously are not anxious to view the contents set before you,...leave my office."

"Very well!" Said Greenburg getting slowly to his feet.

"Wait, Sir!!" Said Emmit quickly. "I have no doubt you are an excellent Lawyer....But, Sir, you are working for Organized Crime at the worst level! You may, or may not be happy with that,...and you may, or may not be an honest man, I have no way of knowing!...But I am an honest man, and I work for the law!...I also work for the Government. In essence Justice will be served here,...and if your New York Client was here today, I would do the same for him! Because crime in Dallas, Texas is illegal!...Mister Greenburg, Sir,...your Clients are outlaws of the worst kind. That Client of yours in New York is a Syndicate Boss, and that makes him and anyone associated with him to be guilty of the same crimes. Mister Greenburg, that man sanctioned what went on here."

Nodding, Greenburg placed both hands on the table. "I am an honest man, also, Your Honor,...and believe it or not, I do understand your feelings about this unfortunate case,...I believe I would feel the same way in your position. But,...seeing as how I have accepted this assignment,...is it possible to see my Clients?"

Emmit cleared his throat then nodded. "Yes, Sir, you may see one of them tonight." He picked up a pencil and wrote on a sheet of blank paper then gave it to Greenburg. "Give this to the jailor, four doors down the hall from here." He shook his head as Greenburg left then shrugged across at Dempsey.

"What do you think he'll do, Emmit?" Queried Dempsey. "You sure gave 'im a reaming,...don't believe I ever saw you in that state a mind before."

"I know, Roderick," He sighed, coming to sit down beside him. "He'll try and make his own defense case I think, it's his job!...He is undoubtedly a very good Attorney and he doesn't anger easily. And because of that, he has probably been paid a large sum of money to come here. But he will not win this one, Roderick. Ralph Phillips has all the ammunition he needs in our case,...and in my opinion, he is the best there is anywhere!

"I sure hope you're right!"

"Roderick,…I would like you to spend time on the streets until the trial, make sure our star-witnesses stay determined. Also, to find out if any of them have been questioned by our Mister Greenburg and associates!"

"Then with your permission, I'll start right now, Emmit."

"Good man!" Nodded Castle. "Oh, Roderick,…check on our Mister McGuire first thing, will you?…Someone will likely tell them he's in the hospital, and that could be disastrous. Now, if he is still unable to be transferred to jail, pull your best man off his watch detail, and place him at the Hospital. No one is allowed into McGuire's room but the surgeons, and I mean that aggressively!…I don't put anything past this Mister Greenburg and Henchmen."

*   *   *

Allan McCleary eased his arm back into the sling and stood as Lyle Greenburg was shown into his cell.

"Are you Allan McCleary?' Queried the Attorney as he came to confront him.

"That I am, Lad,…Who might you be?"

"I am an Attorney at law, Sir, quite possibly your Attorney,…and we need to discuss your case." Greenburg shook his hand as he spoke then sat down on the end of the bunk, watching as McCleary did the same.

"I know all the Attorney's here." Replied McCleary. "Who appointed you, Sir?"

"Jesse O'Riely sent me, Allan,…now please, tell me what happened to put you here?"

"Now, just one minute, Lad. What did Jesse tell you, exactly?"

"Not one thing about all of this, Allan,…this, I'm afraid, was quite a surprise!…I was sent here to go over your books and to offer any legal advice you might need in case of a problem. He has not heard from you in some time, and was afraid you could be in trouble of some kind. …But I do not think he was prepared for this!"

"How did you know I be in jail?"

"People on the street. We went to your establishment and found it all boarded up….And I also asked the Hotel Clerk what happened when we went back. Mister O'Riely doesn.t know about this yet, so I want you to tell me what happened, and be specific,…because I have to tell you, Judge Castle seems to have an air-tight case against you." He listened then as McCleary told him his version of how he was arrested, and why,…and when he was done just shook his head.

"Allan, there has to be more to it than that,…There's a stack of evidence a foot thick on the Judge's desk?"

"That be the honest truth, Sir. This Gunfighter's son was killed in back of me place of business, and me friend Yancy McGuire blamed for it! This Gunfighter killed most of poor Yancy's employees, and then killed him!… And me being Yancy's boss, he set the law on me, and me in the process of sending Jesse three million dollars, too!"

"And this same Gunfighter shot you, is that correct?'"

"On me Mother's life, God bless her,…I was only defending meself!"

"What about the other crimes in the indictment, such as Kidnapping and Rape?"

"All lies, to put us out of business!…This Judge has a vendetta against me, he does,…the Bastard wants me dead!"

"And that's all there is,…nothing more you want to add?"

"That be all I know, Lad."

"Then I'll be in touch." He got up from the bunk as he spoke. "I'll wire Mister O'Riely of this when I leave here. Are you sure there is nothing else?"

"That be the truth, Sir!"

Nodding, Greenburg called for the Jailer and left, and as he was let back into the hallway, he shook his head and went back to knock at Emmit's office door.

"Mister Greenburg?" He nodded as the Attorney entered. "Did you see your Client?"

"Yes, I did, Sir,…and before I say anything else,…I would like for you to tell me the exact circumstances of what led up to, and how Mister McCleary was arrested,…would you mind doing that?"

"I would not mind at all, Sir." Greenburg listened intently while Emmit related the story as it really happened, and ending with. "I was there, Sir, I witnessed everything.…Would you like to read over the indictments now?"

"No, Sir. But this is about what I thought!…Every word from Allan McCleary's mouth was outright fraudulent, and derogatory. He lied with every breath he took!…I had no idea about any of this until I checked in at the Hotel, Judge,…I was sent here to go over his books, nothing more!" He looked Emmit in the eyes then and nodded.

"There's no way I can, or will defend this man, Judge!…You'll need to appoint him another Attorney, Sir,…because I am unavailable!"

"Duly noted…What are your plans now?"

"Back to New York,…I have a retainer to return." He smiled and started for the door.

"What of the two men with you, Mister Greenburg?'

"I don't really know why they were sent with me, Your Honor,...they hardly spoke a word the whole trip!...I thought they were sent to watch over me for some reason, but I don't know,...I guess they'll return with me!...At any rate, I'm on my way to wire my Client now of my findings, guess we'll go from there....Good bye, Judge."

"Greenburg?" He nodded, guessing he had been wrong about the man's ethics as he watched him close the door behind him.

CHAPTER SIXTEEN

The next two days passed without event. Yancy McGuire was finally able to be moved from the Hospital to a cell at the Courthouse, where him and Allan McCleary, between grunts of pain and self-pity, spent their time blaming each other for their predicament. Emmit Castle spent hours with Ralph Phillips going over the case in it's every possible aspect, until they were both confident of its results,...everything was ready. The trial was set for ten o'clock Saturday morning, day after tomorrow.

Marshal Tulane spent his daylight hours watching the Liberty Hotel, and was relieved at night by Derrick Tinsley,...and all they had seen of Greenburg, or the two enforcers, was when one of the men would go out to bring in food for them. However, it was now Thursday, and for the last twelve hours, they had not seen anyone coming out for food,...and when Tulane finally became suspicious enough to go talk with the Clerk, and was told that the two men and Greenburg had checked out already, he frantically withdrew back to the Depot to watch for them,...of course, that was after reporting to Marshal Dempsey of their departure.

No one had seen them leave the hotel, nor had seen them since,...and even though the Sheriff"s Deputy Hurd could not say for sure he saw, or didn't see them boarding the train to leave,...they were all pretty much confident that they had indeed left Dallas and were all pulled from Depot duty, much to the relief of the deputies. Marshal Dempsey, however, being a man of suspicious nature, was not at all sure they had gone. Greenburg had told Emmit they were leaving but they were not seen doing that! He had in fact, sent Tulane to ask questions of everyone on the streets, even shop-owners and Clerks,...nobody could say for sure they had seen them. So,... even though his suspicions were intact, probability caused him to relax the efforts and concentrate on trial security, sending word to Marshal Tulane and Deputy Tinsley to meet him at his office on Friday morning

    *   *   *

"Come in, Marshal!" Grinned Jake Tulane as Dempsey walked in.

"Jake." Sighed Dempsey as he came on to sit down and peer across the desk at him. ""I'd like you and Derrick in that Courtroom during the trial tomorrow,…not that they'll need your testimony, but you never know. Anyway,…I'm not convinced that all is well here, and it's nagging the hell out a me!"

"What do you think it is?"

"Oh, I'll tell ya what it is,…It's Greenburg, and them two enforcers!…Something's wrong about that, Jake, and I don't know what?…But I want you in that Courtroom just in case."

"We'll be there, Marshal,…and I will admit, it's sure been quiet lately!"

"Yeah." Nodded Dempsey worriedly. "Normally, it's th' way I'd like it,…but it's far from normal around here right now!"

"Deputy Hurd's tyin' up outside, Marshal." Said Derrick Tinsley near the window. "Somethin' must be up, th' way he slid his horse in."

They both stood as Derrick opened the door for a breathless Deputy Hurd.

"Marshal?" He panted, staring at both of them. "The Sheriff needs you both at th' Liberty Hotel!…He said to come quick!"

"What's th' problem, son?" Voiced Dempsey quickly.

"We got us a dead man over there, Marshal,…Sheriff think's he's beed dead a couple a days, there's blood everywhere!"

It took several minutes for the three men to run the six long blocks to the hotel, and were all breathing heavily by the time they joined Hurd in the lobby

"Ricky," Gasped Tulane. "Where is he?"

"Second floor, Jake,…you okay, sir?"

He nodded tiredly. "Clear all these people out a here,…keep everybody outside!…Nobody gets in, you got it?" And still out of breath, he followed Dempsey up the flight of stairs to finally gasp for breath again at the open doorway,…but then, almost gagged at sight of the already bloated corpse on the floor.

"Who is he, Jordan?" He asked, looking at the ashen-faced Sheriff.

Hicks removed the kerchief from his nose and mouth. "It's that Lawyer fella, Greenburg, accordin' to th' desk clerk."

"Guess he decided not to leave after all!" Exclaimed Dempsey. "Jordan, go down and send Hurd to tell th' Judge about this,…tell 'im to stay there, too!…Them two Enforcers could still be here somewhere and th' Judge could be a target"

"Wait up, Jordan," Said Tulane. "The Judge will want Greenburg's belongings."

"You think they killed him?" Queried Hicks.

"They got my vote!" Replied Dempsey and sighing again, pressed the bandana tighter against his face and squatted beside the corpse as Tulane began putting the Lawyer's clothing and toiletries into the traveling bag on the bed.

"Greenburg was leaving town," Sighed Dempsey as he gingerly checked the man's pockets. "Judge said he didn't want anything to do with the case!"

"But why kill their own Lawyer?"

"Maybe that's what they were sent here to do!" Remarked Tulane as he brought the valise to the body. "Maybe he was too honest."

Dempsey put Greenburg's personals into the valise and buckled it up before nodding at Hicks, who quickly took it and left the room.

"Th' Judge thinks all three were in th' dark about what happened here with McCleary and McGuire." Said Dempsey, looking up at Jake. "Not till th' Desk Clerk told 'em what happened, anyway…So I'm thinkin' them two old boys was sent here to execute both McCleary, and McGuire,…and this fool here was sent to settle their affairs afterward!…That's what I'm thinkin'!"

"Maybe they're still gonna do it!" Responded Tulane. "That, or break 'em out a jail?"

"But when?' Sighed Dempsey, getting to his feet. "Dallas will be full a soldiers by tonight, they'll never get close to that Courthouse!…And where the hell, are they?"

"I don't know, Marshal," Blurted Tulane. "But I'd better send some help after Mister Hurd, th' Judge could be in danger right now."

"Do that, Jake, but put 'im in with th' jailer, to watch McCleary and McGuire!" He said this as Hicks returned to the room, and nodding at him. "Sheriff,…I'd like you to run down them other two Deputies of Gentry's, see if they want their jobs back?"

"Yes, Sir,…I can do that right now."

"Bring 'em to th' Courthouse, I'll meet you there in a bit."

"Will do,…and I'll fetch th' Coroner on th' way!"

"Good thinkin', tell 'im to bring some help."

"And send Derrick to the Courthouse, Jordan." Said Tulane. "Tell 'im to guard th' cellblock."

Nodding, Hicks left again on the run, leaving both him and Tulane to stare down at Greenburg in distaste.

"You know how he died yet?" Gagged Hicks as he covered his mouth again.

"Knife," Nodded Dempsey. "You can just see the slit in his throat over th' swelling, quieter that way, I guess!...Has the other rooms been checked?"

"Jordan checked their rooms before we got here, they're clean."

"Then you need to ask that Clerk why it took so long to find th' body?"

"He did that already, too!...Th' other two gave orders not to disturb Greenburg, told th' Clerk he was a Lawyer workin' on an important case, and he wanted his privacy!"

"Appears he was, too!" Gagged Dempsey and stepped away from the body. "Maybe you ought a open that window, Jake,...get some air in here!"

"Good idea,...I'm gonna be smelling this for a month, as it is!" He shook his head and went to open the room's only window, and then to drag in a few lung's full of fresh air before coming back. "I still don't know how them two got out a th' hotel without us seein' 'em, I can't recall takin' our eyes off th' place!"

"Not even to take a leak?" Grinned Dempsey.

"Well." Shrugged Tulane, and then nodded. "But it didn't take that long!"

"Just long enough, it seems....And they could a been on to ya, they're professional killers."

"You're right about that!" He sighed, sidestepping the body to move toward the door. "I have got a lot to learn, Marshal."

"You will!...Now, let's get out a here, ain't much more we can do anyway."

"I was wonderin', Marshal?" He said as he looked down at Greenburg again. "I didn't see you put any money in that valise. If he was such a big-money Lawyer, you'd think there'd be a lot of it on 'im."

"If there was, they took it, Jake. Now, come on, there's a lot to do and no time to do it in!" He followed Tulane into the hall and closed the door. "Jake,...on second thought, maybe you better hang around here for th' Coroner, then come on to the Courthouse,...I'm gonna go talk with th' Judge."

*   *   *

"Come in, Roderick, and sit down." Sighed Emmit.

"Thanks, Judge." He nodded, coming on to take a seat by the desk. "I guess Mister Hurd told you what happened?"

"He did, yes,...and it's a shame, too, I had come to like Mister Greenburg. He had ethics I didn't see at first,...any sign of his killers?"

"Not yet,...but I think we know who they are."

"The bodyguards?"

"Yes, Sir,…they checked out of th' hotel three days ago,…and nobody seen 'em get on that train to leave, so,…I think they're still here somewhere."

"Mister Hurd says you think they're here to either harm me, or to break the prisoners out of jail,…why do you think that, Roderick?"

"Yes I do,…that, or to kill 'em! I believe that's why they came here, Emmit,…the Syndicate Bosses would not want this sort of trouble, not if it would point a finger at them!…Why else would they send two enforcers? Greenburg told you they had no idea those two were in jail before they got here and to me,…that could mean that McCleary had become a pain in their nasty ass before all this ever happened!…I think them two was sent here to heal th' wounds,…permanently!"

"And Greenburg?"

Dempsey shrugged. "To disperse of th' holdings, maybe,…but I don't think he knew why they were sent here, maybe he thought they were here to escort McCleary back to New York?…I'm only guessin', Emmit, but I do know th' Syndicate wouldn't want these two talkin' their asses off in that Courtroom!"

"I believe you may be right about that, Roderick!…And the rest of your theory is as good as any I have come up with. So, what's your plan?"

"To protect you and th' prisoners, Emmit, that's number one! Sheriff Hicks is bringin' Gentry's two ex-Deputies here to be sworn in again, I'll place them in th' cellblock till Court time tomorrow, with shotguns by th' way!…Mister Tulane and myself will be relieving each other in th' hallway out here, while Mister Hurd, Sheriff Hicks and Derrick Tinsley work th' streets again."

"Looks as if you have it covered!" Nodded Emmit. "And I surely do not want another Courtroom attempt to break these men out,…or to try and kill them! Once is quite enough for me!" He grinned.

"I remember that one." Grinned Dempsey…."seventy-six. Wasn't it, Judge?"

"It was,…Alex Hayward lost four good men that day!" He sighed. "I was a hero, though, myself, and John Cameron!"

"You shot one a th' outlaws, I remember that, too!…And this, John Cameron,…he was a Sheriff, right?"

"Still is, from Ben Franklin, my best friend, too!" Nodded Emmit. "Not excluding present company, Roderick, because I consider you as one also…. Yes, John Cameron out gunned a very bad gunfighter that day, Roderick,… and I did not believe that he could!"

"Is he as fast as Mabry, Judge?"

"No, Roderick," He sighed. "I don't believe that he is!…To tell you the truth, our friend Seth Mabry has the Devil in his right hand. But then again, so did John Cameron that day. It was something he had to do and he did it!...As did Mabry."

"Well, I ain't never seen his equal!"

"Have you remembered who he is, yet?"

Dempsey sighed then looked up at the ceiling for a moment. "No, Sir, I have not,...and I've been tryin' real hard to forget about it, too!...been losin' sleep over it!" He looked back at Emmit then. "It doesn't really matter none, anyway,...He's a damn good man!"

"That he is, Roderick!...He should be here sometime today, shouldn't he?"

"I expect 'im today, yes, Sir!...To tell you th' truth, I wish he was here already!...He's th' deadliest gunman I've ever seen, and he has a knack for gettin' at things that other men can't."

"That he does!" Sighed Emmit then suddenly looked at the door as the knock sounded. "Come in!"

"Ahhh, Mister Hicks?" He smiled as the Sheriff came in with the two ex-deputies. "And who are these men?"

"Judge, this is Sam Tindall, and Bert Simpson, both worked for Sheriff Gentry. They're both good men, too."

"Very good....Now, Sheriff, would you please go down to the cellblock and bring Mister Hurd back, while I swear these men in,...Roderick has assignments for all of you,...and I have one for Mister Hurd?"

"Right away, Judge!"

*   *   *

"Im so glad I brought my parasol," Commented Laura Mabry. "It's so hot today!"

"Lot a traffic on th' road, too." Returned Seth as he slapped the reins on the horses' rumps. "A lot a dust."

"Where we staying tonight, Daddy?" Queried Greg as he pulled his bandana up to cover his nose and mouth.

"Well, I don't know, son,...but be careful there, one a these cowboys might take you for a Road Agent with a mask on!" He grinned then. "I thought we might stay with a friend a mine, Mason Cooper owns th' Dollar Saloon in town,...th' rooms are fairly clean, too, and it's close to th' Courthouse."

"My, Lord, Seth!" Gasped Laura. "A Saloon?...I have never been in a Saloon in my whole life!...There has to be someplace else."

"There is." He sighed. "But, then again,...you ain't been to town in eighteen years, honey."

"And I haven't missed anything, I'll wager....Except, maybe a store-bought dress, I've always wanted a red one."

"Buy you one while we're here, we got th' time."

"I just might." She sighed. "I found one I liked at Gordon's Store a while back, but couldn't see spending that much money!"

"Probably weren't in style anyway, can't say much about a Tradin' Post."

"I know, they seem to change with the wind....But I would like to look pretty for you once in a while!"

"You always do, Laura. You're th' prettiest woman I've ever seen, then, and now!,...and a red dress wouldn't improve on that!"

She reached her arm through his and hugged him. "Thank you, Darling,"

"How long do you think the trial will last, Daddy?"

"Ain't got a clue, son, never been to one. Not more than a day,...I hope!...Don't worry about it, we got th' time."

"Yes, sir, I know that!...Guess I'm just anxious to put it all behind me."

"Yeah,...me, too!"

"Seth, we don't have to stay in a Saloon,...do we?" Voiced Laura as she raised her head from his arm. "I mean, really!...A Saloon?"

He laughed at the abruptness of her question. "Well, no, I guess not, honey. There's several Hotels in town, we'll stay at one a them."

"Thank you." She sighed. "Seth, did you think to ask Trey along,...he's been so patient with me while you were gone?"

"I did, honey....He's comin' in tomorrow....Said he didn't care about th' trial, though, didn't even want a go."

"Trey's got a gal he's sweet on, Mama."

"He never mentioned that!" She chuckled. "Guess he'll be getting married and moving on one day."

"Naw," Returned Greg. "He told me once was enough for him!"

"That's what every man says, son,...me, too,...till I met your mother!"

"Well," She laughed. "I'm not like just any woman, Sir!...besides,...I think I blame that silly war for the way he feels,...our own Government took it all away from him!...He doesn't even know where his wife and kids are, did you know that?...It's heartbreaking!"

"War ruined a lot a folks!" Agreed Seth, and they all fell silent for a while,...and at mid-day, it was even hotter on the semi-crowded Texas Road as they settled in beneath the large parasol in the sultry heat.

They fell completely silent as the wagon continued to bounce and groan, in and out of the sometimes deep ruts, and were down to speaking only when spoken to, or by passing riders and wagons,...and continuing that way until late in the day, when finally they were crossing the long bridge across the Trinity River. Relieved, Seth rattled the lines on the backs of the horses again to move them along, quickly exiting onto the dusty road on the other side,…and a quarter mile farther on, he was turning the team onto the Main Street road leading in to Dallas, when he recognized Deputy Hurd in the shade of a spreading Elm alongside and stopped the horses.

"Who is that, Seth?"

"That is Deputy Sheriff, Richard Hurd!" He grinned, watching the Deputy lead his horse out to the road.

"How are ya, Mister Mabry?" Grinned Ricky as he stopped at the wheel of the wagon and smiled up at him. "Been waitin' on you, folks!"

"We're doin' well, Rick." Grinned Seth as he reached a hand down to shake his. "Meet my wife, Laura?"

"Ma'am?" He grinned, and touched the brim of his hat. "And how are you, Greg?"

"Still in one piece, Ricky."

Nodding, he looked back at Laura. "It's a pleasure to meet you, ma'am, your husband's a great man, Greg, too!"

"Thank you, I agree with you." She hugged Seth's arm again.

"Now, what's the occasion, Richard,…it's too damn hot to be out in this heat?"

"Oh,…Judge Castle sent me out to wait on ya, said you'd need a place to stay?…Anyway, I was glad to do it,…we're on another manhunt in town."

"Who is it this time?"

"Couple a killers, here from New York!…Them, and a high-toned Lawyer came in on th' train a week ago. Anyway, once they found out McCleary was in jail, two of them killed th' Lawyer and disappeared!…Th' Judge will fill you in on it!…Anyway, Marshal Dempsey thinks they're still in town, he also thinks they're gonna try and kill McCleary,…so, we're lookin' for 'em!"

"My, God!" Gasped Laura. "Won't this ever end,…what if they come after you, Seth?"

"We've been over that, Honey."

"They won't, Mama" Soothed Greg as he put an arm around her.

"No, Ma'am!" Agreed Hurd. "I'm sorry for speakin' out about that, Mister Mabry, I didn't think?"

"That's okay, Richard,…it was me that asked. Now what about this place to stay?"

"Oh, yeah,…Well, up to a couple a years ago, this month, Judge Castle lived at th' Courthouse, he's got an apartment there. He don't use it anymore since he got married and built his house!…Anyway, I'm supposed to bring you."

"Lead on then!" He grinned.

Nodding, Hurd mounted his horse and reined it in front of the wagon as Seth clucked the team in behind him and an hour later, they were coming into the thickly populated residential area of Dallas, Texas, on their way toward the center of the great city.

*   *   *

"Seth Mabry!" Grinned Emmit Castle as they entered, and on seeing Laura, quickly got up and came to greet them. "This must be your wife, Seth!" He took Laura's hand in both of his. "I am so pleased to meet you, lady!"

"I'm Laura, Your Honor,...and thank you." She smiled as he released her hand.

"Call me Emmit, Ma'am,...and not to bring up old pains,...but you have my sincere condolences for your loss,...I am so sorry!"

"Thank you." She nodded.

"And you, Greg," He smiled, taking his hand and shaking it firmly. "You look quite different than when you left here, I'm glad to see it!" He turned to Seth then and took his hand. "Good to see you, Seth."

"Judge?" He nodded. "You sure you want a put us up, Sir,...we can manage elsewhere?"

"I know you can,...and yes, I am sure, in fact I wouldn't have it any other way!" He grinned. "Besides,...my apartment is much nicer than a hotel room, as you will see. I have also taken the privilege of ordering in dinner for you all, table is all set up for you." He turned to nod at Hurd then.

"Mister Hurd," He smiled. "I thank you, sir. Now, if you will bring in their luggage, please?...you know where my apartment is and the door is open,...and when you're done, I'd appreciate it if you would take their carriage to the stables for them?"

"Sure thing, Judge. Good night all, see you tomorrow, Seth?' Hurd smiled and left.

"Now, please," Smiled Emmit. "Sit down all of you, your luggage will be here in a few minutes and you can freshen up."

"Will you be joining us for dinner, Emmit?" Smiled Laura.

"Oh, no, Ma'am,...My Darling wife will have dinner waiting at home for me." He waited until they were seated before returning to his own chair. "Oh, yes,...almost forgot the important part!...There's a spare room adjoining in there, it's got a bath tub, and there's hot water waiting for you. There's also a basin, and a pump for fresh water,...all the comforts of home!...For you, Greg there is a cot, I hope that will suffice?"

"Yes, sir." He grinned. "I can sleep anywhere!"

"So could I,…once!" He shrugged and cleared his throat.

"Judge?' Queried Seth. "What's with this manhunt, Richard told us about?"

"What did he tell you?"

"That some Lawyer was killed a week ago, and you was lookin' for two New York killers,…they involved in all a this?"

"I'm afraid so, though actually how?…I don't know!…Roderick thinks they came here to kill our prisoners,…thinks McCleary has the New York Bosses mad at him for some unknown reason!…He also thinks they are still here waiting their chance. And the Lawyer?…Again, Roderick thinks he was here to settle McCleary's affairs, maybe thinking the two enforcers were here to take McCleary and McGuire back to New York?" He clasped his hands together in thought then.

""Personally,…I think that if that was the case, Mister Greenburg must have gone back to the hotel and told the two Goons that he was quitting, and they killed him for it!"

"Excuse me," Voiced Laura with interest. "Why did he do that,…tell them he was quitting, I mean,…didn't he work for them also?"

"Yes, he did,…but for some reason, after he interviewed McCleary, He came back here and told me he was returning the Syndicate's money!…Said McCleary lied to him."

"I sure opened a can a worms here, didn't I?" Remarked Seth with a frown.

"Can't catch a big fish without them, Seth,…someone had to bait the hook!…If you had not done that, we wouldn't have our city back! McCleary and McGuire had a stranglehold on Dallas, and all you did was break it!"

"All I know is, I'd sure hate to go through it again!"

"And I would not want you to!…Now, to business.…I have reserved the entire front row of seats on one side of the Courtroom, both for you three, and the law enforcement, except for those on guard duty. Security will be in the hands of the Army tomorrow during the trial, some inside, and the rest in the streets outside. So there will be nothing to worry about!…And if those two Syndicate men hope to carry out their plans, it will most definitely have to be before the trial starts,…and Roderick has that part of it covered."

"You will see Justice served, Emmit Castle style tomorrow, Seth!…I will collect your debt for you, you have my word.…And now,…" At that moment, the knock interrupted, him and they all watched as Ricky Hurd leaned inside.

"Excuse me, Judge,…I'm all done, I'm goin' to th' stables now.…Want me to come back here?"

"No, find the others and go have some dinner, Mister Hurd,...you can check with Roderick for assignment. And thank you." Hurd nodded and closed the door.

"I guess you folks are ready!" Smiled Emmit and nodded toward the rear of his office. "That door opens into a hallway, the apartment is at the end of the hall. Sleep well, folks!" He got to his feet as they did and followed them to the door.

"Your dinner will be served in about an hour, Seth....Roderick will come for you in the morning."

"We're obliged to ya, Judge!" Nodded Seth as Greg opened the door. "See you tomorrow."

*   *   *

They were up early, as that was what they were accustomed to, and were all bathed and fully dressed by the time breakfast and hot coffee arrived. But afterward, faced yet another hour of anticipation and boredom, and it passed quite slowly. They were all relieved, however, when the knock finally sounded at the door,...and when Greg opened it.

"Hi, ya, Greg." Grinned Dempsey,...taking his hand and shaking it. "You're lookin' well again, I see!"

"How are ya, Dempsey?" Greeted Seth as he came to shake the Marshal's hand.

"I'll be a lot better when this trial is behind me, Seth." He grinned. "Good to see ya, man....I see you brought th' Missus this time, too?"

"Yes, I did,...my wife, Laura, Marshal." Smiled Seth, stepping aside to allow Dempsey to shake her hand as well.

"A pleasure to meet you, Laura,...but I wish it was under different circumstances!" And when she nodded, he turned back to Greg. "Son, you can pick up your boot-money at Jake's office before you leave for home again."

"Boot money?" Queried Seth.

"Tommy gave me some money to hold earlier that night, Daddy, I told you about it."

"Thanks, Marshal," He nodded somberly. "Take a seat and have some coffee."

"I'd like to, thanks." He came on to sit at the breakfast table then accepted the coffee from Laura. "We got a few minutes yet," He said as he took a swallow of the hot liquid. "We'll be goin' up with th' guards when they take th' prisoners up,...added security, you know."

"I take it, you ain't found your killers yet?"

"Nope,...and it beats me how they can just up and disappear like that!"

"They're professional killers, Marshal, they know their job!...McCleary was right under our noses, too, and we couldn't find him!"

"How well, I know!" He sighed. "And these two might be, as well....If they're still in town?"

"Do you really think they want a kill McCleary?"

"I don't really know why, Seth," He sighed. "But yeah, I really do!...For some reason, I believe McCleary got on his boss's bad side, and when you add th' fact that he's in Federal custody,...and that whatever he might say on that witness stand could be ammunition for th' Government to go after that Boss-man,...then I'd say yes, I think they want 'em dead,...and they want 'em dead before th' trial starts!"

"And in sayin' that,...you think they'll try somethin' between here and th' Courtroom?"

"I do, Seth,...and I hope I'm wrong!...At least, Emmit thinks I am."

"Well, I don't!" Nodded Seth, and suddenly turned to Laura and Greg. "Son, I want you to take your mother and go on up to th' Courtroom,...and stay close to her, Son!"

"You're not coming with us?" Gasped Laura.

"No,...I'm goin' up with th' prisoners, and th' Marshal."

"But why,...They'll have guards?"

"I have to honey, you know that!...Now, please do as I say, Greg'll be with you....If you need to be relieved, do it now and then go."

"He's right, Mama," Agreed Greg.

"Yes," Agreed Dempsey. "You can use th' stairs by where you came into th' building, and Greg,...you might want a leave your gun with your father, that, or th' Soldiers at th' door."

"Emmit said there'd be Soldiers guardin' th' place." Commented Seth.

"Damn near a whole troop of 'em!" Sighed Dempsey. "You'd be surprised at th' people out there who would like to pot-shot those two?"

"Maybe I wouldn't, too." Nodded Seth. "We goin' in th' same way?"

"We'll use th' stairs at the other end of the hall, so, if you're ready we can go out there and wait?"

Nodding, Seth turned back to Laura and Greg. "Son, you and Mother go on ahead now, okay?...And don't worry, honey." He soothed then leaned down to kiss her. He watched them go down the hallway and turn back toward the front doors before pushing Greg's pistol into his belt. "I'm ready when you are, Marshal."

He reached down and removed the loop from his pistol's hammer then followed Dempsey down the narrow hallway and into the larger one, where they immediately walked the short distance to stop at the cellblock's outer doors,…and leaning against the wall there, waited patiently for the door to open.

"Seth?" Sighed Dempsey as he looked up and down the long hallway. "If it was you,…how would you do it?"

"Do what,…kill McCleary and McGuire?"

"Yeah,…this bein' th' last chance you had to do it, where would you hide?"

Shrugging, Seth turned to stare back the way they had come, watching the soldiers at the entrance, as they checked those people entering the Courthouse for the trial. "If that's what they're gonna do," He sighed, looking past Dempsey at the other end of the hall. "It's gonna be between here and them stairs yonder,…what's down there?"

"Locked doors." Said Dempsey. "I must have checked 'em ten times since last night….Me and Tulane spent th' last two nights in this hallway, and nobody got past us!…I don't know, maybe I'm wrong about all this, Seth,…maybe they left after all?"

Seth nodded, still staring down the dimly-lit hallway. "Consider it a blessing, if they did!…I'll tell you what, though….After hearin' your argument about it,…I'm leanin' toward believin' ya! These Crime Bosses got a be plenty smart,…and th' assassins even smarter!…No, I think you're prob'ly right, Marshal." He said, nodding at the darker end of the hallway.

"If they're gonna do it at all, it'll be from one a them doorways there…. And they likely know they're gonna die when they do it."

"Suicide killers?" Blurted Dempsey. "You're kiddin', right?…They ain't that crazy, Seth!…Do ya think?"

"Men go into battle without knowin' he's comin' out,…why not?"

"You scare me sometimes, man!" Just then the cellblock door opened and they moved from against the wall as two Deputies with shotguns exited first, then came the restrained McCleary, his right arm still in a sling and his left chained to his waist. Behind him came Yancy McGuire, shirtless and with his upper torso still bandaged, and both arms in slings. Both men glared hatefully at Seth as they were told to stop in the hallway.

Sheriff Hicks and Jake Tulane squeezed past them into the hall and closed the door behind them, one of them watching the area between them and the front of the Courthouse, while Tulane watched the prisoners.

"Okay!" Said Dempsey, looking at Tindall and Simpson. "You two walk on either side of the prisoners and slightly in front, Seth and me will lead th' way, and men,…be ready for anything." He nodded at Seth and they led the small procession slowly down the half-lit corridor toward the rear stairwell.

Seth felt himself beginning to tighten up inside as they walked, and had just glanced sideways at Dempsey to meet his glance, when from the corner of his eye, he saw the movement. Quickly looking back he saw the man step from the doorway with arm raised, and just as quickly drew and fired as the killer released the stiletto, the slug knocking the breath from the assassin's lungs with a loud grunt as he was pitched backward to fall heavily onto the hardwood floor.

The explosion was deafening in the confines of the wide hallway, and as the second killer emerged from the doorway Seth fired again, dropping this man across the body of the first, and just as he was raising his knife,...all of it happening in the space of an ear-shattering heartbeat, catching everyone off-guard, except Seth.

The echoes of gunfire subsided quickly and Seth, along with Dempsey moved on down the hall to check the fallen assassins, both as yet unaware that Deputy Sam Tindall had taken the thrown knife in the chest. He had unknowingly stepped in front of McCleary and into the knife's path, thus saving the Crime Boss's life. When they heard the commotion, both Seth and Dempsey quickly came back to squat beside the downed Deputy, finding him already dead and the others kneeling in shock beside him.

"GOD DAMN IT ALL TO HELL!" Shouted Dempsey in frustration. "These Bastards was right here all th' time,...GOD DAMN IT!"

Getting to his feet, Seth holstered his pistol and reached to angrily grab McCleary's shirt-front in an iron grip. "You slimy Son of a Bitch!" He yelled, jerking a gasp of pain from the Crime Boss's mouth as he cowered backward into a steadfast, and rigid Jake Tulane. "Everything you fuckin' touch, dies, you filth!"

"Seth stop!" Yelled a robed Emmit Castle, as him and several soldiers rounded the corner from the stairwell.

He released McCleary as Emmit got there, and angrily moved back against the wall while the Judge squatted to check the dead Deputy Tindall. If he'd only been paying closer attention, he thought sadly, he might have saved this man's life,...why didn't he expect it?...But he knew it had happened too damn fast,...and he reluctantly found himself beginning to appreciate the killer's accuracy and ability at throwing a knife that far,...and by his seeing it in time to stop the second man, likely saved someone else's life.

"Let me through, damn you!" Shouted Laura loudly, as a soldier tried to hold her back. "My husband is over there!"

Seth looked up to see her and Greg then, and started toward them,...but Emmit saw them, too and quickly issued orders to let them pass. He met her as she ran toward him and held her close.

"God, Seth!" She gasped as she clung to him. "I was so scared!"

"I know, honey,...but it's over now!" He looked into Greg's worried eyes then and smiled, then all three of them turned to watch the soldiers remove the bodies of the assassins. Two more came to carry the Deputy back toward Emmit's office and the front entrance.

"Okay, people!" Voiced Emmit loudly as they left. "We still have a trial to conduct!...Roderick, you men take the prisoners on up to the Courtroom and seat them, have the Bailiff call the crowd to order, we'll be right up!" He turned to Seth then as the prisoners were ushered past, and shook his head.

"I guess we have you to thank again,...Marshal!" He said the last part with a slight grin. "You make a good lawman, sir!"

"Honorary Marshal, Judge,...and a thanks ain't necessary." He replied tightly. "Another innocent man died!"

"In the line of duty, Seth,...it was his job!...Two might have died, if not for you,...Roderick told me what happened!" He nodded. "Now come on, folks, you can watch me collect the debt these men owe you."

"ALL RISE!" Shouted the Bailiff as they entered. "COURT IS NOW IN SESSION,...THE HONORABLE, JUDGE EMMIT CASTLE, PRESIDING!"